Henry Sutton

Henry Sutton was born in 1963 in Hopton, a small town on the Norfolk and Suffolk border. He began a career in journalism with the *Norwich Mercury* and now regularly contributes travel articles to *The Times*, *Condé Nast Traveller* and *Elle*. He has published two previous novels, *Gorleston* and *Bank Holiday Monday*, and lives in London with his wife, the painter Jane Langley, and their young daughter.

'Sutton's lyrical but gritty prose relates Eleanor's experiences with rare sensitivity'

Tatler

'He wields the house-hunting metaphor and its reality seamlessly together . . . He also convincingly inhabits the mind of a heroine – a rare thing in a male novelist, and something devoutly to be wished'

Hampstead & Highgate Express

'A must for anyone who's about to do it or who has already done it'

Nine to Five

'With the connections Sutton makes between individually sharp "readings" of various houses, he endows the book's naturalism with an eerie sense of fragility. An abortive affair, a sudden death, the revelation of a family secret – the narrative is not lacking in "events". But it is distinguished by the finessed stretches between them, alive with memorable detail'

The Sunday Times

Henry Sutton

THE
HOUSEHUNTER

SCEPTRE

Extract from 'Accepted' by Elizabeth Jennings, in *Collected Poems* (Carcanet), used with kind permission.

First published in 1998 by Hodder and Stoughton
First published in paperback in 1999 by Hodder & Stoughton
A division of Hodder Headline PLC
A Sceptre Paperback

10 9 8 7 6 5 4 3

A CIP catalogue record for this title is available from the British Library

ISBN 0 340 71731 9

Typeset by
Palimpsest Book Production Limited, Polmont, Stirlingshire
Printed and bound in Great Britain by
Clays Ltd, St Ives PLC, Bungay, Suffolk

Hodder and Stoughton
A division of Hodder Headline PLC
338 Euston Road
London NW1 3BH

To Jane

You are no longer young,
Nor are you very old.
There are homes where those belong.

Elizabeth Jennings

Buying any house can be complex and stressful.

Barnard Marcus

38 Whittlesey Street, SE1

She stepped into the house and smelt old air, feeling its thickness, its stillness engulf her. But as she moved further along
the narrow hallway she caught traces of a perfume she could-
n't name, as if its wearer had recently hurried through and the
air had settled after her, leaving loose particles of scent
hopelessly suspended. The hallway was dim and she stopped
to run a hand down a wall. She couldn't tell what colour it had
been painted because of the bad light, but it had been hung
with an indented, patterned paper – the ridges and bobbles
softening as she pressed harder, wanting to make sure that she
was still alive, pushing herself to believe in this moment. That
she was doing the right thing, because she was suddenly
overwhelmed with doubt. She heard the click of a switch
behind her and the hall light came on, removing some of the
dimness but none of her doubt. She had wanted to see clear
space – an unfettered brightness. She had expected, naively, to
see the beginnings of a new life. Instead she faced walls that
were what she imagined a paint manufacturer might call
cinnamon, or coffee, or perhaps burnt almond, already
sensing a terrible bitterness. On her right, just above shoulder

height, were three decorative plates fastened to the wall by heavy wire brackets. *God is Love*, said one in gold letters. *God loves all existing things*, another. And, *In God we Trust*, the third.

'Oh, urrgh, Mrs Mitchell, if you carry on through we could start with the breakfast room and the kitchen at the back,' said the estate agent, consulting the particulars – Eleanor couldn't remember his name. 'You'll appreciate,' he said, 'these houses benefit from having particularly spacious halls. Though I don't think the colour of these walls makes the best use of the available light. I wouldn't say this was a dark hallway at all. There is the window above the front door. Take no time to brighten up the place. This is what I always try to remind people – it's amazing the difference a lick of paint can make. These plates aren't going to remain here either, of course. Ha, I don't think I could live with them. Could you, Mrs Mitchell?'

Eleanor had wandered the short way into what she presumed was the breakfast room. The air here smelt sweet, of food – and Eleanor thought for some reason of baby food, ground into the coir carpet furrows. Of babies in soft clothes smiling lovingly, unconditionally. Learning to wave. But as she looked about her she couldn't see any evidence of small children. There were no high chairs or playthings. No baby photographs among the few snaps tacked to a cork board by the dark mahogany dresser. Eleanor leant closer. In one photograph she saw a late-middle-aged man with thinning, slicked back grey hair, glasses, a pointed nose and thin unsmiling lips. He was standing next to a large woman with round, friendly cheeks and fluffy grey hair. They were outside what appeared to be a country church – swallows and yew trees and tall, fair grass momentarily stilled in the background. Though it might have been a city church taken from a careful angle. There was a photograph of a young woman, also with glasses and thin lips, but plump cheeks and flyaway light brown hair. She looked more like her mother, Eleanor decided – kinder than her father. She was wearing an electric-blue gown with a mortarboard balanced somehow on top of the hair and was holding a scrolled and red-ribbon-tied degree certificate with both hands tightly, proudly, to her chest, as if it might suddenly be taken away from her. Eleanor shivered, feeling a draught, more a fluttering brush her face. She turned quickly away.

'This room, as you can see,' said the estate agent, who had manoeuvred himself past Eleanor and was hovering by the entrance to the kitchen, 'could either be used as a more formal dining room, or as a breakfast-cum-living room as the current occupants have utilised the space. Or indeed as a playroom, depending on your requirements, of course. The garden's south facing, so there should be plenty of light.' He bent down with a slight groan and prodded the floor. 'Good-quality carpet – years of wear left.' He stood, breathing loudly, looking about him. 'The windows are not double-glazed, which is a blessing if you ask me. Much easier to pop them open. Besides, it looks very quiet out the back here, which is amazing if you think how central we are. You could be in Covent Garden in fifteen minutes walking, and the City's not much further. Do you work nearby, Mrs Mitchell?'

'Urrm, not really,' said Eleanor. 'No, not at the moment.'

'Some people might find the kitchen a little compact,' he said, disappearing from Eleanor's view, 'but everything's here. Dishwasher, washing machine, fridge freezer, AEG electric oven – got one myself – gas hob, double sink with stainless steel drainer, waste disposal, NEFF extractor. I'm not entirely sure what the vendors have decided to leave behind, but all this will obviously be negotiated in due course. High-quality cabinets – should last for ever.' Eleanor could hear cupboards and drawers being opened and closed. 'Loads of storage space above the wall units, and I see they've made room for an ironing board and brooms and suchlike in a recess at the end of the sink unit. One double rad. Ceiling- and wall-mounted spotlights. Vinyl floor. Door to garden. Mrs Mitchell?'

Eleanor walked towards the kitchen entrance, having listened to little of what the estate agent had been saying, thinking instead of the family who lived here and who now wanted to move. Quite what had happened to them here. Not being able to get the picture of the daughter out of her mind – the way she was holding on to that scroll, clutching it to her, as if she were somehow clutching at life. Eleanor presumed she was already living elsewhere – she didn't feel enough of her presence in the house – and that the parents, sick of the rising council tax and frightened by the crime – she knew about the crime – had decided to retire to a cheaper, safer place, perhaps by the sea where there'd even be fresh air. Eleanor had finally realised she needed to move that morning, though she knew she didn't want to leave London. Not yet. She was only forty-two. 'Christ,' she said, 'it is small.'

'You could probably get a small table in up at the end,' the estate agent said.

'You must be joking,' Eleanor said. There was barely enough room for both Eleanor and the estate agent to stand. And he was a small man, Eleanor noticed, looking at him properly for the first time – a good few inches shorter than she. She didn't feel threatened by him exactly, though she found his manner was making her nervous. She was quite unsure of what he might do next. He was wearing a cream shirt with faint pencil-thin pink stripes and hard-looking yellowy sweat stains around the armpits, a grey tie, badly creased grey trousers and brown crêpe-soled shoes. 'The kitchen has been well designed,' Eleanor said, trying to lighten her mood, 'given the space.'

'A number of people along the street have knocked down this wall,' he said, leaning past Eleanor and pointing to the wall adjoining the breakfast room, leaving a distinct smell of either antiperspirant or cheap aftershave, she didn't know which, 'forty-seven and fifty-eight, if I remember correctly. We've sold both within the last couple of years. And some have extended over here.' He swung round and indicated through the kitchen window. Aftershave, she thought, because his shirt didn't look as if he used enough antiperspirant, though he didn't smell too bad. 'Then you would lose a bit of garden and light of course, but you could always put on a Perspex roof. The great thing about this property is that it's in pretty much its original shape, leaving you with all manner of options. Nothing's undoable. Shall we go into the garden?' He took a number of tiny steps to the door, as if he were trying to make the room seem larger. He undid the bolts at the top and bottom, turned the handle and pushed, but the door didn't open. He pushed again, as if it suddenly would, but it still didn't so, looking puzzled, he took a bunch of keys from a trouser pocket and started to go through them. 'It must be one of these,' he said. He tried a couple of keys but neither worked. 'Maybe they've left it in a drawer or somewhere.' He put the bunch back in his pocket and began opening drawers again – rustling cutlery and hand tools and pamphlets and bits of paper as he sifted. 'Very strange,' he said. 'I haven't actually shown the property before.'

'Look, never mind,' Eleanor said. 'I can get a pretty good idea from the window.'

'It's obviously well kept,' he said. 'I love a good garden. Have bit of a knack for it myself.' He brushed past her front-on, unnecessarily close she thought, and walked back into the breakfast room, pausing by the dresser. 'Should we carry on through – upstairs?'

'Okay,' said Eleanor, following him. She noticed he had a slight limp, as if one of his legs were shorter than the other. The carpet in the hall and on the staircase was a pale pink, a salmon, and seemed softer and more expensive than the carpet in the breakfast room, except it was badly stained. The stains were dark and sort of smudged, Eleanor thought, as if something, whatever it was that had leaked, had been dragged down the stairs. The landing was split-level, the short lower level leading to the bathroom – the door was ajar – but they left it for the moment.

'Three bedrooms of course, a couple of doubles and a single,' the estate agent said. He moved gingerly ahead into a front room, seemingly afraid of what he might find in there, pushing the door open as he went – it creaked slightly. 'Arrgh, this must be the master bedroom. They certainly go in for the religious stuff. I can't say I'm a churchgoer myself. The wife has been known to on occasion. How about you, Mrs Mitchell?'

Eleanor edged in after him, not answering, feeling suddenly uneasy about going into a strange bedroom with a man she had never met before. There was a neatly made bed with a couple of doll-size pillows positioned on top of the bedspread, which in turn had been pulled over the normal pillows. They were white with blue and pink embroidered words spelling out, Eleanor could just read, *Lord overshadow me with thy spirit*, and, oddly she thought, *Go with me Lord as I leave this place*. A large, simple cross hung above the bed and a Bible was placed on a bedside table. Eleanor suddenly, vividly imagined the old couple from the photograph awkwardly propped up in the bed she was facing – wearing padded dressing gowns that smelt faintly of sick and moth balls. She wondered what comfort they gave each other, whether they still loved each other, how long ago they had last had sex. She looked for some casually discarded item of clothing but saw none. There were no wilting flowers either – no magazines, no books, no alarm clock, no radio, no half-drunk glass of water, no box of tissues. To Eleanor there was nothing seemingly out of place, yet nothing in place. She followed the estate agent out of the room and into a smaller bedroom, also at the front of the house. She thought this room was even more unhomely. There was no cover on the sagging bed, just the shape of its useless springs coming through the floral mattress fabric. The cross hanging above it was smaller than the one in the main bedroom and looked as if it was made of plastic pretending to be wood. It had even been grained and slightly distressed.

'The wardrobe's a good size,' the estate agent said, sliding open the doors with some force, which made the empty wire coat hangers inside jangle. 'Though it does seem to take up a fair bit of room.' He banged on the side with his fist, setting off the coat hangers again, but louder. 'It would come down no problem.'

Eleanor walked over to the window and drew aside the dry, dusty net curtain, immediately wanting to wash her hands, as if she had got chalk on them, or something much more unpleasant, something rotten. But she didn't move and stood looking out on to Whittlesey Street – the pale two-storey houses which had what appeared to be a third floor except the windows were bricked in and the space behind was really pitched roof and attic, the fake Victorian streetlights with their spindly wrought-iron stems and hanging lamps like goldfish bowls, the cars that were neither very smart nor completely clapped out – VWs and Fords, the odd Fiat and Volvo and slightly newer Vauxhall. Above the roofs and the chimneys and the extended aerials there was a sky of fat, fast-moving multi-shaded September clouds and the odd patch of the purest blue.

'Oh, urrgh, Mrs Mitchell? I'm in here,' the estate agent shouted. 'The rear bedroom.'

She let go of the net curtain, watched it smoke her view and slowly stepped backwards before turning. Once in the rear bedroom she immediately knew that it had been the daughter's room, and she felt again a coldness prickle her face – as if whatever had caused it downstairs had now caught up with her here. Boxes of books were lined against one wall. Another had floor-to-ceiling shelves, now largely devoid of books and objects, with just the plastic veneer lifting on a number of the MDF planks. There was an empty desk in a corner, no pictures on any of the walls, no crosses either but, surprisingly, the odd Blu-Tack stain was visible. So she must have been allowed posters at some stage, Eleanor thought. The room didn't smell stale exactly, more long forgotten. A sweetness still lingering in the air – a sweetness that came not from a perfume or flowers but something more human. 'So this was where the daughter slept,' Eleanor said aloud, to herself. And at that moment she noticed a cross had been laid on the single bed where the pillow should have been.

'You have children, do you? Grown up are they?' the estate agent said.

'No, no I don't,' Eleanor said.

'I've just the one, a daughter. She's pregnant in fact. About time too, if you ask me. She's thirty this year and not getting any younger. Women seem to leave it so late nowadays. Still, she's found herself a nice bloke. He's in the building trade. Pretty successful, too.'

The window in this room, like all the other windows in the house, was shut and Eleanor suddenly felt uncomfortably hot and slightly dizzy, that she might even faint. She urgently needed more air and went to the window, unclipped the catch and hauled it up. It was loose in its frame and easy to open. Cool air instantly hit her face and she breathed in deeply, tasting exhaust and, faintly, the Thames – a tangy, oily taste at the back of her throat.

'Are you okay Mrs Mitchell?'

She took a few more deep breaths, her eyes beginning to water. 'Yeah – I'll be okay.' She stayed by the window, blinking, waiting for her eyes to clear, staring into a wavering blur. Slowly her distant vision took shape and beyond three straggly, overgrown gardens to her right, beyond the end of Windmill Walk, as she thought she probably would, she saw her house – its faded green front door, the quiet glinting of the brass letter box and numbers, which she had ceased to polish long ago and which she couldn't possibly read from here but knew said, *89*. 89 Roupell Street. Her and Clay's home for the last fifteen years. The only house they had ever lived in together. Four years unmarried, eleven years married, but there didn't seem any difference to Eleanor now. It had been fifteen years. The longest she had lived anywhere. 'I hope I'm not holding you up,' she said. She had no idea how long you were meant to spend viewing a house.

The estate agent limped out of the room at a speed and with an agility that surprised Eleanor, so she wondered for a moment whether her dizzy spell had unsettled him somehow, or she really was holding him up. She wasn't nervous of him now – she could tell he was harmless. 'Of course you could knock up into the roof here,' he said, descending the split-level while looking at the ceiling, 'and put in a Velux. A number of people have, forty-seven and fifty-eight, if I remember correctly. Why not expose a couple of beams too? That's very fashionable at the moment. I can recommend a great builder. The bathroom's, urrgh, certainly distinctive,' he said, stopping with a foot in the door. 'It's all yours.'

'I see what you mean,' Eleanor said, trying to get past him. The room was a bright red, a vermilion. She caught herself in the mirror above the avocado-coloured sink. She didn't think she looked pale, but then maybe the light in the room was so infused with the red it was giving her cheeks colour. She ran her fingers down one side of her face, from the high, well-defined cheekbone to her jaw, pulling the skin on her face, feeling the slightly sticky film of Roc Melibiose – the cream was a present from her sister. She wondered whether she looked at all pudgy, because she felt bloated. But she didn't think she did – if anything she looked drawn. She was thinner now than she had been for a long time. Possibly since before she gave up smoking. She flicked her fingers through her hair. She thought it was probably getting a bit too long. It fell to her shoulders – the bob having lost much of its shape – and seemed thin and stringy. It was the same colour as her eyes, except there was the odd grey hair also, which she didn't pull, because she believed they came back with a vengeance if you did, like leg hair, or pubic hair around your bikini line.

'Nothing a lick of paint won't remedy,' the estate agent said as she emerged from the bathroom, buoyed by the fact that she at least had good reason to get her hair cut, something she enjoyed doing. 'Airing cupboard and hot water tank's in here,' he said, banging on a small, flimsy door by the bathroom. He looked at his watch and started to descend the rest of the stairs.

'Jesus Christ,' Eleanor thought she heard him say some moments later. She was taking the stairs carefully trying to avoid standing on the carpet stains.

Little natural light made it into the sitting room – the net curtains, the narrowness of Whittlesey Street and the height of the houses opposite doing much to hinder its passage. The estate agent had turned on the main light but it must have had a low wattage bulb because the corners of the room were still in deep gloom. 'As you can see,' he said, when Eleanor had entered, 'everything's in pretty good nick – quality carpet, again.' He didn't bend down and prod it this time. 'Gas fire, solid-looking shelves in the chimney breast recesses. TV aerial point.' The room was small but sparsely furnished. There was a sofa, an armchair with matching foot stool, a side table and a standard lamp. A few ceramic figurines stood on the shelves and a cheap reproduction of a painting hung above the gas fire. It was of Christ on the cross. There was a crown of thorns digging into his forehead so he was bleeding, and a halo above that. 'Yep,' he said, 'not much more to say than that. Shall we take a peek at the last room, across the hall, which would be the formal dining room or study, depending on how you arrange it, of course?' He was already walking out of the sitting room, as if he couldn't get out quick enough. He crossed the hallway, pushing open the door to the final room, Eleanor followed. 'Arrgh,' he said, shaking his head, 'it's a little cluttered. I was warned about this.'

Eleanor tried to see round him, stooping to get a better view. There were boxes everywhere, piles of furniture, pictures, lamps, pieces of crockery, vases, cushions, clothes falling out of bin-liners, rolled-up posters, fraying LP sleeves – things, Eleanor thought, that gave houses character, that made them livable. It was as if someone had cleared the house of its individuality, its character and dumped it all in one room. She knew, of course, that this was the sort of stuff you brought with you and accumulated over years, over decades, over lifetimes, arranging it how you wanted, but perhaps because she had only just begun looking she couldn't envisage the house any other way – cold and lifeless. And that was not how she wanted things to be at this stage in her life. Then she saw it, the tip of the still neatly scrolled degree certificate. She heard herself breathe in.

'This will all be going,' the estate agent said. 'You could even knock right across to the sitting room – open up the whole ground floor. I know a great builder who works locally. Come to think about it, I'm not sure if that was not what they did at forty-seven, or was it fifty-eight? You get to see so many houses in my business, of course, you can't remember every one. Feel free to have a wander about.' He edged out, brushing against Eleanor's breasts, quite on purpose this time she was sure, and made for the front door, limping extravagantly, seemingly aware that he had just done something he shouldn't have.

Sunlight was now streaming through the window above the front door, illuminating the hall walls, which were maybe more a hazel, or sorrel, and making the gold lettering of the ceramic plates glow, so Eleanor had to concede, to herself at least, that the estate agent was right, it wasn't a dark hallway. Not that that made it any more homely. 'I've seen enough,' she said. The estate agent opened the front door to an even greater flood of light and Eleanor followed him into Whittlesey Street. Sun was catching the car wing-mirrors and bouncing on to the pale brick and grimy sash windows. Theed Street abutted Whittlesey Street to the east with a terrace of identical two – but with that fake third bit – storey Victorian houses. It was in shade. At the other end, in the sun, a block of turn-of-the-century Peabody apartments rose five floors. Above and beyond that the limestone spire of St John's could just be picked out against the towering, though even paler,

Shell building. The Shell building was flying its yellow and red flag – a dot of colour, like an exotic bird, from this distance. 'How much is it on for?' Eleanor realised she didn't even know.

'They're asking two two nine.'

'Two hundred and twenty-nine thousand pounds?'

'They're wanting a quick sale. They're moving out of London, I believe, to some place in Kent, or is it Sussex? On the south coast anyway. They're down there at the moment, which is why you've had the pleasure of me showing you around.' He laughed. 'There's been a recent bereavement in the family, I understand – the daughter.' He stopped laughing and looked at his feet, suddenly shy.

'Oh, oh God, how terrible,' Eleanor said. She was shocked, even though she had sensed something had happened to the daughter. She could see her, clearly. Her uncontrollable hair and round, kind face. The air being sucked out of her cheeks.

'They'll take two two five, possibly two twenty. It's in good nick. Nothing a spot of paint won't cover up. It certainly doesn't look like it needs any major structural work. There's no obvious subsidence. No damp, no dry rot, not that I'm able to guarantee it of course. If you ask me, it's as solid as rock – last for ever. Nice garden, bit of care's gone into that. Very sought-after street.' He paused, trying to shield his face further from the sun, which he seemed quite unused to. 'Of course we could get into a bidding situation and who knows where the price might go. We get enquiries every day about properties on the streets round here. Look at it this way, it's not going to hang around. Not much is coming on the market at the moment and prices are beginning to rise again. I'll tell you, another boom's on the way. Have you been looking long?'

Something, a fleck of dust perhaps, flew into Eleanor's left eye. It began to water immediately and she stopped seeing the young woman, the life taken so abruptly from her. She blinked, tilting her head back. With a finger she poked around the corners but was unable to locate anything, or stem the watering – it was far worse than in the bedroom earlier – so she covered her eye with her hand, applying pressure. 'No, no. This is the first house I've seen,' she said.

'Where are you wishing to move from?'

'Oh not far from here – Roupell Street.'

The estate agent nodded slowly. 'Roupell Street. No point in me telling you about the local amenities then. Just fancied a slightly different aspect, did you? Somewhere new to do up? We get a lot of people even staying in the same street.'

'I thought it might be bigger, being double-fronted and with that top bit.'

'Deceptive, isn't it? No, I reckon Roupell Street houses are about the same size, possibly even bigger. They might not be double-fronted but they go back further. Classier street too, if you ask me – it's got the name. Valuable properties.' He nodded slowly again.

'We've been there a long time. I'm sort of sick of being so close to the railway at the back and the scrap metal place and the garage on Brad Street. It's very dark there at night.'

'I suppose Whittlesey might be quieter,' he said. He was still trying hopelessly to shelter from the sun, shifting from foot to foot on the bright pavement. 'Your place is not on the market yet then?'

'No,' said Eleanor. 'We haven't got quite that far yet.' She didn't like the man at all, his over-familiar manner, the way he had brushed against her, but she couldn't help feeling sorry for him – his limp and the way he looked so unused to the sunshine. His worn clothes. Obviously, she thought, not enough houses were coming on the market, that or he was working for the wrong company, or estate agents just spent too long in sad, shady houses. 'Sorry, but I don't think this house is quite what I'm looking for.' She extended her hand wanting to get away from him. Wanting to forget about this house and its occupants, the poor girl, but knowing she wouldn't be able to. Knowing somehow that the threshold she had crossed, the still, heavy air in the hallway that she had first disturbed was going to cling to her. That she had a much bigger step to make before she'd be able to shake it free. 'I hope I haven't wasted your time. Thanks anyway.'

'We've got your details, have we, if anything else comes up?'

'I think so,' she said, knowing they didn't, shaking his moist, clammy hand. Like a child's on a hot summer day, she thought.

A train eased to a halt – the brakes psst, pssting and the doors emitting sharp hydraulic puffs. A shuffle of feet. The tinny, electronically distorted voice of the announcer listing, Eleanor could hear from her kitchen, *Orpington, Sevenoaks, Tonbridge*. And she knew that this train was going to end up at Hastings, before the announcer continued with, *Tunbridge Wells, Frant, Wadhurst, Stonegate, Etchingham, Robertsbridge, Battle, Crowhurst, West St Leonards, St Leonards Warrior Square, Hastings*. Hastings, Eleanor repeated to herself, wondering if that might be where the distraught owners of 38 Whittlesey Street were headed. Hastings, just to the east of Bexhill and slightly further away Eastbourne, according to her *AA Big Road Atlas*, which she kept not in the car but with the cookery books in the kitchen. The heart of the south coast. The train doors shut with more hydraulic puffing and the engine whined a few pitches higher than its stationary murmur and the train began to pull out of Waterloo East with a shudder, leaving an echoey clank clanking of electricity to trail the 19.40 from Charing Cross – 19.43 from Waterloo East – due to arrive at Hastings at 21.17, according to Connex South Eastern's endlessly enthusiastic platform managers. She had never been to Hastings, or Orpington, she had never even caught a train from Waterloo East, and she decided she would, once, before they moved.

'Clay,' said Eleanor, 'do you think it would be worse to lose a child than never to have one?'

'Uhmm. Uhmm?'

'Do you think it would be worse to lose a child, you know, if they died – I don't know why I bother.'

'What, what are you talking about?'

'You heard.'

'How can I possibly answer that?' Clay said. He was angry and he carelessly folded his newspaper and threw it hard across the sofa so it hit the arm with more of a splatter than a flutter. He stood up with an empty wineglass in his hand, a drying red smear circling the bottom, only to pause, shaking slightly, as if he had reached a tricky altitude too quickly and was waiting for enough oxygenated blood to make it to his head and steady him. He walked towards Eleanor, who was leaning against the door to the kitchen. She was motionless, staring at the floor with her arms crossed, her hair falling forward and shading her pale cheeks and eyes, so she couldn't see much more than a column of smoke-tinged air and a patch of scruffy rug slightly forward of her feet. He reached out and caressed the underneath of her chin with his fingers – the way he had always presumed she liked, but she didn't much, finding it somehow demeaning – trying to lift her head. She eventually gave in, looked at her husband, the veined whites of his greeny-blue eyes, his reddening, puffy cheeks, his fleshy nose with the few tough black hairs poking out at odd angles, his receding grey hair, which was still bushy at the back and slightly too long, because he thought that he might as well grow what he had left. He leant forward, clasped her shoulders, raised himself on to the tips of his toes – he was an inch and a half shorter than her – and kissed her heavily moisturised forehead. 'I'm sorry, sweetheart,' he said, his breath smelling faintly of wine and strongly of cigarettes, a metallic smell, before backing away and heading into the kitchen.

Eleanor watched him move to the wine rack – his swelling stomach and chest stuffed into a soft blue fraying shirt, his saggy cords hiding his scrawny bottom – select a bottle, open it, and replenish his glass. And she found herself thinking he was still attractive, at least from a distance and with his clothes on. Beyond the pudginess, which had recently begun to worsen, he had a distinctive, characterful face, and in a way she liked his hair being a bit too long – it gave him an irreverence. He was fifty-three. Then maybe she was kidding herself, looking for something that might once have been there, imagining it still was, if only slightly tarnished. Though, she thought, perhaps self-deception can have its advantages, something like a safety net to keep you from hitting the ground at the low points, to keep you alive and together. Was it so bad to look for something that was not there, believing it was? Because so much had gone into it and it was easier that way. Though there were days when she felt the net just wasn't there and she hit the floor, not fatally but hard enough to wind her and make her not want to go back up and try again. Times when she felt unbearably numb. She was forty-two, jobless, childless, and tired. Life seemed to be rapidly closing in on her.

She stepped into the kitchen where nothing worked properly and everything was coming away from its hinges and the walls, found a glass and poured herself some wine. She didn't drink much, red wine gave her migraines and years of watching Clay had simply put her off it, but she felt she wanted to have a glass now, whatever the consequences. 'I saw a house today,' she said, suddenly buoying her mood with the idea of moving at least.

'A what, sweetheart?'

'A house. It was for sale.'

'Oh yes.' He took a long, slow sip of wine, loudly sucking in air at the same time, as he often did when he was drinking a bottle he particularly liked, or didn't know. 'Why?'

'Because I want to move. I'm fed up with living here.'

'Eleanor, you don't think you're rushing into anything?'

'Rushing into anything? We've been here for fifteen years.'

'Exactly. We can't just up and leave after all that time. Let's think about this properly.' He took another lengthy, gurgling sip. 'Where was this house anyway?'

'Whittlesey Street.'

'Whittlesey Street? That's not much of a move.'

'It's this house I'm fed up with. Not the area.' Though as she said that she wondered whether perhaps she was fed up with the area too – the darkness of the narrow, treeless streets. The commuters who poured between Waterloo and the offices on the other side of Blackfriars Road so at rush hour it could even be a struggle to get out of the house. The nosiness of the neighbours. The fastidiousness of the residents' association, of which Clay was once a committee member but never made it to chairman. The scrap metal man's fork-lift truck. The industrial-strength vacuum cleaner of the garage, worse than any car revving, and the respraying unit. The railway, of course. The King's Arms at closing time. The fact that there was no supermarket anywhere near – or a park. Just a continuous shriek of sound, a high-pitched shuddering, which had long ceased to be exciting.

'What was it like?' Clay said.

'Depressing. Tragic really. I think something awful had happened there. I suppose it was in quite good condition. There was all this religious stuff everywhere. Crosses, pictures of Jesus.'

'What number?'

'Thirty-eight.'

'Thirty-eight, thirty-eight. Must be between Windmill Walk and Theed Street. Don't think I've ever come across the people.'

'It was no bigger than here either.'

'We don't need a bigger house.'

17

'Of course we do. This place is far too small Clay. We're completely on top of each other. And there's so little room for anyone to stay. The garden's tiny. Nowhere for children to play.'

'We don't have any children.'

Eleanor saw she had finished her wine and wondered for a moment whether she should have another, before helping herself. 'We could get a fortune for this house at the moment.'

'Yeah, they say property prices are going up again.'

'Clay, we could get well over two hundred thousand pounds, perhaps as much as two thirty, two forty even. And I could put in some of my redundancy money. Think what we could afford.'

'We've been lucky, we bought at the right time. But Eleanor, we've got to live off something. My business is not exactly booming at the moment. I can't seem to get my hands on the sort of equipment I used to. There are too many people involved. When I started there were perhaps half a dozen serious camera dealers in London. There must be twenty or thirty now. Plus, you know I've borrowed a lot of money over the last few years. The recession hit me hard. It's still hitting me. This house is really our only tangible asset.'

'I'm not going to give up already.' She sipped her wine. It tasted bitter. 'Christ, I've only seen one house. Okay, it wasn't great, but no one's going to find what they want that easily.'

'Sweetheart, perhaps you should concentrate on looking for another job. It might be of more use right now. Maybe it's upset you more than you think. It can't be nice being sacked.'

'I wasn't sacked. I was made redundant. There's a difference. They paid me to go. They thought I was worth something.' She sighed, clutching her glass tighter, wondering how much harder she would have to squeeze it to break it.

Clay stubbed out his cigarette and walked over to Eleanor, put his hand on her shoulder and raised his swelling, loose body to kiss her gently on the forehead for the second time that evening – a cloud of cigarette smoke coming with him, reminding Eleanor why she gave up smoking. 'If you want to move sweetheart, that's fine, of course we will, only please think about the cost. We don't want to be stuck with a bloody great house mortgaged to the hilt. There is only you and me, unless you're planning for your mother to come to live with us. If that's the case count me out.'

'Do you think that's likely?'

'And don't forget my shop's in Clerkenwell. I don't want to spend forever commuting. I'm not the type. It's all right for you, you don't have to go anywhere any more. You don't have that hassle.'

'Clay, give me a bloody chance.'

'It is pretty convenient here,' he said. 'The more I think about it the more I'm not so sure how adaptable I am. I'm not getting any younger. Besides, I'm very fond of this house. Don't you remember how pleased we were when we found it? We knew we wanted it instantly. Maybe it just needs redecorating. A coat of paint here and there. Some new carpet. We could sort the kitchen out.'

'Clay, I'm not happy here any more. I want to move. It's as simple as that.' She left the room as the 21.43 took off with a hiss and puff and a clank, making the window-panes trill, and Eleanor's empty glass shift on the kitchen table, fraction by fraction, towards the edge. She ran up the stairs heavily, a blast of wind, the vortex left by the train perhaps, finding her as she reached the turn in the stairs. She was hungry, but tiredness and a welling dull ache in her womb were more pressing.

She entered the bathroom and ran the taps, hoping the steam would help warm the room. She slipped out of her clothes, which were loose fitting but well cut, unhooked her bra, shook it off her arms leaning forward, stepped out of her knickers and reached for her dressing gown. Steam was beginning to build and the mirror above the sink misted over, softening her face and the surrounding frame of dark hair that fell on to the upturned collar of the ghostly white towelling. She cleansed her face, turned off the taps, felt the water temperature, clumsily getting half her sleeve wet as well. She quickly hoisted the dressing gown around her waist, sat on the toilet, had a long, spluttering pee, wiped herself, checked the toilet paper for blood – there was none – stood up, pulled off the gown and gingerly climbed into the bath, kneeling before unfolding her legs in front of her and sliding under on her bottom right up to her neck, careful not to get her hair too wet.

The hot water instantly relieved the cramp. And she wondered whether her sudden anxiousness to move had anything to do with the fact that her period was coming. She had never really suffered from premenstrual tension and she thought it unlikely, particularly as her periods, which were never large, seemed to have been getting even smaller and more irregular over the last six months or so. She believed this was due to the stress of thinking she was going to lose her job and then actually losing it.

She had worked for a photographic library for nearly ten years, joining shortly after Clay and she were married. The outfit was based in Clerkenwell – as well as Clay Mitchell Collectable Cameras. She was a senior cataloguer and was responsible for buying rights, dealing over time with all the fields the library covered from fashion to food. She was laid off when the place was bought by a larger library and rationalised. This had happened three months ago and she still couldn't bring herself to visit Clay's shop, as she had done almost daily over the past decade, for fear of bumping into old work colleagues in the street who would ask her what she was doing now, or worse express pity on her. She hated having been made redundant. She couldn't help feeling ashamed and angry and was quite unwilling at the moment to look for a new job, or even for freelance work. It was only the second proper place she had worked after college, the other being a small, specialist Chelsea-based auctioneer, where she had first come across Clay. Then Clay had been one of London's leading collectable camera dealers. He regularly bought at the camera, photographic equipment and photography sales, eventually getting to know a shy, pale young woman called Eleanor who was responsible for the illustrations in the auction house's catalogues.

Eleanor sat up, she hadn't yet soaped herself, so her body was perfectly clear. She looked down at her wet breasts, not as firm as they once were but still small and shapely, at her pubic hair floating in the swaying water. She pulled the soap off a ledge by the taps, dipped it in the water and ran it along her arms, the back of her neck, her breasts and gently over her stomach, before sinking her body into the water and clouding it. Eventually she climbed out of the bath, seeing steam rise from her. She dried herself, put on her dressing gown again with its still damp sleeve, cleaned her teeth and covered her face with a thin layer of expensive hypo-allergenic toner, also a present from her sister. The cramp had returned since she had been out of the warm water and resting her foot on the edge of the bath she pressed against her lower stomach. Slowly she curled her index finger into her vagina, wiggling it very slightly. She quickly pulled it out and bringing it up to eye level saw a tiny smear of dark blood on her nail. It had recently occurred to her that there might be another reason why her periods were becoming lighter and lighter. But she couldn't contemplate it seriously. She was only forty-two. And she longed to have a child – suddenly more than ever.

She often thought how odd it was that Clay and she were brought together by photography, that both their careers were intrinsically connected to it, yet neither of them took pictures – she used to but didn't any more. She wondered whether it was because they were increasingly afraid of recording the past, the gaps in it, what they knew they had missed out on.

Before leaving the bathroom she inserted a Tampax, thinking surely the flow will increase. She was too old for accidents.

Wind roars down Roupell Street taking with it the litter and butt-ends, the Coke cans and grit. Leaves blown in from elsewhere. Roof tiles and larger objects start to take off in swirling, unpredictable patterns – clattering and banging against the asphalt and brick and unsteady cars. Streetlights begin to bend and uproot, tearing the pavement, while the bulbs shatter, filling the air with glistening fragments of glass. Doors and windows work themselves away from surrounding sills and mortar with a terrible beating intensity. Purple clouds, picked out by the flaky lights of Greater London, churn and tumble over each other. And out of this storm, this tempest, suddenly appears the young woman, hanging on to her scrolled degree certificate and flat hat, her bushy hair billowing. She loses the hat first, the certificate shortly disappearing after it, then she too is gone in a flash like a cheap magician's trick.

Eleanor took a long, uneasy moment to wake fully. Something hard was pressing against her lower back. She didn't move immediately, not sure what it was, or even where she was. However, Clay's snoring soon filled the room, shaking not just his body but the whole of the bed as he exhaled, and she knew where she was. She reached behind her and felt his erect penis poking through the fly in his pyjamas. It was hot and dry and she could feel the blood pumping through it. She pulled her hand away and smiled to herself, knowing how much he would have loved to have been conscious now. For the last two or three years he had had trouble getting erections. They rarely had sex, but not just because of Clay's impotency – long before this became an issue they had both lost interest. Eleanor's failure to get pregnant had simply put her off, while Clay seemed quietly to acquiesce. Rose, her younger sister, couldn't understand it. She had told Eleanor she ought to have an affair, or even leave Clay, but Eleanor had stuck with him, not always fully understanding why – wondering whether she just wasn't a very passionate person. She didn't think Clay had had any affairs, though she wasn't completely sure, not knowing what she would think if he had – if she would really mind.

However, Eleanor had a feeling this lengthy period of calm and understanding, or perhaps it was really a state of not trying to understand, of not looking at anything too hard, was coming to an end. She turned on to her back and opened her eyes. A streetlight's yellowy haze curled around the curtain and fell on the corner of the duvet in a fuzzy band. She was beginning to realise she had accepted things too easily. That she had somehow lost control of her life.

A wave of heat shot through her, instantly bringing a sweat to her forehead. She climbed out of bed panicking and short of breath, her nightdress twisted and tight around her waist. She pulled it free as she stepped away from the bed, while Clay remained in his noisy, fitful slumber, quite unaware of his wife's erratic departure from his side, her state of mind or his lost chance of a quick, once-in-a-blue-moon screw. Despite the dimness Eleanor quickly found her dressing gown on the back of a chair, where she always threw it, and walked out of the room. As she descended the stairs a silence came with her, deepening step by step. The breakfast room – as the estate agent would no doubt have referred to it, but which had always been so much more than that – was quite inhospitable at this hour. The overhead light didn't improve the atmosphere and she turned on a side lamp instead. She waited for a train, the comforting puff and hiss, the spacy Tannoy call, the clank and after-clank of electricity. But there was just silence and a growing sense that she was quite alone. She walked over to the window, moving close enough so the reflection from the lamp didn't interfere, and peered up at the sky. Watching the swell and echo of artificial light recede as the night, a deep starless black, began to bear down on her.

She suddenly turned and hurried out of the room, up to the bathroom, where she sat on the toilet, leant forward and with her right hand tugged on the Tampax cord. She felt as if she were pulling herself inside out, the whole of her lower body smarting. The Tampax slowly came clear and she closed her legs, squeezing them together trying to dissipate the pain, while she examined it. There was the faintest blot of something that looked darker than blood at the distressed furry tip. That was all. She dropped it in the toilet, stood, and removing her robe dressed in the clothes she had carelessly left on top of the old wicker dirty-washing basket when she had had a bath earlier. She grabbed a coat from the rack in the hall by the front door and let herself out of the house into the still, charged night air – far too early for trains and commuters, and sleepless lone women.

The fake Victorian streetlights, which had recently sprung up all over the Waterloo conservation area, were pretty useless and kept much of Roupell Street in the dark. The murmur and more daunting crack and whoop of the city was beginning to fill the air above the soft scuffing of Eleanor's hasty footsteps. She tried to concentrate on her breathing, calming it, as she turned left into Theed Street, not entirely conscious of why she was going this way. A couple of houses had upstairs lights on, but the curtains were drawn so she couldn't see in even if she moved out into the middle of the road to improve the angle. She wondered whether she might happen to stumble across another estate agents' hoarding she had somehow missed in daylight and which was advertising her dream house – three or four bedrooms, a couple of bathrooms, a dining room, a bright comfortable sitting room, a warm kitchen, a playroom, a large garden with trees to climb and bushes to hide in. Much, indeed, as she remembered the house she had grown up in. But there were none on Theed Street, of course, none anywhere near here, so she cut back to Whittlesey Street, slowing as she approached number 38. She thought the place was in darkness, though as she drew closer she could discern faint light through the curtains in the sparse front room, the room with the picture of Jesus hanging above the mantelpiece. The light was flickering. Prayer light, Eleanor thought.

She hurried on, passing Windmill Walk and reaching Cornwall Road, where she paused. To her right, past St Patrick's Montessori, she could see the odd car traversing Stamford Street, and beyond that a corner of the IBM building and the top of the London Television Centre tower. The river was obscured, though Eleanor could sense its presence – the twang of brine, the way it seemed to suck at the night echoes. Up on her left, stretching over Cornwall Road, were the enclosed walkways leading to the Waterloo East platforms. Something caught her eye below and it took her a moment to realise a light had just come on in Konditor & Cook, the fancy patisserie which stood on the corner of Cornwall Road and Roupell Street. Eleanor headed for it, seeing a couple of men in cooks' whites inside. She waved but they didn't wave back and she thought they probably hadn't seen her. A smell of fresh dough stayed with her along Roupell Street as she walked home, the sky beginning to brighten, thinking she would treat herself to a slice of Konditor & Cook banoffee pie later that morning – well, she hardly ever bought any cakes from there – and then work out where she would look next.

63 Lillieshall Road, SW4

'Mum,' she said, 'I'm fine. Stop worrying. Of course I am eating enough.'

'How's Clay?'

'He's okay. Same as ever.'

'How's his chest? I wish he'd give up smoking. Can't you make him?'

'Mum, he's fifty-three. It's up to him. Besides, I've never been able to make him to do anything.'

'It's such a pity'

'Everything all right with you?'

'Yes, I suppose so. Nothing changes here. When are you coming to visit?'

'I don't know – when we've got time. I think we're going to move.'

'Move?'

'Yes.'

'But I thought you were happy where you are. It's such a sweet little house. And you've been there for so long.'

'Exactly. We've been here forever. We need a change Mum.'

'Maybe losing your job has unsettled you. It would be quite understandable.'

'Don't, you're beginning to sound like Clay.'

'What does he think about moving? I shouldn't think he's very keen on the idea.'

'He's coming round to it.'

'Well, where are you going to move to? You know you can both always come to live with me for a while if you get stuck. There's plenty of room. Seriously, darling. Buckinghamshire's not that bad.'

'No thanks Mum. Clay wouldn't commute, apart from everything else.' Eleanor held the receiver away from her and sneezed.

'Have you got a cold, darling?'

'No, no. It's just some dust or something. I looked at a house near here the other day, actually. But it wasn't right.'

'Eleanor, for God's sake, if you are going to move you might as well move to a decent area.'

'I thought you thought it was okay here. You always said how convenient it was.'

'Yes, but it's so noisy, isn't it? And polluted. And there are so few trees about. I couldn't live anywhere with so little greenery.'

'What do you expect? It is central London, not Buckinghamshire – thank God.'

'There's no need to be rude, darling, I'm only trying to help.' She paused, waiting perhaps for Eleanor to say something, but Eleanor didn't, so she said, 'There are places that are not quite so in the thick of it, aren't there? Like Richmond?'

'That's miles away.'

'But Eleanor you're not working at the moment. Maybe you could find a job out there, or work from home like your sister.'

'Clay still has to get into town. Look, I'm not going to start talking about work. It's a separate issue.'

'Well, what about Clapham – it has a common, doesn't it? Or Dulwich? There's a lovely park there. I had a friend who lived in Dulwich. I thought it was super.'

'I don't know. I can't say either have occurred to me.'

'Perhaps I'd better come up and give you a hand.'

'No, no Mum, really. It's not necessary.'

'Eleanor, you know I can pop up any time. It's no trouble.'

'No, please.'

'How's Rose? I haven't heard from her for ages. I wonder if they've been away? She never lets me know what she's doing – not like you darling. Does she know about your plans?'

'I shouldn't think so – I haven't told her.'

'Surely she can help. She knows all about houses, doesn't she?'

'Mum, I don't want to trouble her with this. She's got the kids and everything.'

'They must be back at school by now.'

'She does work as well.'

'I don't know why she struggles with it. It's not as if she has to, Mark earns so much money.'

'Perhaps because she enjoys it. Some of us like working.'

'I'm sorry Eleanor, that was insensitive of me. Look, I'll pop up soon. We can at least go and have some lunch – you're probably not getting out enough.'

'Mum I've got to go. I'll speak to you soon. Bye.'

Dulwich, Eleanor thought, was probably too far so she looked for Clapham in the index, finding *Clapham Common, North Side, South Side, West Side*, and opened the *A – Z* at the appropriate place. The green triangle was immediately clear and looking closer, wondering for a moment whether she needed reading glasses, the ponds came slowly into focus – *Long, Mount, Eagle* and *Cock*, followed by the *Tennis Courts*,

Bandstand, the *Rec. Grd.*, the *Pav.*, *WC* and *Playground*. She also noticed three schools in the streets to the north of the Common, two south and one west. A library, a post office and a hospice. She couldn't remember the last time she had passed by the Common, they had no friends who lived in Clapham, so she thought it must have been when Clay and she had driven to Southampton to catch an overnight ferry to France for their last proper holiday, three and a half years ago. Maybe they had been to Midhurst or Wittering for the day since then. But they usually just went to Buckinghamshire to visit Eleanor's mother if they went out of town at all, and that meant going via Marylebone Road. Clay's parents had lived in Suffolk, but they stopped going there after they died, within months of each other the year before the French holiday.

She suddenly remembered being in France, driving on one of those typical poplar-lined roads – maybe she was just imagining it from having seen too many French films – with the sunlight harsh and throbbing, flickering through the trees on to the smooth black surface, making it painful to look ahead, because the view promised so much, but in reality was just hard and foreboding and endless. Perhaps, it now occurred to her, she was still on that road. Clay used to inspire her. He was bright. Too bright, she often thought, for running a second-hand camera shop – he didn't believe in struggling for a living, he wasn't career-minded. Maybe that was part of his charm. She hadn't been able to place him when she first met him. He'd seemed so unusual. He'd both unnerved and excited her.

Eleanor closed the *A-Z*, having first folded down the corner of the Clapham Common page, and put it into her bag. She picked up the car keys, which were beside the telephone on a small table in the hall, pulled on her coat and left the house. It was late morning and Roupell Street was as quiet as it ever got mid-week, with the lunchtime rush yet to happen and surprisingly no noise coming from the scrap metal merchant's or the garage, and Eleanor thought maybe it's not so bad here, maybe I'm being stupid wanting to move. But the feeling only lasted a few seconds. The sky was bright with the odd rolling cloud. There was a stiff breeze hinting at the colder weather to come, a seasonal change, but the sun was still strong and warm, playing on the rooftops and the aerials and the lead flashing. The pale London brick. Perhaps Mum is right, perhaps we need green spaces more than we realise.

The Common appeared suddenly on her right as she swept through Clapham Old Town in the ten-year-old, dull red Citroën BX, passing the Croydon-bound double-deckers badly parked around The Polygon, and on to The Pavement in the heart of the one-way system – having taken the back route through the smarter parts of Stockwell and along Larkhall Rise, lined with spectacular turning trees. She flipped down the sunshade as she pulled directly into the path of the sun rounding the scruffy junction by Clapham Common tube. Not knowing where to go she simply stuck in the lane she was in and went with the traffic as it straightened up on South Side – the Common still opening up on her right, but with the sun now falling across her. The air over the Common appeared to be heavily stained with greens, russets and coppery blues, as though it were coming through a stained glass window. People and dogs were walking through this colour, this broad drifting light.

She turned right before Clapham South tube into The Avenue. The road was thick with tyre-pressed leaves and she felt as if she were being pushed on by the low sunlight. She accelerated, and by the time she had to bear left where West Side met North Side in another one-way system she was touching forty-five mph. She braked hard, causing the car behind to hoot, but she thought he shouldn't have been so fucking close. Some children were playing football on the patch of ground she was now circumnavigating. They looked to Eleanor to be about seven or eight. The game appeared to be properly organised, with the children either in blue or red soccer shirts. She spotted the referee, or teacher, just as she was starting to loop back along North Side towards Clapham Old Town, still without really thinking where she was going, where she should start looking – unable to pull out of the flow. The teacher was tall and balding and wore glasses and a thick pullover, and lumbered across the makeshift pitch. The ball shot into the air, much higher than she imagined boys that age could kick anything. But then she didn't know any seven- or eight-year-old boys. Rose's children were five and six and a half – Sarah and James.

The traffic eased and she slowed considerably, passing the grand North Side houses and a gap through which she caught the four gleaming chimneys of Battersea Power Station rising uselessly into clear blue sky, thinking this'll do. But she couldn't see anywhere to stop and before she knew it she found herself back by the badly parked buses. A car on her inside forced her to keep going when she was on the verge of pulling over. She missed a couple of further stopping points but managed to avoid a repeat trip around the Common and keeping left passed an estate agents she hadn't noticed earlier, before finally getting out of the traffic by turning into a side road.

The road, Lydon Road, was full of large, red-brick Victorian houses. There were few trees or shrubs and no parking spaces, and she drove on lightly tapping the clammy steering wheel until she hit a T-junction. Looking left down this road of similar houses she could see the traffic shifting along North Side into the Old Town, the way she had come a few moments earlier, so she turned right, shortly finding herself at another T-junction. She pulled out slowly before stopping sharply in the middle of Lillieshall Road – she was facing the street sign attached to someone's garden wall. Mature trees arched above her while shrubs spilled on to the pavements. She picked out a rowan, an acacia, a mahonia, a cotoneaster, plus a couple of honeysuckles and rosemarys before everything began to blur. Her right eye was suddenly watering. The driver's window was most of the way down and she presumed a piece of dirt or a fly or something must have blown in. Though her eyes had been watering a lot lately and she wondered whether it might have been because she needed glasses, that she had been straining them. She managed to get the car over to the kerb and climbed out, blinking and dabbing her eye with a handkerchief – the quietness of the street taking a while to become apparent. Eleanor even thought she could discern a freshness in the air, because she was sniffing more than looking. It was quite unlike the stuff that drifted over Waterloo, more reminiscent of air found in Buckinghamshire, or even Hertfordshire where she had been brought up, until she was twelve anyway. It seemed almost country air.

Her sight began to recover, the thing dislodged, if it had ever been there. The road was perfect, she quickly realised – the houses being mostly early Victorian, some four storeys, and set back behind small front gardens bursting with greenery. It was a street so unlike Roupell Street and so like where she had been born that she was suddenly nervous of venturing further, wondering whether it was purely by chance that she had found herself here. So quickly.

Virginia creeper fronted the house with the estate agents' board. The board was tied to the gatepost – the rickety-looking wrought-iron gate was open and for a moment Eleanor thought she should go up and press the bell, and that if she did she would surely recognise the trill. The creeper was burnt and brilliant and shot up the building, bouncing light like sunset back on to her and the pale dry pavement. The house where she had spent the first twelve years of her life, in Bishop's Stortford, had been covered in Virginia creeper too, she remembered. She edged forward trying to see into the windows, but she caught nothing of the interior, or any life inside, and she stepped backwards feeling something brush against her, more than a rush of wind. Someone shouted, 'Careful.' It was a female voice, alarmed. Eleanor spun round to see a woman struggling to keep a small pram upright. Two wheels had gone over the high kerb and a crossbar was grating on the concrete as she pulled at it, but the baby inside wasn't stirring, seemingly unaware of nearly being tipped on to the road.

'Sorry,' Eleanor said, moving to assist the woman. But the woman shook her head as if to say, no, I don't need your help, and she quickly got the thing back level on the pavement and hurried off – the pram wobbling from left to right for a time with a faint tickety-tick as the wheels bumped from one paving slab to the next. Eleanor thought the woman was about her age, indeed she had been struck by it, and there was something else about her that had reminded Eleanor of herself. The colour of her hair? Her eyes? Perhaps it had been her mouth – she wasn't sure. She watched them until they had disappeared, the woman still obviously unnerved. Disconcerted herself, Eleanor turned and went in the other direction. However, her mind soon filled with the thought of the house she had just seen, and already knew she wanted.

'Lillieshall Road, Lillieshall Road,' the estate agent repeated. 'It's a house, is it?'

'Yes,' said Eleanor.

'Not a flat?'

'The sign didn't specify.'

'I think you need to speak to Jenny, over there. She deals with houses. I'm flats.' She pointed to a young woman sitting at a desk against the far wall. She was the only other person in the hot, harshly lit office, though there were five or six desks, covered, Eleanor noticed, with laminated maps like table maps. Jenny was talking on the phone, cradling the receiver between her shoulder and chin, so her head was at an uncomfortable-looking angle. Eleanor walked over to her trying to make herself noticed. She stooped a little as if this might somehow raise Jenny's head, but Jenny didn't look up, not registering Eleanor's presence at all. She was using her free hands to order and re-order a stack of paper. Eleanor thought she was about thirty, perhaps younger. Her hair, which had clearly been dyed blonde, was held back by a thick purple hair-band.

'Yep, yep,' she said into the phone, her voice sounding slightly hoarse from smoking or maybe just speaking too much, 'but they're ready to close now . . . No. I don't think they'll wait any longer. I thought everything was in place . . . I've stalled them for about as long as I think possible . . . No . . . I thought the survey was approved . . . Abbey . . . Yes . . . So you're now not sure . . . Great . . . Yes they are going to chuck in the carpets and the freezer, as you requested . . . Good . . . You'll lose this house, and so will I . . . The vendors want to be out by the end of October . . . Have you any idea of what's happening in the market right now? . . . You're very lucky to be in the position you're in . . . Look stop fucking us about and get back to me first thing tomorrow morning with a yes or a no. There might be plenty of other estate agents you can piss around, but this isn't one of them. Okay?'

Eleanor tried to look as if she hadn't been listening and peered down at her feet. She was wearing a pair of black low-heeled lace-ups. The carpet was a pale blue and she followed it to the skirting, then up the walls, which were a darker blue, the wallpaper incorporating the estate agent's logo in yet another shade. The air was close and smelt of crisps and cheap perfume. It suddenly occurred to Eleanor that she should ring Clay, that maybe she could persuade him to take an hour off from work, leave Charles, his assistant, in charge for once, and join her. She obviously had to get things moving as quickly as possible. Whatever was happening in the market right now was not in her favour.

She could feel she was beginning to perspire, her chest and neck and face were tingling, and she thought she must be coming out in blotches. She wanted to take her jacket off but didn't want to draw attention to her condition. She was sure Jenny had noticed her now, and the other woman by the door. She found a seat in front of a nearby, empty desk. The heat seemed almost instantly to dissipate and she could have shivered as she sat concentrating on where she was – thinking about the house, imagining the interior, a copy of the house she had been brought up in. She found she had been clenching her fists and when she opened them the palms of her hands had gone white. She was sure 63 Lillieshall Road was meant for her, because she knew you didn't just stumble upon houses like that, that meant so much. And she felt her body relax further, the temperature regulate, and her mind fill with no thought, but a blank, a light blue blank, many shades whiter than the carpet – like a clear sky at noon when the sun's at its most powerful, taking away almost all trace of colour.

'Yep?' Jenny said loudly, 'can I help?'

Eleanor stood up unsteadily, realising Jenny was addressing her, and moved towards her desk. 'Yes. The house on Lillieshall Road?' Eleanor didn't think the hair-band suited her, it made her look too pale.

'I'm afraid it's under offer.'

'What?'

'Sorry?'

'Under offer?' Eleanor couldn't immediately comprehend what the estate agent meant.

'Yep. It was only on the market for a couple of weeks. Though I'm not surprised, it's a lovely house.'

As Eleanor began to understand the situation, she said, stepping forward so her legs were almost pressing against Jenny's desk, 'But it's just what I've been looking for.' She could feel cold sweat under her arms.

'I'm sorry. We have got a number of other, similar priced properties.'

'What if the offer doesn't come off?' Eleanor was thinking of what she had overheard the estate agent say on the phone.

'Oh, I'm sure it will. We're a long way down the line.'

'Could I at least view it? Surely nothing's completely certain yet.'

'We have stopped showing it.'

'I won't take very long.'

'Look, we're extremely busy. Have you gone through our list? Maybe there's something else you'd like to see.'

'No, I shouldn't think so. I've a very strong feeling about this house – being the right one.'

'Today's chocker.'

'I'm free all week.' Eleanor knew she must have sounded desperate, but she didn't care.

'I'll see what I can do. Let me get you the list anyway.' Jenny stood up, surprising Eleanor by how short she was. She was wearing a tight black skirt and blue blouse, which must have been a company regulation because it was the same blue as the walls, but without the logos. She had a large bottom and thick calves, Eleanor saw, as she went to a bank of metal filling cabinets. She spent ages clanging drawers and files before she came back holding out an armful of particulars. She dumped the pile on her desk and began to hand sheets to Eleanor without sitting. 'Here's our complete list of properties over a hundred and fifty K, and some individual properties I think you should consider. Taybridge Road, just two beds but it's in excellent decorative order and on at a good price.' She paused, waiting for Eleanor to catch up with her, pushing a few loose strands of hair back under the band. 'We've got one on Broadhinton Road, which is just behind Lillieshall. They're smaller houses, but charming. This one's got three beds, retains many original features and they've extended the kitchen. Rozel Road, now here's a good opportunity – it's just off North Street, which runs off Old Town towards Wandsworth Road. It's end of terrace, very light and has recently undergone a sympathetic refurbishment. We've got a magnificent house on Larkhall Rise, it needs a bit of work, but you rarely get anything like it on the market. Though it depends, obviously, on what you can go up to.' She looked expectantly at Eleanor, her eyes slightly red and puffy, as if her contacts were giving her trouble. 'Something's just come on in Orlando Road. But the details aren't quite ready. It's conveniently situated for all the amenities of Old Town and the High Street, plus the tube, of course. Do you work in the City?'

Eleanor looked at Jenny, her sore eyes and purple hairband, which didn't suit her at all, and said, sharply, 'No.'

'A lot of people who live around here do, for the tube, still it's just as handy for the West End. It branches at Kennington. What's your upper limit?'

'My what?'

'Your upper limit – the price you can go up to?'

'Oh, I'm not sure – two hundred and fifty.' Eleanor didn't say thousand, because she thought that would sound as if she wasn't used to dealing with estate agents – they never seemed to say thousand, K, but not thousand – and that she wasn't serious.

'Sorry?'

'I don't know, two seventy.'

'You did realise Lillieshall was on at three five five.'

Eleanor paused. 'Oh. I'm sure that's not a problem.'

'Perhaps you could clear this up before I try to arrange a viewing. We are extremely busy. We don't want to waste everybody's time, do we?' Jenny looked at Eleanor and smiled tightly, her lips pressed firmly together.

'I said, I was sure that was not a problem,' Eleanor said. 'We could go up to that.'

Jenny's phone went and she picked it up immediately. 'Yep,' she said. 'Paul, hi, hi . . . Okay. How's Islington? Yep . . . Yep, love to . . . No, no, browsers . . . Yep, things have been moving pretty quickly here, too. Not as quick as the papers would have people believe.' She started to laugh, sat down and cradled the phone as before, but this time she began playing with her hair, not a stack of particulars, removing the purple hair-band altogether and curling strands around her fingers. 'No, really? God, I loved that film. Excuse me a minute.' She looked at Eleanor, opening her red puffy eyes wide, as if she were expecting Eleanor to say something. But Eleanor remained silent, so Jenny said, removing the phone from her neck and holding her hand over the mouthpiece, 'Why don't you leave your details with Susan over there,' she pointed to the woman sitting by the desk near the door who Eleanor had first spoken to, 'and we'll get back to you?' She returned the phone to her ear, the swivel chair creaking as she made herself more comfortable. 'Paul, sorry—'

'Clay,' Eleanor said, 'I've found the house.'

'That was quick,' he said, 'hang on a minute.'

Eleanor looked through the smudged panes of the phone box. The sun had just gone in – a great bank of dark cloud was moving south, slipping over Old Town and the edge of the Common, making the trees lose colour and rustle, making them seem hostile. The wind had freshened too, and a discernible chill was seeping into the phone box, but it wasn't enough to take away the smell of stale urine and damp tobacco. The earpiece had been warm when Eleanor had picked it up. 'Clay?' she said, suddenly desperate to get out of the confined space. 'Clay?'

'Sorry, sorry sweetheart, I had to deal with a customer. What were you saying?'

'This house, it's perfect. Why don't you come up to have a look, now?'

'Now?'

'Yes. You'll be able to see it from the outside at least and we could have some lunch to talk about it.'

'Eleanor, that's impossible. I've got someone coming to see me at two – he's coming all the way from Belgium. We can have a look at the weekend, surely. What's the urgency?'

'Have you got any idea what the property market's doing here?'

'Where's here, anyway?'

'Clapham.'

'You're joking? Clapham? I'm not living in fucking Clapham. Who do you think I am?'

'Clay,' Eleanor said. 'Don't be stupid. You can at least look at it – for me if nothing else.'

'How much is it?'

'I'm not sure, about three hundred.'

'What, three hundred thousand pounds? Eleanor, have you gone mad?'

'I'll speak to you later, I've run out of money,' she said, watching the LCD display start to flash, INSERT MORE MONEY, INSERT MORE MONEY, and without saying anything further she hung up. Rain had started to hit the smudged panes at an angle so the drops splayed and left trails like shooting stars, which soon began to obscure her view out further. It rapidly became heavier and started to drum on the roof and the pretty patterns on the windows were wiped out by larger splashes turning into trickles. She stepped outside trying to cover her head with her arm. Rain was bouncing on the pavement now and Eleanor thought there was something tropical about it. A car sped through the rising wet with a long, amplified swish. She spotted a café across the road and headed for it, managing to cross quickly, but stepping in a deep run of water just before the kerb. She wasn't wearing socks and she felt the leather of her right shoe become soft and slimy. 'Fuck,' she said loudly.

Other people had had the same idea and there was confusion just inside the café entrance, made worse by coats and hair being shaken – water was spraying everywhere. Eleanor's hair was soaked, which made it look darker than it was and glisten – prettier than she could have imagined. But she found it simply annoying, the way it was sticking to her face, and she wondered why she hadn't got it cut yet. She found a seat and then tried to dry it with a paper napkin, but the paper fell apart and she gave up, letting the drops slide down her face like fat tears, wiping them eventually with her sleeves. Stretching, she could feel how damp the shoulders of her jacket were, and her trousers on her thighs, which were feeling really itchy. Fucking Clay, she said to herself. When do you ever do anything for me?

'Hello – is anyone sitting here?' Eleanor looked up to see a man pointing at the chair opposite her.

'No, no,' she said, quickly looking away, at the people on the adjacent tables, and for a menu.

'I can't believe this weather,' the man said.

Eleanor glanced across to him again. He had dark, wavy hair, about the colour of hers. It was long, slightly longer than Clay's, and swept back, kept there by the wet, or some lotion – she couldn't tell. He had blue eyes and looked as if he hadn't shaved that morning. He was wearing a brown leather jacket over a faded blue shirt, the same blue as his eyes. Eleanor reckoned he was about her age, perhaps a couple of years younger. She immediately found him attractive – the clearness of his eyes, his fine, strong face, the way he held himself.

'Do you mind?' he said, reaching across for the menu that Eleanor had failed to notice and was face down in the middle of the table.

'No, of course not,' she said, suddenly embarrassed because she didn't normally look at men in such a way and thought she must have been staring. Jazz was coming out of some hidden speakers and she tried to listen to it. But she didn't recognise the piece, jazz wasn't her thing – Clay liked it. There were posters on the walls advertising famous exhibitions by painters such as Miró and Kandinsky and Braque. Thick condensation had built up on the inside of the front windows so it was hard to tell what was happening outside, though people were still clambering in soaked.

'Are you ready to order?' A young waitress had appeared by Eleanor's side. She was wearing jeans and a tight-fitting top, and held a pad and pen ready.

'Oh, just a coffee.' But as soon as Eleanor had said that she realised she was hungry. It was getting on for two. She saw the man opposite was still looking at the menu. 'It's not too late for lunch?' she said, before the waitress had disappeared.

'No, course not. Specials are on the board up there. Shall I come back?'

Eleanor could see the board, though she couldn't quite read what had been handwritten on it in multicoloured chalk. 'Urrgh—'

'I recommend the baked aubergines,' the man said, holding the menu away from his face. 'If you like cheese.'

Eleanor smiled at him, sure her cheeks were flushed – she felt so itchy. 'Okay,' she said to the waitress, 'I'll have the baked aubergines.'

'I have lunch here most days,' the man said.

'Oh,' Eleanor said, quite uncertain whether she really wanted to talk to him.

'I work at home, a couple of streets away. Is this your part of town?'

Eleanor thought she recognised the music now, she'd heard enough of Clay's collection over the years, though the name of the track still escaped her. 'No, but I'm thinking about moving here.' She immediately wondered why she had said, *I'm thinking about moving here*, and not, my husband and I, or we. 'Do you like Clapham?'

'It's been okay. It's good for families. The schools, the primary schools anyway aren't bad – I've got a couple of kids, three.' He said three as if he'd just remembered that he had a third child – raising his eyebrows. 'And there's the Common. Plenty of shops, bars, cafés, that sort of thing. It's handy for the tube. I've been here a while. You know, I'm moving myself. My domestic set-up has changed recently – to say the least – and I'm not going to need such a big place, even if I could afford it. I need the money.' He smiled at her, a smile she didn't quite understand, but it betrayed sadness, or regret anyway.

'I don't have any children,' Eleanor found herself saying, perhaps because he was smiling at her in that way – it unnerved her.

'They certainly make life complicated. No, I love them really. It's who you have them with that's the tricky thing. That's where I went wrong.'

Not wanting to talk about children, not with this man, and certainly not wanting to talk about his relationships, or her own, Eleanor said quickly, 'So where are you going to?'

'I'm not sure. Wherever, it's got to be soon – I think I've just sold my place. It's not easy looking when you're busy. I had thought about going north of the river – you know, somewhere like Islington, or Camden perhaps. A complete change. But I don't know, the more I think about it the more I go off the idea. South London's probably too ingrained, and I don't want to be that far away from the kids. They're moving to Balham – two of them anyway. I wouldn't mind moving a little nearer town, though. It's easy to lose touch working from home.' He paused. 'And I could happily give up the Common – all that dog shit.'

'Don't put me off,' Eleanor said, 'I've just seen my perfect house.'

'Location's the key, if you ask me. You can make a flat, a house into anything you want, given a bit of time and money, and imagination, surely?'

'Not me, I'm crap at that sort of thing.'

'You might have found what you think's this perfect place – if such a thing exists – but you still have to step outside. You can't shut yourself away in it for ever. If the area's not right, forget it. There's not much you can do with a location.'

'No,' said Eleanor, 'I suppose not.' The waitress brought their food, but the baked aubergines were so hot she couldn't tell whether they were any good or not. She had to blow on each forkful for ages before putting it in her mouth. They didn't talk for most of the time they ate, Eleanor blowing on her food and the jazz tinkling away stupidly, and she thought that they had probably spoken about enough already. She found the man rather forthright, oddly sort of how Clay used to be, and she wasn't at all sure how to react to him. His looks, finding him so attractive, making it much harder.

They had coffee and while they were finishing the man said, 'I didn't ask you, where do you live at the moment?'

'Waterloo. Sort of between the station and the South Bank. It's fine, very convenient. Though it's a bit noisy and grimy, and I've been there too long. I need a change.'

'I hadn't thought about Waterloo. Maybe I should have a look there,' he said.

Eleanor laughed, getting up. The man was tall, a good three or four inches taller than her, and slim, without being too skinny. They walked out of the café together. The sun had returned and was playing on the wet road, making it glisten. The Croydon-bound buses were sparkling away as they dripped-dry in the cool after-rain air, and Eleanor blinked in the brightness, suddenly aware that she didn't know this man's name and would probably never see him again. 'Well,' she said, 'I hope you find what you're looking for.'

'Wait a minute,' he said, 'if you've got a place you're selling in Waterloo maybe I'd be interested. You never know – we could always cut out the estate agents' nonsense.' He started to laugh. 'I didn't get your name?' He held out his hand.

Eleanor shook it lightly, still unsure of how to react to him – his manner quite unsettling her. 'Eleanor,' she said.

'Eleanor, I'm Steve. Look, here's my card.' He pulled a card from an inside pocket and handed it to her. 'I should be there for a few more weeks.'

She took the card, but stuffed it straight into her bag without looking at it – because she still felt unnerved and excited in a way. *Eleanor*, the way he had said it. 'Thanks,' she said, trying to smile. She turned and walked in the direction of the car realising that it was herself he was really interested in, not her house in Waterloo, not possibly, not with that tone in his voice and those pale blue eyes. And she wondered how much else of what he had said was actually true, because she was hopeless at judging people, or their real intentions in these situations – they happened so rarely. She knew she should have been pleased that someone so good-looking had, she presumed, tried to pick her up – she wasn't young any more – but she just felt frightened. Some twenty paces on she thought she heard him calling something out, her name? She didn't look over her shoulder, because she knew that unlike before, unlike the few other occasions when someone had flirted with her over the last fifteen years, she couldn't now be sure where it might lead, where she would stop. It was this that scared her, this sense of recklessness, of a growing, wayward excitement – it was so unlike her. Her left shoe was still damp, but her feet tapped on the patchy pavement none the less, audible just to her as the cars and trucks and buses drowned them out for anyone further afield. Steve wouldn't have heard her stepping away. Her heart, her breathlessness, a reluctance, that went with the footfalls.

She kept thinking about the Virginia creeper. The six steps leading up to the front door. The wrought-iron gate with black paint flecking off it and the catch no longer catching. The mahonia and the cotoneaster and the rowan. The airy sway of the road steeped in autumnal foliage. And birdsong. And the distant hum of cars circumnavigating Clapham Common, with its makeshift football pitches and ponds and bandstand, and children's play area crowded with toddlers clambering over the municipal climbing frames. The wavering light playing on the leaf-strewn grass, through trees no longer capable of creating quite the thickness of shadow they could a week or two ago. The four colossal chimneys of Battersea Power Station sometimes glowing and numinous depending on the strength of the sun and the clearness of the backdrop.

The interior of the house was something Eleanor was not yet prepared to run through. She knew exactly what it would be like, of course, but she was saving it – like you might save a happy memory for a time when you didn't have to hurry over it, for a time when you needed it most. She was suddenly aware of Clay entering the kitchen and she moved over to the table and the shopping she had dumped there.

'So,' said Clay, clearing his throat, 'tell me about the house.'

'It's set back from the road, which is tree-lined and seems really quiet. There are steps up to the front door. There's a big bay window and it's covered in Virginia creeper. It's lovely.'

'Okay, and the inside?'

'I thought we could see that together. The estate agent was very busy.'

'You mean you haven't seen it properly?'

'No.'

'And you were going to drag me all the way up from work?'

'I told you on the phone we'd only be able to see the outside. Christ, you can get a pretty good impression from that.'

'I didn't realise you hadn't actually seen it.'

'There's an offer on the place. But it might not go through. There wasn't a message from the estate agents when you got in was there?'

'No, just your mother again, oh and Rose.'

'I didn't think they'd ring. Why are you back so early anyway?' Eleanor started to unpack the shopping. She had thought she would make something special for dinner, even surprise Clay and have it ready by the time he got home. She realised she probably hadn't been easy to live with recently and she wanted to make things better – particularly as she knew how much work she was going to have to put in to get Clay more interested in the idea of moving. Then, as she stood there looking at the food she had bought, thinking of the effort she was going to, she felt Clay hadn't exactly been that easy to live with over the last few months either. Perhaps neither of them was being understanding enough, but at least she was trying to break the impasse – with a couple of poussin and some potato dauphinois, Clay's favourite dish. She didn't know why it was always up to her to try to sort things out. He had stopped buying her flowers ten years ago.

'I had a busy day, what with this guy coming over from Belgium, and to be quite honest I just felt rather tired. I haven't been sleeping well lately.'

'No? Well neither have I.'

Clay moved over to the wine rack. It was three-quarters empty, how it always was. He bent down, groaned, and started to pull bottles out and slide them back again. He went through every one, some twice before making his decision and standing up with it, his face a deep red. He saw what Eleanor was unpacking, sighed, making a sound like a piston, and opened the bottle, pulling the cork out with a pop. He poured himself a glass and said, 'Want some?'

'No, not at the moment.' She was pulling the plastic wrappers off the poussin. Once free she placed them on a baking tray. She knew Clay was watching her and she took her time quartering a lemon and stuffing the pieces into the birds, before lining them up on the tray and sprinkling them with olive oil, dried basil, pepper and salt.

'Sweetheart,' Clay said, 'we can't afford it. There's just no way. I'm sorry.' He took a large sip, a gulp really, not bothering with the swilling and gurgling routine, and swallowing it immediately. He lit a cigarette, knowing Eleanor didn't like him smoking in the kitchen when she was cooking. 'I don't think you quite realise the state of our finances.'

Eleanor looked up from what she was doing. 'What exactly are you saying?'

'How much did you say it was on for?'

'About three hundred – thousand. Perhaps a bit more.'

'We just don't have that sort of money to go throwing around on a new house – whether it's got a bloody bay window or not. To be honest, we'd be pushed to be able to afford something for half that.'

'I don't understand,' she said, 'This house is worth about two hundred and thirty thousand, more probably, and there's my redundancy. We could extend the mortage a bit, surely? Christ, it's not as if we've got any children to look after.'

'Sweetheart, you know I've had to borrow money against the house to keep the business going. You see, as the value has increased I've borrowed a bit more, here and there. At the moment we probably owe more than it's worth, and the business for that matter. We won't be able to get a bigger mortgage, particularly as you don't even have a job at the moment. Anyway, we wouldn't be able to pay it.'

Eleanor looked at the food she was about to put in the oven, watched it go out of focus as her eyes misted over, as she felt a wave of anger, or perhaps it was just a wave of violent, uncontrollable depression, sweep through her. She dropped the baking tray on to the floor and the baby chickens bounced on the worn lino, skidding across it, until they finally came to a stop by the bottom of the cooker, as if they somehow knew where they were meant to end up – a glistening trail of basil-and pepper-speckled oil showing their path. She rushed out of the room, Clay shouting behind her, 'I'm sorry, sweetheart. Please. I'm sorry.'

She could hear him following her, the creak of his joints chiming with the creak of the floorboards, his panting – he was always out of breath. She thought about locking herself in the bathroom but carried on up to the bedroom – she had to lie down, she was dizzy and every muscle in her body ached. She left the light off and flung the door closed behind her, knowing Clay wouldn't come into the room. Her body collapsed on to the bed, which had grown softer over the years and now eased up around her, so despite her exhaustion she had to fidget for a while to get comfortable. But the bed still seemed unsteady, as if it were made of jelly. 'Eleanor, please,' she heard Clay saying from the other side of the door. 'I'm sorry. Look, let's talk about this properly – work out exactly what we've got. It's not that bad. Compared to most people we're extremely lucky. Fuck it. Eleanor?'

After a while Clay went away and the wobbling stopped, and there was a lightness, an ease of movement somehow, and Eleanor found herself being pulled though the interior of 63 Lillieshall Road by Jenny, or another similarly rude estate agent with sturdy little legs moving twice as quick as normal legs did walking – because every second was valuable house-selling time, seeing as the market was really hot right now. And the house was not at all how Eleanor had expected it to be. It was some other people's house. Their things. Their decorating. Their lives.

'Okay,' the Jenny-like estate agent says, 'this is the double reception room.' Her voice coming across with a swiftness, an immediacy. 'As you can see the room has been opened out to maximise both space and light – it now makes a superb entertaining area. Two matching fireplaces, both with gas coal-effect fires. Dwarf cupboards to alcoves with fitted shelves above. TV and telephone points. Ceiling cornicing and mouldings, picture rail. Sash windows to front and rear with shutters. Stripped pine floor.' She taps the floor with the hard leather soles of her brown loafers before bounding out of the room. 'Mrs Mitchell, please, this way.' But Eleanor doesn't follow immediately, her eyes are stuck on the mantelpiece, on a wedding photograph in a stand-up silver frame.

She sees herself in the picture, not how she was when she got married to Clay, not in her early thirties, but how she is now, a decade or so later. And the man she's standing next to, the man she's just married is not Clay. He's so much better looking, standing there in a linen suit and opened-neck shirt, a good few inches taller than her.

'Mrs Mitchell, do hurry please, we haven't got all day.' She's already at the half landing and is calling back. 'Mind the pushchair by the bottom of the stairs. Yes, up here, that's right.' Eleanor starts to climb after her – it is no effort and she feels as if she is floating. 'I'm always keen to get to the bedrooms,' the estate agent laughs, scampering out of Eleanor's view, her voice fading behind her. 'Forget kitchens, you learn more about the occupants of a house from the bedrooms than anywhere else. Believe me.' *Believe me*, she said in a hoarse whisper.

Eleanor follows where she thinks the woman has gone, finding herself in a darkened room at the front of the house. The curtains are shut but daylight is seeping through the fabric and around the edges giving the air a pink, smoky tinge. The estate agent, however, is not in the room. Sure she is nowhere, Eleanor moves over to the bed. A man is lying under the duvet, only his head and bare shoulders are visible. He is asleep. Eleanor is not startled because she knows, somehow, she is in a dream. She stares at him for a long while – his dark hair curling on to the pillow. Slowly he opens his blue eyes. Eleanor starts to undress. Her clothes fall silently to the floor – jacket, trousers, top, underwear. And even though she knows she's dreaming she feels a tightness in her chest as she edges towards the bed – a surge of fear, of excitement. The man lifts the duvet and she slips in naked and their thin bodies reach for each other.

Eleanor felt a hand caressing the back of her neck. She needed to be touched, she needed that comfort, so she let

Clay continue. 'Eleanor,' he whispered. 'Eleanor. Are you awake?' She didn't answer but shifted slightly closer to him so he knew she was. His hand began caressing more of her, trailing lightly down her back, and up, and running on, running down her legs, reaching the backs of her knees, nestling in there, perhaps trying to part her legs. 'You've still got your clothes on sweetheart,' Clay said, his hand moving round her bottom and up her side, his fingers brushing a breast. And despite her top and the looseness of his touch, she could feel her nipples were already hard, and that there was a tingling warmth between her legs. Clay's fingers began to circle her nipple – squeezing it gently. Squeezing it harder.

'We'll find something,' Clay said. 'I'm sorry about the money, but business has been really tough. Even my Belgian mate didn't buy much today and he'd come all that way. I can't seem to get people interested in my stuff any more. Maybe I've lost my touch, that or I'm in the wrong business. I should call it a day and do something completely different.' He coughed, trying to cough lightly, but it came out loud and phlegmy. 'God knows what,' he said swallowing. 'I don't know what I'd be capable of doing. At my age.' He paused, but his fingers continued to play with her nipple. 'Though I have to say I still get excited now and then. I still get that feeling when something really special turns up, like this great IIIa with an unused motor-drive that came in last week. Did I tell you? It's a lovely piece of machinery. The Germans really used to build some fantastic cameras.' Eleanor made no more noise than that of a breath being exhaled and another hurriedly drawn. 'Original boxes and everything.' Clay moved his hand over to her other nipple and began rubbing it between his thumb and forefinger, sandwiched in her clothes. 'I didn't know house prices were going to slump as much as they did. They don't warn you that that's a possibility when they lend you all this bloody money. But I'm pretty well insured up, I've at least seen to that. If I die you'll be okay – don't worry about that. Probably be the best thing to happen.' Eleanor rolled on to her stomach, forcing him to pull his hand away. 'What's the matter?' he said. 'I thought you were enjoying it.'

'No Clay.'

29 Druce Road, SE21

She didn't know whether it was her or Clay – she'd never been pregnant, and as far as she knew Clay had never got anyone pregnant – perhaps it was both of them. They had never found out. They hadn't tried fertility treatment because Clay had a phobia about hospitals and clinics – he hated even going to the doctor. Besides, she knew he wouldn't have been able to address the fact that they had a problem, he had trouble facing up to any adversity. Not that Eleanor ever knew how much Clay really wanted children, they rarely talked about it now – Eleanor didn't see the point, she had long believed that they weren't going to have any. Every so often she felt a sense deep within her that something was missing – more a feeling that she wasn't quite whole – but it wasn't crushing and she thought she'd come to terms with the situation. Until recently. Until the last six months or so when her body started to reject this state and crave something else – wholeness, completeness, children. The full intensity of her longing, stifled and calm for years, had surged forward. Losing her job, she realised, had only exacerbated it. She hadn't said anything to Clay because she had no idea how he would react. Plus she was embarrassed, as if it was quite unnatural, as if she were going mad. She was forty-two and he was fifty-three and she thought couples their age just didn't start families, not after being together for fifteen years.

God, she hated getting older. It wasn't so much the way her body was changing shape, or the proliferation of grey hairs – of normal-coloured hairs in strange places – or the wrinkles and the way her skin was losing its elasticity and starting to sag on her cheeks, and her wrists and her knees, but what went on inside, the stuff she couldn't see that woke her up at night. And it wasn't a gradual thing. It was a shock. It suddenly happened. One moment, she thought, you're in your twenties with everything wide open to you, the next you're fast approaching fifty with great barriers falling all about you. It was like arriving somewhere without remembering how you got there, or even setting off. She wasn't prepared.

She had been flicking through a fashion magazine without taking anything in and she put it down noticing it was months out of date. She didn't pick up another magazine but sipped her coffee which was cool and had an oily film on the surface. A neatly cut hair about a centimetre long was resting on the edge of the saucer and she blew it off, inadvertently in the direction of the girl behind the reception desk. Eleanor hadn't seen her at the hairdressers before. She was very skinny and had short, spiky black hair, which suited her face, making her look even younger than she probably was. She had beautiful cheekbones.

An assistant approached Eleanor, and said, 'Mrs Mitchell, Tina won't be much longer. Can I get you another coffee?'

'No,' said Eleanor, nodding her head, 'no thank you.' The reception area was at the front and Eleanor looked out into Earlham Street. It was windy and the wind was picking up grit and rubbish, swirling it about. People were clasping their coats tighter together, desperately hanging on to bags and flapping newspapers, and Eleanor suddenly thought of the young woman from Whittlesey Street – knowing she shouldn't feel so angry and hopeless about getting older when many people never even got as far as she had. But that thought didn't lift her mood much, because she knew it wasn't the point, because she knew that she couldn't be the only person who felt the way she did. She was sitting awkwardly on an uncomfortable, trying-to-be-trendy bright pink bench – the pile of fashion magazines littered over a matching bright pink coffee table in front of her. She felt foolish and out of place. The hairdressers had recently been revamped and she wasn't at all sure about its new look. She shut her eyes for a moment listening to music she didn't recognise, with the hair-dryers going in the background, plus the shower heads, the phone and the receptionist's squeaky voice announcing the name of the place, proceeding on to days and dates and names of individual stylists who happened to be free when.

'Hello Mrs Mitchell,' Tina said, holding a light blue gown open for her. 'We haven't seen you for a while. Everything all right, is it?'

'Yes,' said Eleanor, standing. 'Yep,' the colour of the gown reminding her of the estate agents in Clapham.

'Why don't you just slip this on,' Tina said, and Eleanor held out her arms obligingly. 'That's the way. Lovely. And if you'd just like to follow me through.' Tina was short and slight and had long blonde hair which fell almost to her waist – Eleanor had always thought it was too long for her. Eleanor was seated in a fancy, state-of-the-art chair at Tina's work station, which was towards the end of the room. Tina stood behind her and said, 'You really haven't been here for some time have you?' Eleanor nodded in agreement. Tina began running her fingers through Eleanor's hair and then with her palms held out cupped the hair, pushing it up, trying to make it look an inch or so shorter the whole way round. 'You normally have it up to about here, don't you?' Eleanor didn't nod this time, or say anything but bit on her bottom lip, thinking. 'A couple of inches or so off should get it back into shape. Shall we get you washed and conditioned?'

'Actually,' Eleanor said, 'I thought I'd try something different.'

'Oh, okay,' said Tina. 'We can certainly have a look. What had you in mind?'

'I'm not sure. I think I'd like it much shorter than usual.'

'If that's what you want.' Tina started to push Eleanor's hair up again, but much higher.

'And so it isn't so neat, I suppose. Sort of, urrm,' Eleanor reached up and tried to ruffle her hair, 'not exactly like this – sharper.'

'Yeah,' said Tina slowly, 'I think I know what you're getting at. Spiky and coming forward slightly. Yeah, I see. You have a great face for it. Okay, let's give it a go. Lovely. Shall we get you washed then?'

Tina led Eleanor to the hair-washing basins and left her there with the assistant who had brought her coffee earlier and who made her sit back in another fancy, state-of-the-art chair, which reclined electronically. With the back of her neck resting on the cold, hard edge of the basin she found she had nowhere to look but straight up at the tiny halogen lights suspended across the ceiling on thin wire tracks, so she shut her eyes and shortly felt the warm water on her scalp, still seeing the pattern of the lights – tiny bright orange flares. Because of the running water and the water collecting in her ears she couldn't hear the music any more, or the hair-dryers, or the receptionist on the phone. There was just a gurgling, swishing, sandy noise as the assistant began gently to massage her scalp, working in the shampoo. Eleanor shivered, enjoying the sensation, wondering whether her body, whether older bodies, needed to be caressed and touched more. That the outward pressure, the gentle moving of hands over skin, the softening and sensitising, would in some way attune, if not arrest what was happening inside. She had always been shy of her body.

'Been working hard?' Tina asked, combing Eleanor's wet hair. 'You do something with photographs, don't you?'

Eleanor thought that Tina must have had a cigarette while she'd had her hair washed – she could smell it on her hands. She nodded, catching Tina in the mirror. Tina had a pretty face and she looked tanned and glowing, with the halogen lights ablaze around her. Tina dropped the height of the chair and the chair made a short, hydraulic puff – a sound not unlike the train doors made opening and closing at Waterloo East. *Orpington*, *Sevenoaks*, *Tonbridge*, Eleanor imagined hearing. Hair began to fall on the light blue gown, clumps curling slightly. Tina said nothing further, though her scissors sort of whispered. A few strands got on to Eleanor's nose and she tried to blow them off, angling her breath, seeing the hair scurry away and slow in the hot, sticky air. She saw herself in the mirror, and her hair that no longer fell to her shoulders. Hair that was once nearly as long as Tina's. Hair that Clay used to say was the first thing that had attracted him to her. *You have wonderful hair* – he'd said it countless times. He would run his fingers through it, brush it behind her ears. He would smell it and bury his face in it. He had loved her hair. Tina raised the chair, but this time it barely made a noise – a short, faint wheeze, as if it wouldn't rise as high as it was meant to. As if it had run out of puff. *West St Leonards*, *St Leonards Warrier Square*, *Hastings*.

'Don't mention it Mum, okay?' Eleanor led her mother into the kitchen. 'Coffee?'

'Eleanor, what have you done?'

'Mother.'

'But why? You had such lovely hair. It's the sort of thing I would have expected Rose to do, when she was younger anyway, not you.' She tutted. 'And you have such lovely hair.'

'It will grow back. It's not even that short.'

'What does Clay think? I bet he hates it.'

'I'm not sure he's even noticed.'

'Of course he has.'

'Look Mum, it's up to me what I do with my hair. I quite like it. I think it makes me look younger.'

'You didn't exactly look very old before.'

'Well I felt it.'

'How do you think I feel? I'm nearly seventy.'

'Yes, but you've got two grown-up children, you've got grandchildren – besides you've been married twice, nearly three times,' Eleanor said, turning to fill the kettle.

'What do you mean by that, exactly?'

'It doesn't matter. Sorry. I'm tired.'

A train swept through Waterloo East without stopping, the electricity clanking and fizzing loudly after it. It had rained earlier in the morning and perhaps that had made the current sound sharper than it normally did. Water still clung to the freesia just outside the back door – Eleanor thought it had never quite done as well as it might have, perhaps because there was insufficient light there – and the coral-red berries of the small barberry, which seemed to have remained stilted too, probably for the same reason as the freesia, or maybe because of the pollution, or the fact that the soil was too alkaline. I'm not like Rose, Mum, Eleanor said to herself. She's much more like you than me. You can't see it, can you? You would have chopped your hair off, had you felt like it. You did whatever you felt like, regardless of what anyone else thought. I might not be as strong as either of you two, but at least I haven't hurt anyone as much – certainly not as much as you hurt Dad, Mum. Another train pulled in with a slow screech.

'I think it's brightening up,' Eleanor's mother said. 'Perhaps we should go out. How's the house-hunting going?'

'Terribly,' Eleanor said. 'I found this lovely house in Clapham, but apart from it being about double what we can afford, it was under offer. Apparently the housing market's beginning to take off again.'

'There must be other houses, dear. And estate agents.'

'Oh sure, but this house was really special.' She didn't feel like telling her mother why.

'I think you're going to have to be a little more flexible. A house is only a house after all. Surely it's the area that's important.'

'Mum,' Eleanor raised her voice, 'I'm the one who has to live in it. I'm the one who has to spend all day in it.' She handed her mother a coffee. 'I'm sorry, I didn't mean to shout. I haven't been sleeping well lately. God, I don't think I'm cut out for trawling around London looking for somewhere new to live. I'd much rather be at work.'

'Maybe you should give up the idea of moving for the moment and concentrate on looking for a job.'

'Mum I can't go on living here, this house is driving me mad. I want to sort out moving first, at least while I've got the time.'

'Did you think about Dulwich? It always seemed very nice to me.'

'No. Well, yes, for about two minutes. It's too far.'

'You think so, darling? We could always pop along there today. It is clearing up.' She walked over to the back door and peered through the dirty glass. 'We could have a walk in the park at least, and some lunch. It would be good for you to have some air. You don't look as if you're getting out enough. You're awfully pale.'

Eleanor stared at her mother blank-faced, at the kitchen which hadn't changed in fifteen years and was steadily packing up – the lino having rotted at the edges and worse in front of the fridge and the cooker, the cupboard doors now badly warped and coming away, only two out of the five spotlights working despite all the bulbs having been replaced recently. One of the ones that actually worked was angling on to her mother's face, showing a thick layer of foundation and how thin her grey hair was. She'd carefully fluffed it up, as she always did, to make it look thicker. Eleanor got her hair from her father, whose had remained thick and dark right up until he died – shortly after a heart attack at the age of sixty-four, nearly nine years ago. The heart attack was quite unexpected. He survived it, just, but three days later he slipped into a coma and then his liver and kidneys packed up because not enough blood was getting through, apparently.

He hadn't married again and Eleanor and Rose were the only people with him when he died. Eleanor remembered the doctor leaving them and how afraid and helpless she felt. She and Rose remained in the brightly lit room for a long while not speaking, with only the air-conditioning grinding away and a blind caught in the down-draft, flapping like a trapped bird. The oxygen mask, which had been attached for his last few hours, had been removed and there was the faintest smile spread across his face. Eleanor was glad she had witnessed his last moments, but knew she never wanted to experience anything like that again. The release at the instant of dying, the exhalation of his failing breath on her left hand, the tiniest flutter of warm, stale air. The fact that she couldn't do anything about it.

They had been on the eighth floor of St Thomas' and she remembered going down in the lift with Rose and the two of them getting lost trying to find the exit they had entered by. They eventually found themselves on Westminster Bridge Road. It was late March but could have been May. There was no breeze, as if everything had suddenly lost its breath too. The sky was hazy blue and the sun, pouring through the stillness, hot. They crossed the road and walked over to Albert Embankment. The tide was out and the mud glistened, showing the haphazard tracks of scavenging birds. Tiny waves washed to the gentle bank as empty sightseeing boats and full waste-barges, keeping to the middle, motored past – their thick, spluttering exhaust soon distilling into the hazy sky, a sky which seemed to have sunk to earth. The sun was picking out the green-tinged copper flashing of the Ministry of Defence building across the water, and slightly further away the glass panels arching high above Charing Cross Station, more like a place of worship from where they were than a train terminal. The South Bank was busy with tourists not quite believing their luck with the weather. The young trees were in bud and the benches packed. The hum of the West End drifted over the river, and with it came an air of excitement and rejuvenation.

Eleanor said to Rose, 'Why did he have to die today? It's not the sort of day people should die on.'

Rose said, 'Is any day? I think I'd rather die when the sun was shining than not.'

'Maybe,' said Eleanor. But she hadn't been paying much attention to the perfect weather, she couldn't stop picturing her father's face at what must have been the very moment of death, the way he seemed to relax into nothing. And she wondered whether he had been relieved to die, because that, she decided, was what it had looked like. He hadn't had an easy life and during his last years he had appeared increasingly haunted, as if he were bearing some terrible weight, as if there was something he'd never come to terms with. He liked to think of himself as someone who was strong and independent – at times he could come across as almost impenetrable, such was the wall he erected around himself, his silence. But that was all shattered now and Eleanor knew he'd never managed to escape some terrible sorrow, some great regret while living.

As a young teenager she had witnessed him suffering when her mother had left him and this suffering had escalated in her mind as she had grown older so all she could believe, on the day that her father died, was that her mother was somehow to blame – for splitting up their marriage, for the one thing she thought he'd never really accepted. And as she and Rose continued along the South Bank, reaching the Festival Hall, the clatter of skateboards echoing from the shady underpasses, Eleanor vowed that she would never treat Clay, whom she'd only just married, in the way her mother had treated her father. She wouldn't betray him, she wouldn't walk out on him. However bad it got.

Eleanor looked at the patch of damp creeping up the inside of the kitchen wall. It had first appeared last winter, stabilised during the summer, but seemed to be spreading again, the backing paper beginning to lift, showing salt crystals like frost on the sodden plaster. It was now a couple of feet or so across. She sighed, thinking she was never going to manage to get herself and Clay out of Roupell Street, how they seemed to be stuck here, how they were a part of the kitchen, the rotting walls and indelibly stained lino. Maybe that was it. Maybe she shouldn't expect anything more.

Eleanor's mother burped quietly. She had a habit of doing this after drinking warm, milky liquid. 'Don't sigh, dear,' she said.

Eleanor felt cold air on her ears and neck, prickling the down. She wasn't used to the sensation. She looked at her mother, her thin hair flattening out in the breeze. Eleanor was pleased she no longer dyed her hair blonde – it had never looked very convincing. She was much shorter than Eleanor, but as slim. She was wearing her favourite camel-hair coat, which had once been smart but was now shabby, and a pair of navy trousers. It was noon and there was a crowd of parents and young children outside the Montessori on Cornwall Road. More children were being led out of the school by one of the teachers and taken as far as the gate where they were handed over to their mothers, or nannies, or the odd father. Some of the children were clutching drawings they had obviously just completed. Eleanor and her mother kept to the other side of the road, cutting back up Whittlesey Street to where she had parked her car. She could rarely park it on Roupell Street, there weren't enough resident permit bays.

'Poor little mites,' Eleanor's mother said. 'It can't be much fun going to school around here. There's nowhere proper for them to play.'

'I'm sure they're fine,' Eleanor said, unlocking the car.

'It's just as well you and Clay never had children. This wouldn't have been the place to bring them up. Whatever happened between your father and I, you can at least be thankful for the fact that you were brought up somewhere decent, with plenty of space to run around in and fresh air. I can't see how people can have children in London. It seems so cruel.'

'Maybe they don't have any choice,' Eleanor said. They both spent some moments getting organised before Eleanor turned the ignition, hoping the car wouldn't start so she wouldn't have to accompany her mother to Dulwich, but this time it did. She slammed it into first, reverse, first again and pulled out. She did a loop, passing 38 Whittlesey Street, which she noticed was still for sale, on to Theed and back down Roupell and left into Cornwall, thinking she really must get their house put on the market, despite the fact that it was in a terrible state – they were never going to do it up first. The traffic was fast flowing until the Elephant, where they quickly became snarled up. Eleanor aggressively nudged the car forward, ignoring her mother telling her to be careful, and that they weren't in a rush – she was still angry and wanted to be moving, not stuck behind some bus, and she thumped the horn as a car tried to cut her up while she was turning into Walworth Road. 'Fuck you,' she shouted.

'I suppose this is what happens to people when they live in London too long,' her mother said.

Eleanor looked at her, and said, 'Yep.' She accelerated quickly only to have to brake sharply as the lights by the first pedestrian crossing shifted from amber to red, and nobody crossed. Eleanor had always hated Walworth Road and today it was as bad as it ever got, with buses pulling out regardless of what was in their way because numerous cars had clogged the bus lanes. The kink just before Burgess Park was solid. Some cabling works were going on and the pavement had been dug up and pedestrians were being channelled along a coned-in path on the edge of the road, except most people had veered further out, knocking over the cones, as the path was too narrow for their number.

Pulling up Denmark Hill the traffic eased and passing King's College Hospital and then Ruskin Park the sky suddenly brightened, and the trees in the park reminded Eleanor that it was still autumn – it wasn't winter yet. They were a deep russet and seemed to be fluttering in waves, making a smoky grey-green light only seen in autumn – and which followed them to the top of the rise, engulfing the pre-war mansion blocks of the Denmark Hill Estate. Eleanor was not thinking, swamped by the light, driving on impulse, and it was her mother who pointed out the sign for Dulwich Village just in time. Eleanor braked and swung the car left into Red Post Hill and they started to descend at a cautious pace, because Eleanor realised she had not been concentrating and could have had an accident, and that she was driving away from the south London she knew into a place that seemed quite different. She wondered whether she had actually been to Dulwich before.

Semi-detached and small crescent-shaped terraces of Edwardian family houses lined the road behind trees and shrubs and drifts of sodden, coppery leaves. The road continued to descend, past housing of more varying ages but still predominantly two or three storeys and well set back. The BBC transmitter at Crystal Palace came into view just as they were passing North Dulwich train station, pushing up between a bank of trees on a distant ridge, seemingly piercing the slow drifting clouds, and Eleanor's mother said, 'Doesn't it look like the Eiffel Tower?'

They had to stop by some lights at the Village Way junction where Red Post Hill turned into Dulwich Village. A house on the corner was covered in Virginia creeper and Eleanor said, her anger having dissipated, 'There's something I've been meaning to ask you – our house in Bishop's Stortford had Virginia creeper running up it, didn't it?'

The lights had turned to green and they were moving forward by the time Eleanor's mother answered, 'No darling, I don't think so. No, I'm sure it didn't.'

'That's odd. I was sure it did. I must have been confusing it with somewhere else.'

'Well Derek's and my house in Cambridge certainly didn't. He would have been far too concerned about the damage it would have done to the brickwork. Mike's didn't. My house now doesn't, as you know. Perhaps it was one of your father's places.'

'No, I'm sure it wasn't, not that he would have minded about the brickwork.'

'You must have just imagined it. Look, there's an estate agents.' It was at the far end of a row of shops and they came to a stop almost level with it because a second set of lights ahead were on red. 'Eleanor, see if you can park, we might as well pop in. It's not quite one. This is rather exciting.'

The lights changed and the traffic started to shift and Eleanor saw the deep piles of leaves which had been blown against the kerbs of the junction by speeding cars, and she said, 'Please, let's just have lunch or something first.' On the far corner of the junction was an old school with tall iron-framed windows – the sort that only opened a fraction at the top or bottom. They reminded Eleanor of her first school. 'I don't think I want to live in Dulwich anyway,' she said, passing it, continuing through Dulwich Village. 'It takes forever to get here. Clay would hate it.' She felt it seemed so removed, like somewhere from a different time.

Past a pub, a café, a florist, a Pizza Express, a boutique and a newsagents, Eleanor's mother shouted, 'There's a space, Eleanor, there.'

Eleanor pulled over, knowing her mother would only go on and on otherwise. They were in front of a large, detached house set well back from the road. It was much older than most they'd seen so far, probably Queen Anne. And getting out of the car, disorientated, Eleanor scanned the skyline for something familiar, but there were no tower blocks, no cranes, no columns of heating vapour in sight, just trees and tiled, period roofs, and a low, wide sky. She knew why her mother had suggested Dulwich, because it was so safe-looking, so suburban.

'Hello there. Can I help?' The woman stood up and walked round from her desk. She was probably Eleanor's age, but looked older because of the clothes she was wearing – a long, shapeless beige skirt, with a white blouse underneath a maroon cardigan – and her large glasses and mousy hair, which had been pinned to the back of her head so it was almost in a bun. Though she had a lovely smile which immediately made Eleanor warm to her. Eleanor was also taken with the way she had stood up so quickly and come out towards them. She was the only person in the small office, which had been decorated in a sickly brown and cream. Spotlights were making the gloss paint on the woodwork gleam and were reflecting on the rack of chrome-plated frames, supporting the details and photographs of the properties for sale or to rent. The light bouncing around the chrome was such that it made reading the material, set behind thick Perspex, almost impossible.

'My daughter's looking for a house in the area,' Eleanor's mother said. 'We wondered whether you had anything suitable.'

The estate agent looked at Eleanor and smiled again before she turned to her mother. 'To be honest,' she said, 'we don't have that much of anything at the moment, but let's see what we can do. Perhaps I can take some details?'

'Yes, of course,' said Eleanor's mother. She turned to her daughter, 'Eleanor, what exactly are you looking for?'

Eleanor moved forward, not wanting to be difficult. 'I don't know. Urrgh—'

'The price bracket?' the woman said.

'I suppose something in the one eighty to two thirty region.' She avoided her mother's eye.

'Two or three bedrooms?' the estate agent said.

'Oh, it doesn't really matter,' Eleanor said. 'Three?'

'I can't see why you need three, Eleanor,' Eleanor's mother said. 'I'd have thought two would be sufficient. Think of all that extra heating.'

'Any streets in particular?' the estate agent said, seemingly ignoring Eleanor's mother.

'No – I don't know the area at all.'

'Well, within that price range we've got two or three things quite near to the village.' She went to a filing cabinet at the back of the room and opened a drawer.

'What's the crime like?' Eleanor's mother shouted. Whispering to Eleanor, she said, 'You can never be too careful.'

The woman straightened. 'There's the odd break-in, of course. But I live here and I walk home at night. I feel pretty safe.' She went back to the opened drawer.

'And the shops?'

'Oh, there are plenty of shops,' the woman didn't turn round this time and continued searching for what she wanted, pulling out pieces of paper and then putting them back – 'and quite a few cafés and restaurants.'

Eleanor looked at her mother, as if to say shut up. She walked over to the window and watched a swirl of leaves take off from a patch of grass in front of the school and spiral away. 'Mum,' she said, 'don't you want to call your friend, seeing as we're here?'

'Oh no, darling, I couldn't possibly. I haven't spoken to him for years. He's probably dead by now.'

'Who was he?' Some of the leaves were blown back into view, though they might have been different leaves from trees much further away.

'A friend.'

'Here we are,' the woman said, shutting the drawer having hung on to some details. 'Not much, I'm afraid.' Eleanor turned towards her. 'We've a period cottage on Boxall Road. It has three bedrooms, though it is small and the bathroom's on the ground floor.'

'Where's that exactly?' Eleanor's mother said.

The woman walked over to a large map pinned to the wall next to her desk. 'It's just off Dulwich Village by the florists, here,' she pointed. 'We're here.'

'How much?' said Eleanor's mother.

'It's on for one five nine, five hundred, but as I said it's pretty small.'

'It would be cheap to run,' Eleanor's mother said.

'You'd probably want to move the bathroom upstairs and then you'd lose a bedroom,' the woman said.

Eleanor said, 'It sounds too small. Where we are is too small for us, Mum.'

'Eleanor, I didn't think you were in a position to be extravagant – you're not working at the moment.'

'Mum, if anyone knows anything about being extravagant it's you.'

'We've got something on Aysgarth Road,' the estate agent said handing Eleanor the details. 'Aysgarth runs parallel to Boxall. They're the same period but slightly bigger. However this one only has two bedrooms and it does need a certain amount of refurbishing. I don't think it's been touched since the seventies. It has a large, open-plan ground floor which could be nice.'

'I would rather have three bedrooms,' Eleanor said.

'We have a semi on Court Lane, which is here.' She turned to the map and and traced her finger along a road. 'It is under offer at the moment, but we're still showing it. They were asking two thirty five, which is an excellent price for the road. It has four bedrooms.'

'Looks like a busy road to me,' Eleanor's mother said, peering at the map.

'Not really,' the estate agent said. 'There are sleeping policemen right the way along.'

'Oh God that's worse.'

'Mum,' Eleanor said, 'please.'

'And,' the estate agent said, handing Eleanor another sheet of details, 'we've just been appointed to handle this property on Druce Road. It's on at two five nine, which might be a bit beyond your limit, but it's well worth looking at. We haven't shown it to anyone yet. It's a solid, semi-detached Edwardian villa, typical for the area. Three/four bedrooms, large garden and many of the original features. It needs some redecorating work, though there is a new kitchen. Druce Road is exceptionally quiet.'

'I think we should see that little cottage,' Eleanor's mother said.

'Thank you, Mum.' Eleanor didn't think any of them sounded particularly suitable and was still totally unsure of the area, but she didn't want the estate agent to feel they had wasted her time, and she supposed the more houses she saw the better idea she'd get, so she said, 'Perhaps we could see the last one you mentioned – Druce Road?'

'I don't know what you want with four bedrooms,' Eleanor's mother said.

'Most people, of course, move here for the schools,' the estate agent said. 'We have a very good state-run junior school which acts as a feeder for the College—'

'I really think it's up to me, Mum,' Eleanor said, 'and Clay.'

'I don't have the keys, but if you wait a minute I'll call them. You'd like to see it today presumably?' Neither Eleanor nor her mother answered and the woman went to the phone on her desk, opened a large diary, found the number with a finger and started dialling.

Eleanor's mother said, 'Why don't you take your jacket off darling, you look awfully uncomfortable. Your face has gone all blotchy.'

'I'm fine,' Eleanor said, feeling terrible. The restaurant was stuffy and she was too hot and nauseous to eat any more and she pushed her plate away.

'Do you mind?' Eleanor's mother immediately transferred her daughter's half-eaten pizza onto her own plate. 'I don't know,' she said, 'but I'm still hungry. Of course I'm lucky, I never put on weight. You get that from me.'

The cloud had thickened so there was no trace of blue, no colour at all, and they stepped into the gloom. Car sidelights trailed long and the air was breezy and cold and Eleanor felt it run right through her. Few people were about and those that were were either hurrying out of cars into shops, or the other way round. And the shops soon petered out leaving even gloomier, quieter space for Eleanor and her mother to fill – wholly inadequately. However, this hard emptiness was interrupted every sixty seconds or so with the loud, uneven whine of a descending plane, which seemed to follow them from the Pizza Express, past the turnings for Aysgarth Road and Pickwick Road, and on along College Road to the entrance of the park, where they appeared to bank away and fade into a hum then a murmur then nothing.

Eleanor and her mother paused by the elaborate iron gates and her mother looked up at the sky, the thick cloud hiding yet another banking plane, and she said, 'Perhaps we'd be better off wandering round the Picture Gallery. How long have we got to wait?' She looked at her watch and answered the question herself, 'A good hour. It's just up there to the right – there's the sign. It's not a very nice afternoon. I think it might rain.'

'Oh no,' said Eleanor, wanting to be outside. 'Come on, let's go into the park. You never did like walking much, did you?'

They entered the park with leaves falling silently from the broad trees about them. There were no other people in view, though a few cars were parked along the wide, unmarked road which led in. Cold damp air stung their noses and the pavement was dark with wet. They said nothing again for a while, a tension building, and the trees making sounds like someone coughing lightly, trying to clear their throat, coming up behind them. The low pressing cloud made a beautiful background to the fading autumn colours, but only to the naked eye. It was a light a camera would never have been able to pick up, Eleanor thought, not even one of Clay's vintage Leicas.

A woman came into view. She was pushing an empty pushchair while a small child walked some paces behind. They were getting closer and Eleanor suddenly pictured the woman with the pram she had bumped into outside the house in Clapham. The woman who had reminded Eleanor of herself. And an uneasy, disconcerted feeling came back too. Eleanor and her mother stepped to the side of the pavement to let this woman and her child, a boy, pass. Eleanor thought he must have been about two and the woman not much more than twenty. Some paces on Eleanor looked over her shoulder to see the woman bending down to the little boy and doing something with his jacket, and she knew that unlike the woman she had nearly knocked off the pavement in Clapham, she would never think of this mother and child again. Or see the trees they were walking under in quite the same way.

The road had curled round in front of them and they crossed it taking a narrow, railed-in path, which led to and ran beside a large pond with an island in the middle. Willows and silver birches hung over the path and Eleanor's mother said in the thick, wet, amplified quietness, 'If he's making you very unhappy you don't have to stay with him, you know. You can always leave. You've been with him for a long while. Marriages do come to an end.'

'It's not that. It's not him, especially. I don't really want to talk about it. I'm fine.'

'Eleanor, you haven't been quite yourself for a long while. You don't look very happy. I'm worried about you.'

'I'm fine, really.'

'Is he having an affair?'

Eleanor laughed. 'No. No, I'm sure he's not.'

'Are you?'

'Mum, for God's sake.'

'How old are you? Forty-two. I wasn't much younger than you are now when I left your father. You know, it's not too late. You could marry again. You're still very attractive – or would be if your hair was a little longer.'

'I'm not like you. I couldn't just leave Clay. I don't know how he'd cope by himself. He doesn't see many other people. He doesn't have a family any longer. There's just me. Besides, look what you did to father.'

Eleanor's mother took a deep breath – the air smelt of rotting leaves. 'I don't know what you mean by that exactly, but what went on between your father and me was a lot more complicated than you think. We couldn't have stayed together any longer.'

'Because you went off with someone else.'

'It wasn't as simple as that, Eleanor. There were things that came to light – look, the relationship was over. It had been for years before we finally split up. If you must know we stayed together for as long as we did because of you and Rose. You and Clay don't have any children. You don't have that responsibility. Fond as I am of Clay, you have to do what's right for you. It's your life darling – it's up to you to make the most of it.'

'Christ, Mum, I never realised quite how selfish you are. Dad always loved you – you destroyed him.' Eleanor felt a pressure behind her eyes and saw a milky sheen come over the near foliage and the pond, so everything became a smudged grey. She realised she had said something she had never said before, and she immediately regretted it.

'Eleanor, don't be so naïve. I didn't destroy your father. He destroyed himself. His problem was that he spent his whole life deluding himself and it eventually caught up with him. You know he could never face up to things. Just look at what happened to all his business ventures. He'd bury his head in the sand – you know how uncommunicative he could be – he thought that if he didn't talk about his problems they'd just go away. Okay, he had his pluses – he was never aggressive, he could be charming – I married him, I did love him once. But he was totally divorced from reality. And totally unreliable, you knew that. He lived in a dream world. And that's not to mention his drinking and smoking – he didn't know how to look after himself. Eleanor, darling, I only ever had your and Rose's interests at heart. And it wasn't always easy, I can tell you. If I've over-protected you, if I tried to shelter you from your father's failures, then I'm very sorry.' She took another deep breath and let it out with a shiver.

Eleanor thought her mother might be about to cry. She hated seeing her mother cry and she regretted saying what she had just said even more, but felt unable to say anything else, to try to put it right, so she said nothing, feeling a tightness in her head and shoulders – an anger, really, with herself, an anger she knew she wouldn't be able to dispel for a long while, because it went so deep.

The path broadened out as they came to the end of the pond and the trees shrunk back. A little further on was a café with a small mechanical dolphin rusted-up outside. The windows were thick with condensation, making it look warm and cosy inside, and Eleanor's mother said, 'Why don't we just have a cup of tea, darling?'

'Okay Mum,' Eleanor said, wiping her eyes with her sleeves before entering the café. The café smelt of fried food and cigarette smoke and was indeed warm and cosy, the condensation blanketing out Dulwich Park so they could have been anywhere.

The large woman behind the counter was facing the other way, talking through a hatch to someone in the kitchen. She laughed, a loud throaty laugh which made her whole body shake. She turned round eventually, still chuckling, and seeing Eleanor and her mother, said, 'That bad, is it?'

'I mean, you're still having sex, aren't you?'

'Mum, that's none of your business.'

'It's amazing what these fertility clinics can do nowadays. You're always hearing of women your age having children – people a lot older than you. Only don't go and have six or something.'

'Stop it Mum, it's too late.'

'Nonsense. It must be Clay. Rose didn't have any problems getting pregnant. I didn't. Your father certainly wasn't—'

'Mum—'

Children were coming out of school and the leaf-blown junction by Turney Road was heavily congested. Waiting cars curled back into Dulwich Village. Eleanor had to stop well short of the junction and she began to get anxious because she hated being late. 'We shouldn't have had that tea,' she said, 'it's nearly four already. We were meant to be there at three thirty. What if she has to go out?' She had the *A-Z* open on her lap and could see they weren't far, but the traffic wasn't moving. It was dusk and the road looked wet with the rear car lights shining on it – it hadn't rained when they were in the park and Eleanor thought that maybe it had just rained very locally. The traffic started to move eventually and they made it over the junction, turning sharply into Court Lane.

Court Lane was full of sleeping policemen, as the estate agent had said, and lined with large semi-detached houses set back from the road behind hedges and built-up flower beds – most of which were bare, though there was the odd rose bush and the odd flower. The houses were Edwardian with boxy bay windows and Tudor-style gable ends – the thick cross-beams showing. The road was on a gentle slope but the outlook didn't improve as they climbed and in the short time it took to reach Druce Road Eleanor knew she didn't want to live anywhere near Dulwich. She knew that she wouldn't fit in here. She wasn't organised enough, her life didn't consist of enough elements. She turned left into Druce Road hoping Mrs – God, she couldn't remember the name of the woman whose house it was – would have given up waiting and left to pick up her children from school or gone shopping or whatever people did around here at four o'clock in the afternoon. The houses on Druce Road were not as set back or hidden by foliage or built-up flower beds as those on Court Lane, but they were much the same architecturally. There were no sleeping policemen, the road was clearly not a cut-through, and Eleanor found the house too quickly and parked slowly with a childish sinking feeling growing in her stomach.

'You couldn't do much better than this,' Eleanor's mother said. 'I thought Dulwich might be the answer.' She smiled at Eleanor, a smile that said, I'm always right. She leapt out of the car and strode up the short path of 29 Druce Road, her thin frame looking terribly fragile, though Eleanor knew it wasn't.

A woman opened the front door a crack and Eleanor's mother said, 'Mrs Wilson?' The woman nodded, opening the door wider. 'We've been sent by the estate agents – we've come to view the house?'

'Yes, of course. Come in.'

'I'm sorry we're late,' Eleanor said. 'We were held up by the school traffic.'

'Happens to everyone,' the woman said. 'Still, that's why most people live here. How old are your children?' The woman edged backwards into a bright, peach-coloured hall, making way for Eleanor and her mother.

'I don't have any,' Eleanor said.

'Oh,' the woman said, 'that's unusual – I mean most people seem to move here because of the schools. I couldn't live anywhere else now, with my two boys. I'm only moving a few streets away – hopefully. It's not at all easy finding houses in this part of Dulwich – people tend to either hang on to what they've got or sell to friends.' She was younger than Eleanor and had highlighted blonde hair, which was pinned up in various places so it was impossible to tell how long it was. She wore leggings and a tight-fitting sweatshirt with the words Naf Naf written on the front. She wasn't tall and had a nice curvy figure, reminding Eleanor slightly of Rose. 'My eldest's at the College. He got a scholarship. I'm awfully proud of him. Should we start in here?' Her voice was accentless, but strained.

Eleanor and her mother followed the woman into a large room which looked as if it might once have been two rooms, though there were no signs of a previous partition. The front portion was the reception/living area with an ornate, tiled fireplace, a glass-topped coffee table, a vast TV with a video player and a stack of videos piled next to it, a sofa and a couple of worn armchairs. The room looked well used, but the carpet had obviously recently been vacuumed and things dusted and tidied-up. The other half of the room was the kitchen, which, from where Eleanor stood, also looked tidy. Cabinets – faced with a light wood, a beech, or an ash, or perhaps a plastic veneer made to look like wood – lined one wall and came out from another creating a short breakfast bar. There was a marble-effect work surface, a microwave, a hob, a smoked glass-fronted oven and a large extractor fan. The room smelt not of food but pot-pourri.

'You can have the TV on while you cook,' the woman said.

Eleanor moved closer to the bay window in the front of the room. The air outside was a deep blue and made Eleanor feel wistful. She turned back to face the room, thinking this could have been her life, had she been blonder and a little more curvy, and married to a lawyer or someone who worked in the City, rather than being dark and bony, and hooked up with a second-hand camera salesman who was probably infertile. But she didn't want to be this woman any more than she wanted to be herself at the moment – she didn't look at all happy.

'If there's anything you need to know, do by all means ask,' the woman said. 'We only had the kitchen fitted a year ago – the cooker will be staying of course.' She led Eleanor and her mother back into the hall from a doorway in the kitchen end of the room. 'That's the utility room,' she paused, pointing to an adjacent door, 'with the washing machine et cetera.' She stood to the side so Eleanor felt obliged to have a look, especially as her mother had already wandered further down the hall. The room smelt of clean washing and drying on a rack were an assortment of odd-coloured bras and knickers and children's vests and brightly patterned Y-fronts. 'Please excuse the washing,' the woman shouted. When Eleanor emerged she pointed out the downstairs toilet, which also led off the hall. Eleanor opened this door, thinking she was going to have to see everything. The toilet was pink and the room was tiny and airless and smelt of stale urine. 'Okay?' the woman said quickly, moving towards the stairs. 'Do you want to see the upstairs first or the back room and the garden?'

'I don't mind,' Eleanor said, 'whatever's easiest.'

'Oh the garden I think,' her mother said, 'before it gets too dark.'

'Upstairs?' Eleanor said.

'Maybe we should whip upstairs first – it's been pretty wet out and I'd rather not get mud on the carpet if we can help it.'

There was a wide smudge of dirt on the wall, which followed the stairs to the top at waist height. The carpet on the landing was beige and badly stained and there was a film of faint grey dust edging the skirting. The tidiness, the cleanness of downstairs did not carry on upstairs, Eleanor realised as she followed the woman into the front bedroom – it could have been a different house. Clothes were heaped all over the bed and slung on the back of a chair and a full-length mirror on a stand. As far as Eleanor could tell they were women's clothes. Some attempt had been made to order them, but there were just too many. Eleanor caught the woman's eye, but she looked away and Eleanor didn't say anything because she didn't know what to say. The room had a large bay window, the same proportions as the window in the sitting room, and yellow light from a nearby street-lamp was drifting in – the inert gases picking up the dust-fall on the bedside tables and the alarm radio, which blinked bright green in the dimness because it hadn't been set properly. A half drunk glass of water was on the bedside table nearest the door they had entered by. It was thick with stationary bubbles. A box of tissues was next to the glass, a used tissue stuffed a short way back into the box.

'I'm sorry about the mess,' the woman said, turning on the main light, either because she'd just realised how dark it was in the room, or because she had been waiting for Eleanor and her mother to get used to the mess first so it wouldn't come as quite such a shock. 'I managed to get downstairs in order, then I ran out of energy.' The strain in her voice had given way to an audible wavering. 'I used to have a cleaner but they're so expensive – what with everything else, I can't afford it.' She took a deep breath. 'Things haven't exactly been going my way recently.' She took another deep breath, almost gulping for air, and Eleanor caught her mother's eye. Her mother was raising her eyebrows, as if to say, here we go. The woman swallowed, steadying herself, and said, 'I'm sorry. There's a small bedroom through here.' She opened a door in the far, inside corner of the room. 'We used this for my youngest when he was a baby. His bedroom's at the back now, with his brother's. They get on pretty well, considering their age difference and the fact that they're both boys.' Eleanor and her mother walked over to the door. 'We haven't used it much since.' There was a small single bed, a light blue chest of drawers and wallpaper depicting Disney characters. There were no curtains and the blue outside had turned to black. 'The problem with this room is that you have to go through the main bedroom to get to it,' she said. 'My husband had thought about turning it into a studio. He's an architect. Well he thinks he's an architect. He's a property developer really.'

Walking back through the main bedroom to get to the landing, Eleanor said, 'The house is lovely and quiet.'

'Yes,' said Eleanor's mother, coughing lightly.

'When the children aren't at home,' the woman said. 'They're a bit of a handful at the moment.'

'How are the neighbours?' Eleanor's mother said.

'Fine. We've never had any problems. If anything they're the ones who have had to put up with us. I should think we've been the neighbours from hell. This is the bathroom. God, I'm sorry it's a bloody tip too.' Towels were draped over the bath and squashed on to a radiator. A squeezed out toothpaste tube hung on the rim of the sink and dried toothpaste speckled the taps like limescale. The door had come off the cabinet above the sink, displaying a vast array of pill bottles and medicine packets. 'I'm going to have to get that fixed,' the woman said, ushering them out of the bathroom. A few paces down the corridor she opened a bedroom door and went in, waiting for Eleanor and her mother to join her, before saying, brightly. 'This is my eldest's. He's actually pretty tidy. Takes after his father.'

Eleanor's mother, seeing the computer on a desk beside the bed and an alcove full of books, said, 'I've a grandson who's not even seven, he has a computer – he's very advanced for his age.'

'It's going to be quite a shock for them when we move,' the woman said. 'We're not going to be able to afford anything like the space we've got now.' She led them quickly out of the room and to the last bedroom at the end of the landing, which had got grubbier as they had progressed down it. Shreds of backing paper were coming off the walls. 'This is Jonathan's room. He takes after me I'm afraid. His room's always a bloody mess.' There were posters of cars and footballers on the walls and clothes and toys all over the floor. 'He's nearly ten. I don't know whether it's his age or has anything to do with his father pushing off, but I can't seem to control him at all at the moment. His brother was never this much trouble when he was ten.'

'The garden?' Eleanor's mother said. 'Before it's too late?'

Clay said, 'How was your day?'

'Wonderful.'

'Your mother okay?' He coughed and his eyes started to water.

'Same as ever.'

'Your sister rang again. You should ring her back.'

'Maybe you're lucky not having any family left.'

'I've got you.'

'Clay, we're not much of a family.'

19 Ufton Grove, N1

Frost lay hard and even on car windows and the empty pavement – the side of the road with the sun just hitting it sparkling white. There were no people about when Eleanor leant out of the bedroom window and it seemed earlier than it was. She found the air tasted thin, as if she were at a high altitude, and she sucked it in wanting more of it – the coldness numbing her face. She wasn't dressed yet so she quickly came away from the window and the frozen air flooded into the room around her, somehow making everything look crystal clear for once. She felt determined and rejuvenated, even if she didn't feel quite like herself.

'Christ, Eleanor,' Clay shouted. He was downstairs. 'There's more of this fucking estate agents' crap clogging up the hall. Do you even look at this stuff? I mean, let's face it, we're not going to move before the end of the year now, are we? Please, tell them to lay off for the time being. It's driving me mad.'

Eleanor heard him kick the envelopes, a muffled clattering sound, and she heard the front door being opened and slammed shut and his footsteps hurry away on the icy pavement, and she found herself wondering whether they would be visible, a trail of Clay's size eights nearly the length of Roupell Street, mucking up the white. He used to walk to work but for the last couple of years he had usually taken the bus from Blackfriars Road, because, he said, he just wasn't as fit as he once was. Eleanor thought that her husband was simply becoming lazier and lazier – he seemed unable to sort his business out, he didn't want to move, he didn't want to go anywhere. He was holding her back.

Downstairs she picked up the thick, half-crushed envelopes and hurriedly leafed through them walking to the kitchen. They were from estate agents in Clapham and Dulwich, and when Eleanor got to the kitchen she dumped the lot in the bin, most unopened. Dulwich was definitely out of the question and she didn't have the inclination to go back to Clapham – the woman had never rung her back about the house on Lillieshall Road, and Eleanor was beginning to think that that was perhaps just as well. The interior was probably nothing like she wanted it to be, how she expected it to be – what was she doing anyway, looking for some piece of her past, some comfort in familiarity? And it would have been far too large, besides the fact that they couldn't have afforded it. Plus there was the Common with all the dog shit and that stupid one-way system, and dangerous men making passes at you when you were feeling far too vulnerable. It wasn't a way forward.

A train came into Waterloo East and Eleanor could tell from the swoosh and shudder that it was travelling into London. She looked at her watch, which said nearly ten, but the thing was always fast and she listened out for the Tannoy to see if that would enlighten her further. It was a perfectly still day and yet she couldn't make out the voice clearly enough, which was unusual unless a gale was blowing, or the platforms were really crowded – people, like the wind, seemed to hold the announcements up there, everything but the faintest, inhuman crackle. So she didn't even know where the train had come from, whether it was Dover Priory via Ashford, or Gillingham via Rochester, Gravesend and Dartford. Tunbridge Wells via Sevenoaks and Orpington, perhaps – late because the points had been frozen up. Eleanor heard in the back of her mind the man from Clapham, with his fine, strong face, blue eyes and dark wavy hair, saying, *Location's the key*. Echoed by her mother, *Surely it's the area that's important*.

Eleanor wasn't convinced they were right. Though that morning she felt she had had it with south London. It wasn't distance from Waterloo that she craved so much as a totally different perspective – a place with different aspirations and agendas. She decided she was going to try across the river. In Islington, because that was where Rose lived, and the place she knew best in north London. Where people seemed to be doing things with their lives, like living, like getting on. Not moving apart, or letting time just run away. Perhaps it was because they were on higher ground. That they had a better view and the air was purer and more plentiful and they were able to breathe more easily. In Waterloo when the tide went out life seemed to be sucked with it – following the curves of the Thames, past Borough, Bermondsey and Rotherhithe.

The day had warmed considerably by the time Eleanor stepped outside. The sky was a deeper blue in the centre, and a whiteness that had been creeping in from the edges was beginning to turn a fuzzy orange. A high-pressure system had hung over Greater London for the last couple of days trapping the pollution. The frost had disappeared and with it, if they'd ever been there, Clay's footsteps. The pavement was dark with wet, as far as Theed Street, where Eleanor picked up the car. The windows of the car were smeared with melted ice – the side windows remaining clouded until she had reached the lights just before the Express building on

Blackfriars Road, when the water seemed to lift off in an instant completely clearing her view. The heater was on full blast and the car was suddenly achingly hot. Eleanor wound down her window a little and an inch of deep, refreshing coldness flooded in.

Sun was falling on the curved façade of the Express building in harsh balls of glare, fracturing on the tinted glass and metal panels. As the lights changed to green and Eleanor depressed the accelerator she felt the car shudder as if there was a momentary blockage in the carburettor. She gained speed slowly, stuck behind a bus, the 63, which Clay would have taken today and which she used to catch to work when the weather was bad, though not usually with Clay because she had to be at work much earlier. Going over the river now she felt sure she was seeing things in a new light – St Paul's, the Bank of England, the NatWest Tower, Southwark Bridge, Canon Street, the cranes swinging like giant clockwork toys, steam rising, the flash of an aeroplane. The lower sweep to her left taking in Middle Temple Garden, Victoria Embankment and the party boats *President* and *Wellington*. Again she had a feeling she wasn't quite herself, that she was someone else – registering things on a different level, on a higher, more connected plane. And a brightness charged through her, like a current, like electricity.

The traffic snarled up once she was over the bridge, Unilever House putting her momentarily in shade. But she could feel there was a greater sense of impatience this side of the river. A trilling, shaky reverberation. And she edged forward, riding the clutch.

'I knew it,' said Rose. 'I knew you'd come round to the idea eventually. What did I tell you ages ago? The children will be delighted.'

'Look,' said Eleanor, 'I haven't seen anything yet – I don't know whether we can even afford it. Besides, Clay's always said he would never live in Islington. He doesn't think it's him.'

'Nonsense. It's exactly him – those old corduroys and cameras and ambivalent politics.' She laughed. 'Or perhaps it was. Things have changed here so much over the last few years I'm not sure who fits in. It's now full of supermarkets and fake French cafés.' She laughed again.

Eleanor didn't answer. She said instead, 'I must just use your loo. I seem to be going all the time at the moment.' She stood up slowly because her back ached and she walked to the toilet, which was at the end of the large basement kitchen and through a utility room. There were drying clothes everywhere, smelling of Comfort. The door didn't have a lock and despite Rose's children not being in the house Eleanor felt oddly vulnerable, so when she sat on the toilet she stuck her foot against the door – even though she knew she was being ridiculous. She peed and there was a slight burning sensation – not like cystitis, it was more tingly than that, almost an itch.

'Oh, by the way Eleanor, I love your hair,' Rose said when Eleanor reappeared. 'Where did you get it cut?'

'Where I usually go, that place in Covent Garden. It's growing out a bit now.' Eleanor suddenly felt self-conscious because Rose didn't often compliment her. Though Rose had always been jealous of her hair. Hers was not as dark or thick, more like their mother's. She was also a little shorter and fuller than Eleanor, but she carried herself well and Eleanor had always seen her as being so much more self-confident and independent than herself that she couldn't imagine Rose was jealous of anything else. Besides she had Mark and the two children, her own career, a place in Islington. At that moment, to Eleanor, it seemed Rose had everything she wanted.

'Though I'm not quite sure I would have had it quite so short,' Rose said. 'Maybe a few years ago.'

'Mum hates it,' Eleanor said.

'It's exactly the sort of thing she would have done. It makes you look much younger. God, I feel so bloody old myself at the moment.' She turned away from Eleanor towards a cork board behind her. Children's drawings and other pieces of more official looking paper were pinned to it and she appeared to focus on something on the board for a moment before turning back. 'It's true what they say, having children really takes it out of you. You're lucky. I thought I'd got over the hard part. Christ, I'm tired.'

'You look pretty good to me – really. You're glowing. Has anything happened? You're not pregnant?'

'Oh God no,' she said quickly. 'No. Two's quite enough.' She paused, dug some sleep out of an eye as if to emphasise her tiredness. 'That would be all I need right now. Come on, look at me properly – don't tell me I don't look exhausted.'

'Well you hide it pretty well.'

'I'm so bloody busy at the moment I don't know whether I'm coming or going. I've got this project on to refurbish a huge house miles away in south London somewhere, I've got something else coming up in an old hospital, and James is being really difficult. Sarah's okay, but James is playing up at school – the head teacher even rang me up about it – and he's being a right pain in the arse at home. I can't control him.'

'How's Mark?'

'Mark? He's been away so much recently I sometimes wonder whether the children forget they have a father. That's probably got something to do with James's behaviour – he needs his father to play football with and do all that other stuff boys do with their dads. Anyway, I'm not going to go on about that. This is much more exciting. The kids won't be back until five, they've got swimming. There are masses of estate agents on Upper Street, why don't we have something quick to eat and I can come with you to have a look. I'm not going to get done what I was meant to do today – I need a break. The children are going to love it with you being up here.'

'Thanks Rose, but I want to go on my own.'

'What? Eleanor, I know all the streets around here and everything. I know where you want to be looking. Besides, I am an interior designer, I do know about houses. I can save you masses of time, and money.'

'Rose, you don't know what we can afford. It's certainly not going to be very near here. These houses must cost a fortune.'

'We've been here a long while, and you wouldn't believe the size of our mortgage.' The phone went and Rose got to her feet immediately and ran out of the room and up the steep, narrow stairs, ignoring the phone in the basement, shouting, 'It's probably a work call, I'll take it in my office.' Her office was on the ground floor in a small room at the back of the house.

Eleanor stood also and alone in the large, well-equipped kitchen she started picking up pieces of paper and cards that hadn't been pinned to the cork board and were littering the work surfaces. There were things from Sarah's and James's schools, take-away menus, something from a video club, bills, unopened letters for Mark – she could hear Rose on the phone upstairs, the tone of her voice, quick, agitated, but she couldn't make out what she was saying – toast crumbs, tea stains, flecks of onion skin. Thinking how full Rose's life must be, she moved on to the cupboards. The doors were solid-feeling and a burnt orange or terracotta colour. She opened the three above the main work surface, which ran along the back wall. They were largely empty, which surprised Eleanor because Rose was normally organised and kept things well stocked. The shelves were also covered in a greasy film of dust. However, the tiled floor seemed pretty clean, with toys heaped in one corner. And there were no damp patches or fittings falling to pieces like in her kitchen at home. The lights all worked.

Rose finished on the phone and shortly Eleanor heard her coming down the stairs so she returned to her chair. 'Sorry,' Rose said, once she, too, had found her chair, and she continued talking to Eleanor as if she hadn't been interrupted. 'Of course, there are some parts you just don't want to consider.'

Though her face was flushed. 'Public transport can be a problem and crime. It's not all great up here. Let me help you.'

'I know it sounds stupid but I'd rather go on my own, initially anyway,' Eleanor said. 'I had this dreadful day with Mum in Dulwich. I just think I might find it easier on my own.' She took a deep breath. 'I don't need anyone's help.'

'Dulwich, God, what were you looking there for?'

'It was Mum's idea.'

'I thought people only lived there for the schools. And that park's not so brilliant.'

'I didn't know you knew it?'

Rose stood and went to the sink with her empty mug and ignored what Eleanor had just said, saying, 'Eleanor, I do think you're being a bit stupid. I mean, how do you know where to start?'

'I'm not that useless.'

'Of course you're not. I just wouldn't want to see you making a mistake.'

'Yet another one you mean.'

'Eleanor, please.'

'Look, it's not as if I'm going to buy anything this afternoon.'

'Here's my card,' the estate agent said, handing Eleanor his card. 'Give me a ring if you fancy seeing anything. As I said, the place on Ufton Grove has just come on. It probably won't hang around for long, though we usually have one or two similar properties. Go home and have a think about it. You've got all the bumf.' He smiled. 'Take your time.'

Eleanor looked at the card momentarily, reading, PAUL MORAN, and ANAEA under that in smaller capitals. She put it in the matching brown and green folder of details she had been given, smiled back at the man and rushed out of the door without saying goodbye. Since she had been in the estate agents Upper Street had sunk into a deep, dreamy whiteness, as if the air had become muslin. Eleanor's gaze was drawn to the low, faint sun seemingly hovering over the Angel. In between was Islington Green and a row of brightly lit shops. Small trees hung with fairy lights lined the wide pavement in front which was packed with a mass of slowly shifting people. Eleanor blinked, not focusing properly, and when she thought she was seeing straight again she saw, in the middle distance, the young estate agent who had just given her his card – his fresh, unlined face and solid, powerful-looking frame. He appeared to be coming towards her, having noticed her also. She shut her eyes for a long, tight moment, letting the freezing air fall on her like lead, and when she opened them he had gone and the near distance, at least, was clear. She crossed the road and entered a café, because she was shivering and needed to sit down and steady herself.

The café was deserted and a waiter appeared at her table almost instantly. Eleanor ordered a cappuccino, still thinking about the estate agent, why he had appeared like that, closing in on her, as if he could have touched her. She couldn't stop feeling cold and thought her teeth might chatter. She had visited four or five estate agents on Upper Street that afternoon and must have talked to at least three other men. She tried to recall everything Paul Moran had said to her, his manner. What he looked like exactly. But nothing really enlightening came to mind, except perhaps a feeling, an intuition, that he was somehow different from the other estate agents. That there was more to him, that he had interests and concerns beyond selling property – and his commission. *Go home and have a think about it*. She could have been wrong, misled by a too low blood sugar level, or the fact that she was having trouble orientating herself today. It was this sense of seeing things new, from a different perspective. Of things shifting right out of context.

The coffee was weak and not very hot and Eleanor drank it in one. She got up to pay while dabbing the froth from her mouth, leaving a trace of lipstick on the damp white paper napkin. Outside, the folder of details firmly under her right arm, she glanced quickly in the direction of the last estate agents she had been into, seeing only a bright shopfront – it could have sold clothes or jewellery perhaps. She went the other way – the milkiness now a dank, uninspiring grey with the sun having sunk from view – and left Upper Street, taking Theberton Street to her car. The meter had nine minutes left on it, five minutes by the time Eleanor pulled away, the car slow to respond because of the cold. She briefly considered going back to Rose's and going over the details with her, but she had already reached Liverpool Road and she knew that she shouldn't, that she must do it for herself. Besides she had a good enough idea from the estate agents she had visited of what she could afford and where. And Paul Moran had been especially helpful and unpushy, and she knew that she could trust him. *Take your time*, he had said. Plus, he had a young, honest face – a face that was still expectant, that hadn't yet become bitter through failure or loss, through letting slip what was close to you. And it had somehow stuck in her mind.

Turning left off Rosebery Avenue into Farringdon Road she was sure she could get Clay to reconsider Islington – it was even nearer his work. She should have listened to Rose ages ago. Christ, there was so much more going on there than in Waterloo. There was a cinema for a start. Sainsbury's and M&S. Numerous antique shops and bars and restaurants and French cafés, even if they were fake. There was a Waterstone's. Fairy lights. A vibrancy on a mid-week winter afternoon. The traffic grew worse by Ludgate Circus and diesel exhaust chugged from the lorries and the buses and the taxis. The traffic was slow moving and the fumes thickened, rising into something of a barrier between New Bridge Street and the river – seemingly blocking Eleanor's way home. But she eventually edged forwards, and the lights in the offices across the river – the Express building and Sea Containers House and the renovated Oxo Tower – beckoned suddenly, warm and bright, and Eleanor found herself ensnared by them and hauled across the river, or perhaps she was just in the slipstream of the 45 bus. Seeing for an instant the lights on the blackened water – playful and thrilling. Youthful.

'Eleanor,' Clay said, 'I thought we were going to wait until after Christmas. With all this other crap to buy, I can't believe people still go out looking for houses.' Eleanor watched him walk into the kitchen. His neck was red and he moved slowly, arching his back slightly, as if something were pressing on his kidneys. 'For fuck's sake,' he said. He refilled his glass and leaning against the sink drank most of it. He lit a cigarette and exhaled slowly. 'Look, Eleanor,' he said, 'we've just got too much on at the moment.'

'Like what?' Eleanor said.

He kicked out at the damp patch, but he couldn't quite reach it without moving, and he didn't move any closer to it so he wiped his forehead with his hand instead. 'Oh, do what you want to do. You always do.'

'Really? That's the first I've heard of it.' Eleanor turned back to the estate agents' particulars she was going through on the pine table in the back room, while Clay remained in the kitchen looking at his diminishing glass of wine, smoking two cigarettes one after the other straight down to the butts. A train passed through Waterloo East without stopping, making the house shudder, like something unsaid. Eleanor could not concentrate on what she was looking at – she couldn't get Clay out of the corner of her eye, wherever she looked, and she was now looking out of the window, trying to see through the blackness. The curtains hadn't been drawn and she could see herself, faint, almost transparent, though Clay was in the window also, more solid somehow, filling much of it. He was propping himself against the kitchen door and the light on him was coming from a different angle, so perhaps that was why his reflection was so much bigger. Or, Eleanor thought, he is just more real and living than I am. 'Rose has asked us over for Christmas,' she said, knowing this would annoy him.

'Oh, great,' Clay said, 'another happy family Christmas. Aren't they fed up with us?'

'Why can't you just be thankful for the fact that you've actually been asked somewhere? What's wrong with you tonight?'

'Tonight? Nothing.' He paused. 'Sorry.' He pushed himself away from the door and walked back into the kitchen and over to the damp patch. He didn't squat exactly but sort of stooped and ran his foot along it, leaving a faint trail in the sodden, blistering plaster. 'We've got to fix this place up. We're never going to sell this house how it is.' He straightened himself a bit and looked around the room. Eleanor had leant back in her chair so she could see him clearly. 'These cupboards have had it. So has the lino.' He started to bang on surfaces and pull at the things that were coming away. Looking up, he said, 'And these stupid lights, I've always hated them. How much does all this stuff cost to replace?'

'How do I know?' said Eleanor. 'It's been fifteen years since we did anything here.'

'Yeah,' he said, 'I suppose it has.' He refilled his glass again. 'Want some?'

'No,' said Eleanor.

He left the kitchen and came through to the back room. He moved round behind Eleanor so he could look at what she was looking at. 'So where are we moving to now? Islington? Islington. Christ Eleanor, what's got into you? We can't afford Clapham. How much do you think houses in Islington cost. I get it, it was Rose's idea.'

'No, for once it was my idea.

'Can't you see, she only wants you up there so you can help look after her bloody kids now you've got time on your hands, while she goes off and does whatever it is she does.

People don't really use interior designers, do they? Not for normal houses?'

'Clay, it was my idea – how many times do I have to tell you – not Rose's, mine. Sometimes I do have my own ideas.'

'Don't I know it.'

'And stupid me for thinking of you and your bloody work. Islington's much nearer to fucking Clerkenwell than here.'

'I don't think I want to live right on top of the shop, thank you very much. And anyway that depends on what part of Islington. If you're way up in, say, Stoke Newington that's not exactly near Clerkenwell. You might as well be in Acton, or somewhere.'

'I wasn't exactly thinking of Stoke Newington.'

'So in Barnsbury, or Canonbury with Rose then. Canonbury, hey, that's going to be cheap.'

'Look Clay, there are places we could afford that are not in the middle of nowhere. Okay, not exactly where Rose lives, but not so far away.' Eleanor flicked through the pile of places she thought might be worth looking at and which she had separated out from the rest. The house on Ufton Grove was at the top of this pile, but her hands suddenly began to itch terribly so she let go of what she was holding.

'Don't you see enough of her?'

'Who? Rose?' She turned her hands over, bringing them closer to her eyes, getting the light on them, but there was no sign of a rash or any blotches or anything unusual.

'Besides, Eleanor, I just don't think we'd fit in with the people up there – we're not fashionable enough. I've always had a real aversion to Islington. I don't know, but it seems to me the sort of place where people are always trying to do one better than their neighbours. They're never content, are they?'

'Like Rose and Mark, you mean?'

'Always after bigger houses, more children, better jobs. The latest designer gear. Exactly, yeah, look at Mark – let's all bow down.'

'They've lived in that house for nearly as long as we've lived here,' Eleanor said. She was sitting on her hands now and the pressure was relieving the itch. 'They moved there because it was convenient for their work, and because of the shops and restaurants and schools, and because it was pretty safe and there are some lovely streets. Things people generally aspire to.'

'If you want my opinion, Islington's full of pretentious fakes. And what really sickens me is that they're all trying so bloody hard at it – conning themselves they're having such a good time. Underneath it I bet you they're all bloody miserable. You know why? Because you can't have everything. It's pathetic. That's the middle classes for you – the great bourgeoisie.'

'What are we then?'

He ignored her, saying, 'Life doesn't have to be like that.'

'You don't have to be so bloody stubborn. What's wrong with a little compromise.' The itch had stopped as suddenly as it had begun and Eleanor pulled her hands from under her and started to shuffle the roughly stapled sheets of details again. Some had photographs attached, others photocopies of photographs, but most weren't illustrated, with the space for the picture remaining blank. 'There's this bit, De Beauvoir, which we could afford.'

'De Beauvoir – I'm not going to live in a fucking place called De Beauvoir. De Beauvoir. Don't tell me, it's got to De Beauvoir Village, or is it Town? Old Town? Why do estate agents have to make everything sound so bloody suburban – as if it's not inner London at all, but somewhere in fucking Buckinghamshire?'

'Well you can fucking well stay here on your own then,' Eleanor said getting up. She left the room, her eyes smarting, and felt her way through to the hall. The moment she was in the hall the phone went. It was right by her so she picked it up without thinking. 'Yes?'

'Okay,' Rose said, 'how did you get on?'

'Rose, I'm tired. This isn't a great time. I'll call you back.'

'Quickly – did you get anywhere?'

'I don't know. Maybe. Look, I'll call you back.'

'Where, where?'

'Rose, Clay's being a complete wanker right now.'

'When's he not? Eleanor, calm down.'

'Sorry.'

'So, have you come across anything worth seeing?'

'Clay says there's no way he's going to live anywhere near Islington. I don't know whether it's worth pursuing this.'

'Oh come on. You're not giving up already. Keep at it. Men always come round. Tell him you'll move without him.'

'I have.'

'He couldn't manage without you – give him time.' Rose paused, waiting for Eleanor to say something, but she didn't so she said, 'You must have come across something?'

Eleanor felt calmer. 'Oh, I don't know. There's a house on Ufton Grove or somewhere that might be okay.'

'Ufton Grove?'

'It's in De Beauvoir'

'De Beauvoir? Eleanor you can't live there. It's miles away, it's virtually Hackney. The public transport's crap – there's no tube anywhere near.'

'Rose, that's about all we can afford. I'm not asking you to move, too. You're as bad as fucking Clay.'

'Sorry,' said Rose. 'I'm sure it's fine. When are you going to see it? I'll come with you, if you like?'

'I told you, I really want to do this bit on my own.'

'I do know about houses, you know.'

'Rose, I haven't even made an appointment to see it yet. Look, come with me if I think it's a possibility – just let me go on my own first. Of course I'd like your help doing a place up – if it ever comes to that, which quite frankly is not very likely.'

'Mark wants to know whether you've made up your minds about Christmas?'

'Already? He's back then?'

'He rang from Hong Kong.'

'I can't think about that now, not with Clay being so bloody difficult.'

Clay walked into the hall at that moment, hearing her. 'What, and you're not?' he said.

'What did he say?' Rose said.

She was dreaming she couldn't get out and she woke suddenly, finding the duvet twisted round her feet. She couldn't recall what or where it was she hadn't been able to get out of, just being unbearably cramped. Her nightdress was damp with sweat, which had seeped through to the sheet and the duvet cover so everything about her was sticky too. She tried to calm her breathing by taking long, deep breaths, and untangle her feet without disturbing Clay. She got her arms out from under the cover and the air felt cool on her skin. Her breathing began to slow and the sound of the draught sweeping through the rotten window-frame and under the bedroom door became louder – a rattling, swooping, plangent noise which seemed somehow human. With her feet free and lying on her back she crossed her arms, but she found they pressed heavily on the duvet, packing it around her, so she felt she couldn't breathe again and she gasped. She lifted the duvet away from her, heaping it on to Clay's side of the bed. He was snoring unusually quietly and the draught became more plaintive, and Eleanor felt a growing tightness behind her eyes and in her throat, as if she were about to cry, and she had no idea why.

The air was now making her nightdress feel cold and stiff, so she swung her legs round and climbed out of bed. Moving quietly across the bedroom floor, she reached the window and pulled back the edge of the curtain just enough to be able to look out. The street-lamps were making little impact on the darkness swirling about the parked cars. She looked up and couldn't see the moon or any stars, but thought the sky might be clear because there was a big sense of depth there. She found her breath was clouding the window, taking away the depth, so she opened more of the curtain and shifted along a bit and the moon came into view in the gap between the roofs Windmill Walk made. It was about a quarter full and the light it gave off was too weak to have any effect on the other shades in the sky – it seemed to hang there isolated. And feeling pathetic and inconsequential herself, Eleanor said quietly, 'I can't let this go on. I'm worth more than this.'

With a spluttering snort Clay shifted fitfully in bed. Eleanor braced herself, waiting for him to wake, but he didn't. Still she didn't dare move.

She didn't know how long she stood by the window, with her nightdress like cardboard, her arms covered in goose pimples, her lips trembling, and the dim view blurring under the condensation. A bell sounded three times, deep and resonant. Big Ben. She let go of the curtain and the room sank a notch darker. She turned towards Clay. He was on his back and she could see the duvet rise with each breath. She walked over to her side of the bed and eased herself under the covers – because it was too early and too dark to be unattached from what she knew. Clay rolled towards her and his face pressed against her shoulder and his snoring evened out, as if he were conscious of his wife's presence. Eleanor reached up with her left hand and stroked his hot, rough cheek before she closed her eyes and prayed that sleep might descend on her quickly and take away a feeling, a terrible urge to hurt Clay, because he was hurting her so much, and that was all she really had to fight against.

But sleep didn't come immediately or for a long while – the room eventually beginning to brighten and the outline of the window-frame becoming clear behind the curtains.

He went first and she stepped after him, catching his scent. A soapy, fresh but peculiarly male smell. Like there was something, some essence of himself he couldn't entirely wash away, or cover up. Eleanor closed the front door behind her. There was a small window above it, though more natural light seemed to be coming from a window – the bottom of which could just be seen halfway up the stairs – so he was in silhouette for a moment before he switched on the hall light. He was taller than she remembered and perhaps slightly broader across the shoulders. It was a narrow hallway, cosy with the light on. There was some sort of matting on the floor, a greeny tan colour. He was wearing black jeans and a smart jacket. The hall had been painted an off-white and there were a couple of abstract prints in simple frames on the walls. There was a door on their right about halfway down. It was shut. He got as far as the stairs, which were just beyond the door, before he turned to face her. She thought he was about twenty-six, maybe slightly older. She ran her fingers along the hall radiator. It was still warm but the heating had obviously gone off. It was shortly after eleven and Eleanor wondered when the occupants had left for work, or wherever they went. The matting continued up the stairs with metal rods to hold it in place and rubber edging the steps – Eleanor could see it would be pretty treacherous otherwise. Paul Moran had pale green eyes and he was looking at her intently.

'All right?' he said, smiling. 'My first time too.' He was holding a clipboard with the details of the house attached, along with a pen in the same company colours as the heading on the details – the chocolaty brown and green. 'Some estate agents like to start with the bedrooms and work down. Others, the kitchens and up. It doesn't bother me either way – I usually start with the first door I come across.' His accent wasn't strong, but Eleanor could tell he came from north London. He went for the door and held it open for Eleanor to walk through, under his arm. He had a jaunty, almost springy way of moving – as if he weren't totally in control of his limbs, as if he were brimming with energy. 'I suppose it's like people saving their favourite bit of a meal until last, like the chips, or whatever.' He laughed. 'I sort of think you have to just get on with things. I don't see the point in leaving the best bit until last – something might happen to you before you get there.' He laughed again.

Eleanor was wearing her black trouser suit. It was made of merino wool and had been her favourite thing to wear for a long while. It was comfortable and loose fitting, but still showed her figure off well. Underneath she had on a thin blue-grey cotton jersey. She had made an effort with her appearance because she'd had such a bad night – she didn't want to look as terrible as she felt. And there was another reason hovering at the back of her mind. But she didn't want to dwell on it. 'Thanks,' she said, stooping under his arm to get into the room, catching his smell again. He followed her in, close behind.

'No,' he said, 'I always go for the plum stuff first. Life's too short.'

'This is nice and bright,' Eleanor said. It was a double room and there was a large sash window at the front and a French door at the back. There were two fireplaces, which looked to Eleanor to be original. They had marble mantels and encased cast-iron grates. Cards and photographs, some in silver frames, were crammed on to the mantelpieces. There were also flowers in vases, though most of the flowers had had it and drying petals littered the grey-white marble, which was already stained and dusty, the dust looking stuck on.

Eleanor walked over to the nearest fireplace, spotting what she presumed was a wedding photograph. It was an informal shot of the bride and groom leaving a building – a hotel perhaps – surrounded by a group of friends. It was night and the flash was centred on them so the edges of the photograph receded into darkness. They were ducking slightly, as if they were about to get into a car, except a person was blocking where the car might have been in the picture. It was this person that really caught Eleanor's eye, because she was the largest figure in the photograph and, even side on to the camera – the curve of her body was sort of cleverly framing the shot – and not fully illuminated, she reminded Eleanor of herself. Her bobbed hair and high cheekbones and slim, curving body draped in a long, tightly-fitting dress. And what Eleanor could see of her face showed an expression of almost pure disbelief, as if she were witnessing the most extraordinary thing. How Eleanor knew she looked when she was surprised – she'd been caught like that on camera before. Some people thought it was an endearing expression but she had always been embarrassed by it. The likeness shocked her.

'Arty, aren't they?' Paul said.

'Sorry?'

'The pictures on the walls and stuff – the vendors are obviously into art. Looks like they know what they're doing, too. Makes a change.'

Eleanor stood back a little. There were two big paintings above the fireplaces and a number of others on the opposite wall. They all appeared to be abstracts and seemed to be connected – either because they were by the same artist or artists from the same movement. 'Yes,' said Eleanor distractedly, thinking about the photo, wanting to have another, closer look, but not with the estate agent still in the room because she thought she'd probably appeared too nosy already.

'I enjoy looking at art,' he said, 'not that I ever seem to get the time.'

Eleanor wondered when the picture had been taken. From what she'd been able to tell from the clothes and the fact that the photograph didn't look old – the colours weren't bleached or hadn't bled into one another – not long ago. The woman was obviously a little younger than her though. 'Who does?' she said.

'Fireplaces are original,' Paul said, 'though I shouldn't think those French doors have always been there.' He walked over to them and rattled the door handle. 'Oh I see, they've built a sort of balcony out from it with steps down to the garden.' Eleanor remained where she was at the other end of the room. 'They've done an okay job. Must be nice in the summer.' He paused for a moment. 'My thing's photography.'

'Really,' said Eleanor. She turned to look out of the front window, stepping closer to it. She thought about telling him who she used to work for but she didn't want to have to explain why she no longer worked there. It had been drizzling all morning and the air was thick with water. The parked cars were wet and the windscreens cloudy and the road was like pewter. Ufton Grove was much wider than Roupell Street and the houses seemingly lower. There was a far greater sense of space and light, even though the atmosphere that morning was so dim and heavy. The trees were bare and there were a few evergreen shrubs looking black. It was quiet with little sound of traffic and no trains in earshot. She stared at the opposite terrace of flat-fronted three-storey Victorian houses, thinking she could have been looking in a mirror, except her face was not visible behind a pane of drizzled-on dark glass – like she had simply been removed. A van went slowly past obviously looking for an address. It was white and had Zanussi written on the side. Eleanor watched it until it turned left at the end of the road and disappeared.

'I take all the photographs for work,' Paul said. She heard him walk away from the French doors and into the centre of the room. She felt her pulse quicken and wondered whether she was blushing. 'It's not exactly the greatest photographic challenge, I know, but you learn stuff all the time.'

'Yes,' said Eleanor, still looking at the empty street, trying to squeeze her insides together and restrain what she was increasingly sure was about to happen, 'of course.'

'It's better than writing up the details. I hate that. That's really boring. Sash window to front, feature fireplaces, double radiator, alcove storage cupboards, picture rail, French doors to rear aspect – it doesn't give you anything like a clear picture. I don't see why we can't say things like – draughty double room with a few shabby original features and out of place French doors. It's currently a dirty cream colour and the carpet's had it along with the light fittings. That's pretty fair, don't you think? Some properties I see all you'd want to say is forget it, the place needs fire-bombing. It would save everyone so much time. I don't know, estate agents – we're not meant to make things easy.' He paused momentarily. 'When you're ready.'

The Zanussi van came back into view retracing its path at an even slower pace. It hadn't reached the house before Eleanor turned to see Paul motioning her through into the hall. 'Right,' she said. She hadn't exploded with heat and she relaxed her body thinking perhaps she wasn't going to. She walked towards the open door smiling, relieved.

'Is downstairs okay?' he said.

'Sure.' She followed him to the back of the hall where there was a short flight of dark, narrow stairs. He found a light switch at the bottom and she could suddenly see where she was going. 'Wow,' she said, stepping down into the kitchen.

'Well, there's certainly everything you'd ever need.' He moved over to the main work surface, which was topped with zinc or maybe stainless steel and crowded with built-in chrome-plated gadgets. 'Juicer, electric tin opener, knife sharpener.' He named everything as if he were reading from a list. 'Extractor fan, halogen spots, stainless-steel splash back.' He made to shield his eyes from the glare coming off the fittings. 'Shaker-style cabinets – it's right up there.'

'Perhaps it's a little, urrm, overdone for me,' Eleanor said. 'I doubt if I'd know how to use all this stuff.'

'People always go over the top with kitchens,' he said. 'They think it's a house's best selling point and will help push up the price. What they forget is that not everybody has the same ideas.' He reached over and ran a tap. The water shot out, splashing him. He turned it off and it dripped loudly for a while. 'Of course there are people who see a place like this who think great, they won't have to do anything to it. But in my experience there are more people who are sooner or later going to get sick of it. This stuff's usually so badly made anyway.' He turned the tap on and off again and the dripping lasted longer this time. 'I reckon there's thirty thousand pounds' worth of kitchen here.'

'I was thinking of getting my kitchen redone before I sold my house,' Eleanor said.

'Forget it – life's too short. Get the next place right.'

'How long have you been working for who you do?'

'Long enough to know that no one's ever going to find exactly what they want. Five years. I somehow managed to get a job when everyone else was getting sacked – straight out of college. My father pushed me into it really, that's why I'm trying to do something with the photography. You know, trying to do something I want to do, for myself. But it hasn't been too bad. It's all right around here. I was in a branch in Clapham for a while. That place really got me down. Everybody who came in seemed to be totally unrealistic. It was like, where have you been? You know, they were all under this illusion that Clapham wasn't really next to Stockwell, or that because Clapham was next to Stockwell the prices would be really cheap.' He quickly looked under the kitchen table for some reason that was not apparent to Eleanor. 'If you ask me most people move for the wrong reasons anyway,' he said. 'Do you want to see the rest of the house, or perhaps you've seen enough already? Don't feel obliged.'

'I wouldn't mind,' Eleanor said. She glanced at her watch, not reading it. 'I'm not in a hurry.'

'Whatever you say.' He sprang towards the stairs, his limbs jerking.

'What are the right reasons?' she said, following, flicking the switch after her.

'Sorry?'

'For moving?'

'Oh God, don't ask me that. Mostly the ones that people haven't thought about.'

'Nothing to do with kitchens then?'

'Not usually.'

'I don't think I have an idea of what my perfect kitchen would be like anyway. I'm not very good at things like that. My sister's into it, it's her job. She's an interior designer.'

They reached the hallway and carried on up without stopping. The stairs creaked as they went and the window on the half landing cast blank light on the greeny tan matting, making it look softer and not quite so treacherous. Outside there was no sky but something else, something grey and thick which had sunk on to the roof tops and was spilling over into the dismal gardens.

'Of course,' Paul said, slowing as he neared the top, 'I take other pictures, too. More serious stuff. But it's still buildings and streets that really interest me. Places, I suppose – the changing light, the way you can pick up warmth and coldness, the patterns and distortions.' His voice had raised a pitch and become slightly hoarse – Eleanor thought he sounded embarrassed. 'You know, things like that. I go all over London with my camera. I suppose I should make more of an effort with people, with faces and bodies. I'll get round to that one day, I imagine – if I ever get the right equipment.' He was on the landing looking back at Eleanor as she was coming up to his eye level. She looked away, noticing a metal rod was missing two steps from the top. 'It's so bloody expensive,' he said, 'even the second-hand stuff.'

71 Battledean Road, N5

Rose said, 'There are only two bedrooms?'

'Yes,' said Eleanor, 'I did tell you.'

'That's because the bathroom's up here too,' Paul said. 'It's the old toss-up with these houses. You either have them in the basement, or lose a bedroom. Though I have seen them crammed into the ground floor. Not a good idea. Personally—'

'I suppose you don't need any more,' Rose said.

Eleanor caught Paul's eye. She smiled briefly before looking away.

They walked back into the main bedroom. 'Good light at the front,' Rose said. Sun was slanting across Ufton Grove, the late rays catching a mottled film of dirt on the windows, as if it had once rained mud, and the light coming into the room was diffused and hazy and thick with drifting motes. 'With a space like this I'd get rid of the curtains,' she said, 'and put up some Roman blinds. They're so less cluttered. I'd also paint the walls brilliant white. I'm sick to death of off-white. Ivory, honey, pearl, apricot, clotted cream – it all looks terrible. Sharpness is the thing now.' The carpet was a light green, a sage, and there were sun-bleached patches below each window a couple of feet in from the wall beginning to look almost burnt. 'This carpet's got to go too. In fact all the carpets. The sisal on the stairs could probably stay.'

'Rose,' said Eleanor, 'I haven't bought the house yet.'

'I thought you wanted my advice.'

'Yes, but—' she tried to catch Paul's eye again. He wasn't looking at her.

'You don't have to take it,' Rose said. She walked over to the boarded-up fireplace. 'I bet you could open this up pretty easily.' She bent down, tapped the board with her knuckles. It was screwed into place, though the screws were loose and she managed to get her fingers around a corner. The board started to come away with a splitting sound.

'Rose,' Eleanor said urgently, 'can you look at the bathroom again with me, please. There's something I'm not quite sure about.'

'The grate's still here,' Rose said, ignoring her sister. She was kneeling, having got the board, or the corner of the board a few inches away from the surround, and peering into the gap. 'Why on earth did they cover that up? People really are mad.'

'Because of the draught, perhaps?' Paul said.

'Rose,' Eleanor said, walking out of the room. There was the splitting sound again but more sudden and much louder. Eleanor rushed back in. 'Christ Rose, what the hell have you done?' Rose was standing, holding a triangle of board, the sides jagged and splintery.

'Sorry,' she said to Paul.

'Rose,' Eleanor said once more, shaking her head.

'It's okay,' Paul said. 'It doesn't matter, really. These sorts of things happen all the time. You wouldn't believe what we have to cover up. Here.' He put his folder on the bed and took the piece from Rose and tried to fit it back into place. He managed to wedge it in, but it didn't look very convincing.

'I'm sorry,' Eleanor said.

'Really,' he said, 'it doesn't matter. Don't worry. They're pretty relaxed people.'

'You wouldn't think so from looking at all these pictures around the place,' Rose said. 'I mean, look at that thing above the bed. How could you sleep with that in the room?'

'I quite like it,' Eleanor said.

'What the hell is it?' Rose said.

'It's a pupil,' Eleanor said, 'an eye, blown up. It's a photograph.'

'Yuk,' said Rose. 'Are they young?'

'Not especially,' Paul said. 'I'd say she's a bit younger than he is.'

'I think it's rather beautiful,' Eleanor said, 'the way you can see right into it. There's so much texture there. It's clever.'

'I wonder where they're moving to.' Rose said.

'Clapham,' Paul said. 'They're buying a property through our office there.'

'That fits,' Rose said. 'I've never come across anyone with any taste who lives in Clapham.'

'They're getting pretty desperate to get rid of this place,' Paul said. 'I'm surprised it hasn't gone already, it's been on for nearly a month, though I suppose Christmas got in the way.' He moved closer to the photograph, and Eleanor. 'Yeah, you're right,' he said to her, 'it is a photograph – I should have seen that. How did you know?'

'I noticed it last time,' Eleanor said. 'And to be honest I've seen one very like it before.'

'Her husband sells cameras,' Rose said.

'I used to work with photographs, for a photographic library,' Eleanor said. She walked out of the room, saying sharply, 'Rose, can you just look at this thing in the bathroom for a minute – please?' She waited until they were both behind the bathroom door, before saying, 'Why did you have to tell him that?'

'What?'

'That Clay sells cameras.'

'Eleanor? Why the hell not, he does doesn't he – second-hand ones anyway?'

'You didn't have to bring him into it – he knows nothing about photographs.' Eleanor stopped, seeing her face in a mirror set in the door of a stainless-steel cabinet above the sink. 'He doesn't know much about anything.' She ran her fingers through her hair trying to make it more lively – how it was after she first got it cut.

'Well leave him then,' Rose said. 'He wasn't exactly a ball of fun at Christmas.'

'Oh sure, simple,' Eleanor said. She thought it needed cutting again.

'It's about time you did something for yourself, Eleanor. How old are you, forty-two?' Rose paused, looking around the bathroom.

Eleanor was conscious of how loud Rose talked and she didn't want to have a discussion about Clay, or her age within earshot of Paul, so she asked calmly, 'What do you think of the tiles? They are a bit too austere-looking don't you think, going right up to the ceiling?'

'At least they're white. No, actually, I quite like the way it's been done. It works. I'd leave them. In fact the bathroom's about the only room I wouldn't change. This is nice.' She opened the stainless-steel cabinet above the sink with the mirror on the front. Inside the shelves were piled with pill containers and shampoo, conditioner and bath oil bottles – some of which were made of indigo-blue glass. There were other perfume bottles, a packet of Lil-Lets, a couple of new toothbrushes and a press-on thermometer in a hard plastic case. Rose reached for one of the perfume bottles, turning it so she could read the label. 'I love this stuff,' she said. 'You should try it. It's bloody expensive.'

'Rose,' Eleanor said, 'don't break anything else, please.'

'I'm sorry to rush you two,' Paul said, edging into the room, his thick brown hair falling across his forehead. Eleanor thought he probably hadn't shaved that morning and that he looked rougher, more tired than when she had seen him a couple of weeks previously, before Christmas. He had had bags under his eyes then, but they had been faint, boyish. Now they appeared heavy and she wondered whether he had been ill, or whether he had just not got much sleep over Christmas. She felt strangely jealous, thinking about what he might have got up to – what he did when he wasn't showing people around houses, or taking photographs. 'There are only two of us working today and I've got an appointment in Highbury at three. I didn't want to cancel coming here. Everyone else has got flu or something – it's the time of year I suppose.' He looked at his watch. 'I'm going to have to get going pretty soon. If you'd like to see it again just give me a call.' He stepped away, awkwardly, the way he moved, like an adolescent – that was it, Eleanor thought – like someone who wasn't yet used to the length and strength of their limbs.

They followed him out and Rose said, after she had already gone a few steps, 'Hang on a minute, I just need a pee.' She turned and went back up into the bathroom and closed the door, locking it. Eleanor carried on down with Paul – the garden appearing briefly through the window on the half landing. It was in sharp contrast with the sun hitting the end square on – suddenly brilliant on a piece of broken glass or something highly reflective stuck on top of the garden wall. Whether this set it off, Eleanor didn't know, but her left eye suddenly began watering, so she covered it with her hand and reached the hall feeling unsteady. And annoyed because she thought this problem with her eyes had cleared up and that she really would now have to get them checked. 'Can I just have another quick look in here?' Eleanor said, already making her way into the reception room with her eye still covered, wanting to wait for it to clear before going, not wanting Paul to see it red and watering.

'Be my guest,' he said, staying in the hall.

Eleanor walked over to the front mantelpiece, the one

with the wedding photograph on it. She could just see out of her good eye. The other was slowly beginning to feel less irritated. Rose was suddenly behind her, so Eleanor turned towards her not wanting Rose to see her looking at the photograph, at the person who resembled her so much, because she was embarrassed by the similarity. But Rose looked over Eleanor's shoulder anyway, saying, 'God, I don't think I could go through all that again.' She was still arranging her clothes and smelling strongly of a perfume Eleanor hadn't noticed before and couldn't place.

'What?'

'A wedding.'

'That's hardly likely, is it?'

Rose didn't answer exactly, instead saying, 'I always rush into things. You're much more sensible than I am. How long were you with Clay before you got married, four, five years? It must have been longer, you lived with him for at least four years before getting married.'

'Yeah, but sometimes I wish I was a little more impulsive. I've always been so bloody sensible.'

'I don't know about sensible – you've just stuck with what you've known. You didn't have to marry someone quite so like Dad. I can't remember, when did you finally get married, was it just before or after he died?'

'Before, Rose, come on.' Eleanor could see clearly with both eyes now. 'Clay's not like Dad was. He's tougher in a way, more single-minded. Okay, he's not exactly brilliant at the business end of things either, but he has a very different attitude to it. Dad wanted to succeed. Success has never bothered Clay.'

'Has anything? Are you all right?'

Eleanor was aware that Paul had come into the room. 'I had something in my eye,' she said. 'It's fine. We should go.'

'I'm sorry,' Paul said, looking at his watch again, 'I'm going to have to get moving.'

Just beyond the Post Office on Essex Road a hardware shop had stacked a load of galvanised-steel dustbins outside on the pavement and they were catching the sun, gleaming madly. Eleanor thought it was more like April or May than January and her feet felt light on the pedals, driving towards the Angel.

'I liked that estate agent,' Rose said. 'He was sort of awkward, wasn't he?' She paused, scratching her top lip with her little finger, sucking the skin taut over her front teeth. 'Funny – as if he hadn't quite been finished properly. Made you want to put your arms around him. Lovely hair. At least it was not all shaved like everyone else his age seems to have it at the moment.'

'He's got nice eyes.'

'Yeah. How old do you think he is?'

'I don't know, twenty-eight, thirty?' Eleanor said, knowing he looked younger than that.

'Oh younger, I reckon.'

'Rose, you shouldn't have helped yourself to that perfume.'

'He didn't notice.'

Someone stepped on to a zebra crossing. Eleanor only saw him just in time and she had to brake hard, the seat belt snapping tight across her chest. 'So what do you reckon?' Eleanor said.

'It's okay. It's not brilliant. It doesn't make you think, I've got to live here. Though you wouldn't need to do anything major to it, at least nothing structural.'

'That's what appeals to me.'

'Great bathroom and kitchen. But it's expensive for just two bedrooms. What's it on at, two six five?'

'I thought that was cheap for the area?'

'It is nearly Hackney, Eleanor.'

'We probably couldn't afford it anyway.' The man had got across and Eleanor pressed on the accelerator. There wasn't much traffic, no buses or rubbish trucks blocking the way and they soon reached Islington Green. The shops on Upper

Street were bright and busy but the trees in front of them, which before Christmas had been strung with fairy lights, stood in stark silhouette.

'Clay would hate it, I suppose,' Eleanor said.

'You don't know,' Rose said.

'He'll hate it.'

'Look, it wasn't great. I'd keep looking. I think you can do better. Wait until you find somewhere really special before you even show him anything.'

'Let's face it, I'm not going to find exactly what I want, am I?' she said thinking of Paul. 'Yeah, maybe you're right. It just seems to take forever.'

'You haven't seen that many places, have you? Maybe you should try to concentrate on one area a little more.'

'I haven't come across anywhere that I really fancy living.'

'Can you drop me here? De Beauvoir's fine. All right, it's not quite Canonbury, but I'm spoilt. See, it's not so far in the car. By that café, there, on the left. Speak to that estate agent, he seemed helpful. Find out what else they have.'

'Here?'

'Yeah, that's great. I've got to see this guy about some shutters. Oh God, and I've got to get a birthday present for a friend's son. What on earth do you buy a ten-year-old?'

'Don't ask me.'

'No.' Rose undid her seat belt and gathered her things.

'Thanks for coming,' Eleanor said. 'You've been very helpful.'

Rose got out of the car. 'Keep looking,' she said. 'You can do better.'

Eleanor watched her sister hurry down Charlton Place, turning almost immediately into Camden Passage. She was about to pull out when a bus swooped in tight just in front of her and she had to wait for it to move again before she could get her car out and back on course, still surprisingly unhindered by traffic. So much so, and perhaps because she wasn't concentrating as hard as she should have been, thinking instead of the house she had just seen for the second time, thinking of Paul, she missed Rosebery Avenue, which she had intended to take, and kept on St John Street. She swept past the depressing City University buildings and The Peasant where some people still appeared to be eating lunch, and had to swerve to avoid an *Evening Standard* van U-turning. Shaken, she slowed considerably and she came into the Clerkenwell she had once known like the back of her hand going well under thirty. She used to work on Great Sutton Street and she slowed even more as she approached the turning, wondering whether she might just drive past her old building, and that even if she saw someone she used to work with they probably wouldn't see her behind the wheel, not expecting to see her. Besides, she could always put her foot down. But she had forgotten that Great Sutton Street was one-way, going the other way, and she couldn't turn into it or stop anywhere near because the *Evening Standard* van had caught up with her and was urging her on across Clerkenwell Road – the lights having just changed from green to amber – the man in the van frantically shooing her ahead, in her rear-view mirror.

An estate agents looking like a fancy boutique had opened on the south-east corner of Clerkenwell Road and St John Street. Eleanor also noticed that many of the old office buildings and former small factories and workshops along St John Street and the streets leading off it were covered in scaffolding or there were cranes and skips about, or buildings had been recently spray cleaned and were clear of grime and crisp, even in the thickening dusk. Plus there were numerous spotlit hoardings advertising residential leases or studio lofts. Signs saying, *Acquired for Residential Conversion*, or, *Live/Work Apartments*. The traffic was stalling as cars pulled out of metered spaces and others replaced them – the great block of Smithfield Market stuck in the middle distance, like something from a different era, an anachronism. Pedestrians crossing the road shimmied around the reversing cars –

helmeted-builders and smart-looking executives. Eleanor couldn't believe how much Clerkenwell had changed in half a year. It had become urgent – emanating a shifting, edgy self-importance. And Eleanor suddenly, strongly, felt not being a part of it, of this transition. Clerkenwell was moving on without her. Even Clay was in the middle of it, she thought, not that he would be appreciating it.

As she was approaching Charterhouse Street a car came out of a bay directly in front of her and she found herself indicating and parking. There were forty-three minutes left on the meter, so feeling lucky she locked the car and clasping her coat tight around her headed for Clay's shop on Cowcross Street. It was hard to tell what daylight was left because of the brightness of the shops and sandwich bars packing up for the day, the windows of which were casting odd patterns on the narrow pavements. But it was bitter and a dampness she hadn't felt in Islington was present now – perhaps, Eleanor thought, because Clerkenwell was that much lower than Islington, that much nearer the Thames. There was a rank smell also, but it wasn't the river's smell. Eleanor knew it was coming from the meat market. She caught herself in the window of a newsagent's – a thin, translucent figure, looking a little stooped because of a kink in the glass. She wondered how a camera would have caught the image, giving some sort of solidity, some sort of permanence to it.

Clay's shop was flanked by an Italian café and a pub. It was the dimmest shopfront on Cowcross Street, looking, oddly, like it had always been there. Despite the dimness, or maybe because of it, Eleanor always thought it attracted your attention, drawing people in. One window displayed stereoscopes, magic lanterns, hand-crank projectors, half-plate, quarter-plate and tailboard cameras, while the other window contained only Leicas, from the earliest mark 1 to a limited edition gold M6, laid out in tiers. The low lighting was simple and shone warmly on to the dusty brass and concertinaed leather, the titanium and the thick convex lens glass, which looked as if it had been wiped with petrol so that it was awash with tiny rectangles of purples and greens.

The place smelt of furniture polish and oil – Eleanor had forgotten quite how strongly. 'Clay,' she said, having stepped into the shop, not really expecting Clay to be listening, 'I'm going to start taking pictures again.'

'Eleanor?' Clay said, getting his breath having rushed from the back room because the bell had rung automatically when Eleanor had opened the door, 'what the hell are you doing here?' They got to within a couple of feet of each other before backing away slightly. They didn't kiss, or touch each other.

'I was passing. I've just seen Rose. Christ, what's happened to St John Street in the last six months?'

'What do you mean?'

'The scaffolding everywhere – the fancy estate agents?'

'Oh, all that. I think it's become fashionable. Not that it's been any good for my business. You weren't sacked that long ago, were you?'

'The shop's a bit dusty,' Eleanor said, walking over to an antique class cabinet full of Leitz lenses. 'Are you on your own today?'

'Yes,' Clay said. He lit a cigarette, inhaling deeply.

'Where's Charles?'

'He's only coming in a couple of days a week at the moment.'

'Is he happy with that?'

'Delighted, I think. He's got other work. There wasn't enough for him to do – besides I couldn't afford it.'

'How long has this been going on?'

'Not very long. A few months.'

'Why didn't you tell me?'

'Why should I have? It doesn't make any difference to you.'

'What do you do at lunchtimes when he's not in?'

'I close the shop for ten minutes or so. I usually manage to get out. Garfagnana's only next door.' Eleanor walked over to another cabinet which housed the more contemporary camera bodies. 'Is this to replace the house-hunting?'

'What?' Eleanor said.

'Taking pictures.'

'I didn't think you were listening.'

'I always listen to you sweetheart. So what exactly are you going to photograph? We don't go on holiday any more.'

'Ha, ha. I don't know – buildings, places perhaps. I'm being serious Clay. I've got that old Olympus at home somewhere. Maybe I might be able to borrow something a little better from here, with a decent lens?'

'Eleanor, most of this stuff's worth a lot of money. It's not even meant to be used. They're collectors' items.'

'Thanks Clay. You've got a shop full of stuff that's been sitting here for years and you won't even let your wife borrow one bloody camera because it's so bloody precious it can't be used.'

'Eleanor, calm down. I don't need this. Look, take what you want.' Clay lit another cigarette and walked behind the old pine counter at the back of the shop – there was another cabinet of yet more lenses above him – and started flicking through an auction catalogue, ignoring her.

'Sorry,' Eleanor said, 'I've got a headache.' She paused, studying the camera bodies. 'I just thought that maybe, oh I don't know—' She tried to open the cabinet she was standing by. 'That maybe it might be a way of making some money. I've got lots of contacts.'

Clay laughed. 'You're trying to tell me you think you can make some money taking pictures? I shouldn't think you could even remember how to focus a camera properly.'

'I did do a course when I was at college. It'll come back. I'm sure there are other courses I could do. I'm not stupid. I thought all cameras came with auto–focus now anyway.'

'How many people do you think there are trying to make money out of photography? Thousands, hundreds of thousands? Christ, I should know, most of them troop through here – without spending anything.'

'Yes, but they don't all have the contacts I have. Perhaps you've forgotten where I used to work.' Eleanor was suddenly sure Paul had been in the shop. She wondered whether Clay had been rude to him.

'You can have the best contacts in the world but you've still got to be able to take decent pictures. I'll tell you, it's easier selling the equipment. Or was.' He put the catalogue down. 'The people with money who come in here don't even take pictures. They've got more sense. They know what's really worth what. They're into the craftsmanship, the mechanics. Palpable stuff – you know, series' numbers, whether it's got the maker's original case. They don't give a shit about the aperture or the perspective, or the lighting. They don't need subject matters.'

'How do you open this cabinet?'

'Eleanor.'

'I'm being serious.'

'Look, why don't you just stick to finding somewhere new to live? It will be a damn sight easier.'

'Maybe I don't want to do something that's easy – what's wrong with a challenge? Perhaps things have been too bloody easy for too long. Perhaps that's our problem.'

Eleanor turned off the taps, removed her dressing gown and stood in front of the mirror. Condensation slowly began to clear from the glass while the bath, getting used to the weight and temperature of the water, began to tick. She saw, first, her shape, her chest rising and falling and, once there was virtually no condensation left, the odd hair on her arms picking up the draught coming under the bathroom door and waving slightly. She leant forward to look closer into her eyes, seeing her pupils dilating, because she was cutting out light from the fixture in the middle of the ceiling. She was reminded of the photograph in the bedroom of the Ufton Grove house – except her pupils appeared to her just surface, just a sheen. And she thought of the estate agent with his odd, jerky way of moving, and his green eyes and brown hair, and smooth-looking, young-looking skin that smelt so particular, so particularly of him – like a musk. She moved her head back slightly, letting direct light on to the mirror. She was blinded for a moment and when she regained her focus she saw rectangles of light on her pupils, as if she had thick Leitz lenses for eyes, like those in the window of Clay's shop, though there was no trace of purple, or anything oily. And the longer she looked into her eyes the more she was disturbed by getting nowhere. She wanted to see their real depth, what was behind them. The shape of her thoughts, her feelings – that she was still capable of loving, of passion. She wanted to know.

She stood further back and checked her breasts in the mirror, something she hadn't done for a few months. She lifted her arms slowly, turning from side to side looking at the outline. They were still about the same size, one wasn't lower than the other – seeing the nipples harden because of the chill and watching them rise as she stretched her arms above her. There was no puckering or dimpling, there were no rashes and she hadn't had any pain, and as she brought her arms down the relief she felt at the fact that her breasts seemed to be okay was not as great as it should have been, because she couldn't help thinking that her breasts were obviously the breasts of a woman who hadn't had children. It didn't matter that they looked liked the breasts of a much younger woman.

She climbed into the bath, which wasn't as hot as it might have been – Clay had had a bath earlier and had already gone to bed because he had said he was feeling very tired and achy and thought he might be coming down with something, though she believed that that was just an excuse to get out of her way. They had a row over supper about the house in

Ufton Grove, Clay saying that he would have to be dead before you got him anywhere near the place, and Eleanor saying she wished he were. So the water was not comforting when she needed it to be and she washed herself without soaking for long – quickly, distractedly feeling her breasts with a soapy hand for any lumps or swellings. She slipped under the water up to her chin, her body slightly twisted to one side to get her knees covered, and shut her eyes briefly, thinking, fuck it, if I've got the tits of a much younger woman, they might as well be appreciated.

'I'm worried,' said Eleanor's mother, 'about Rose.'

'You always have to worry about something,' Eleanor said.

'Mark's been away an awful lot recently. I just hope they're all right. What's that noise I can hear?'

'It's a train, Mum,' Eleanor held the receiver away from her so her mother could hear the train more clearly, 'on its way to Ramsgate.'

'That's nice.' She paused for a moment, as if she had forgotten what she was saying. 'She's so tired all the time. It's not like her.'

'She's busy and I think James is playing up at the moment.'

'Why's that?'

'How do I know? Maybe it's just his age.'

'Has Clay's chest cleared up?'

'He went to the doctor this morning to get some antibiotics.'

'I thought he never went to the doctor?'

'Maybe he was feeling particularly bad.'

'You should look after him better. He's not as strong as you think.'

The snow was fine and dry, coming down at an angle in a steady breeze. It was not settling for long but Eleanor felt it on her face, like sand, and tasted it on the scarf covering her chin. She didn't push the scarf away because she felt more secure behind it, and less recognisable. Cars were moving along Upper Street at a crawl with the traffic backing up in both directions. Shop lights caught the falling snow and the patterns the flurries made when a bus or a lorry managed to pass at some speed. People were hurrying along the pavement with their heads twisted away from the oncoming snow. It didn't bother Eleanor, however, and she walked slowly, knowing where she was headed but not entirely sure whether she would go in. Or what she would say if she did, if she saw him there.

She stopped by the window of the first estate agents she came to – two short of his – thinking she should really pop in here. She looked at the photographs and details of properties in the window, taking nothing in. Her mind was still moving up the street. She left the window and walked a few paces on, stopped and returned to the window, pausing again, thinking, what the hell am I doing? Still she couldn't concentrate on what was behind the glass and she set off again, increasing her pace, striding firmly, as if that were the only way she was going to get anywhere. With pace and conviction. And it was suddenly easy and she passed the other two estate agents without bothering to even glance at their windows, slowing only as she approached Paul's, trying to bury her face deeper into her scarf – her heart was suddenly skipping. He probably won't be there anyway, she said to herself, or remember who I am. But he was. She saw him immediately, sitting at a desk three back. He was wearing the same jacket she had seen him in the other day. The snow was thickening and it no longer stung her face, building up on the ledge her scarf made, melting on her skin. He looked up and straight out of the window, at her, though seemingly not seeing her. She shifted along the window a little way anyway. There were two other people in the office, Eleanor saw, occupying the desks between the door and Paul's. There were no customers.

The snow was getting stronger and she thought, if ever there's an excuse for just going into somewhere this is it. So she entered and the heat of the fan above the door bore straight down on her, instantly making her cheeks flush. It wasn't until she had unwound her scarf and was unbuttoning her coat that she realised that the blast of heat moving through her was not in fact from the fan-heater, but was building inside her, and flowing out through her capillaries. She closed her eyes for a second, cursing, feeling pins and needles in her neck. She opened her eyes, looking down, seeing her navy sweater and black jeans, which she didn't often wear because they were uncomfortable, but had decided to wear today because she thought they were her youngest-looking clothes. The sweater was a V-neck and she had on a long-sleeved striped T-shirt underneath. She wasn't wearing a vest or a bra. She wasn't wearing enough clothes for outside. But inside, now, she felt she had on far too many.

The boy nearest the door was staring at her, not even looking like he wanted to help. She found she had clenched her fists and that they were moist with sweat and her fingers were slipping against the palms of her hands as she stood there fretting. She uncurled her right hand thinking this boy was as young, if not younger than Paul, but he was thicker set with short cropped hair and not at all attractive. He was wearing a grey double-breasted suit that made him look even bulkier. Eleanor pointed to Paul, as if to say, it's him I've come to see. Paul had noticed her and she stepped towards him as he was standing up and coming round from behind his desk to meet her. The woman at the desk in between watched them lazily, smiling at Eleanor – a sly, knowing smile. She looked older than the boys and had a hard, angular face with shoulder-length dyed blonde hair. She was wearing a lot of make-up and her skin looked almost yellow. She was smoking a cigarette like it was the first cigarette of the day, making the most of it.

Paul said, 'That's a coincidence. I just tried you on the phone.' Eleanor thought he was blushing also – though it might have been the harsh lights – and she tried not to look at him, looking briefly behind her catching the boy by the door making a face at Paul she didn't see enough of to fully understand. Paul said, 'Come and sit down.' He motioned for her to sit at one of the two chairs arranged in front of his desk. Sitting, she hadn't realised how heavy her limbs had become and almost immediately her heart slowed and the heat waving within her lessened. She let out a breath like a sigh. 'Disgusting day,' he said.

Eleanor looked over her shoulder again, but the fat boy was on the phone, not making faces. 'Yeah, it's foul,' she said, struggling with her coat.

'We've had an offer on the Ufton Grove house.'

'Oh,' Eleanor said, managing to get it off her shoulders and on to the back of the chair.

'It hasn't been accepted yet. I've managed to stall the vendors – in case you were still interested.'

'Thanks, but actually I've decided that it's not quite right. I was wondering if there was anything else which might be suitable – that's why I've popped in.'

'Have you not been getting our lists?'

'No, I don't think so.'

'That's strange. Have we got your address down wrong?'

Eleanor saw that her hands were shaking. 'The post has been a bit erratic recently.' She didn't want to say that her husband had taken to binning any mail he saw from estate agents. She didn't want to mention Clay at all.

Paul noticed her hands were shaking and said, 'Can I get you a coffee, or something?'

'No, no thanks.' She grasped the sides of the chair. 'I think I just need something to eat. I was up very early this morning and I didn't eat much breakfast.'

'Do you want to come back, or do you want me to quickly run through what we've got?'

'I'm here now, I'm not going to faint or anything.' She forced a smile, swallowing hard, trying to get something into her stomach, even if it was just spit – she was determined not to faint.

'It won't take a minute.' He got a folder from a tray on his desk, opened it and started to go through the particulars. 'There isn't much. We've got something on Mortimer Road, but there's an offer on that. We had somewhere on Tottenham Road, but they're close to exchanging. There's a house on Lawford Road, though it might be beyond your limit. The market's just gone mad over the last couple of weeks, and nothing's coming in. I haven't been out of the office for two days.' He kept shuffling the papers, losing his place and having to go back. 'Arrgh, here's what I was looking for – Battledean Road. Have you thought about Highbury Fields?'

Eleanor shook her head.

'No? Smashing place to live, and parts of it are still pretty undervalued. Battledean's at the top, a couple of streets in. Some of the families have been there for decades. You won't get any trouble, trust me, I was born around the corner.' He passed her the details. 'We've got a place on Stavordale Road, but you're getting much nearer the Arsenal, and unless you don't mind the football crowds I'd forget it. We've also got a two-bed house on Monsell Road – no, I don't think that would be right.' He paused, lined the remaining particulars up and put them back into the folder. 'I'd think about Battledean. Three beds. It's only on at two twenty, though it's going to be a big undertaking – the place practically needs rebuilding.'

Eleanor looked down at the details he had passed to her. The photograph, which she supposed he'd taken, showed a tatty two-storey late Victorian terraced house with double bay windows, one on top of the other. 'Maybe it would be good for me to do something like that,' she said, thinking, if Rose can do it, I don't see why I can't.

'You're not going to get a location like that for that price again.' He looked at his watch and suddenly stood up, all arms. 'I've got to get something to eat myself. There's quite a good place I sometimes go to that's not far. Do you want to come?'

Eleanor stood, too, unsteadily. She also looked at her watch. It was ten to one 'I don't know, urrgh—'

'Come on, we don't have to be long.' Paul got his coat from a stand behind his desk and shot out in front of her, his body springing awkwardly towards the door.

'Okay,' she said brightly, grabbing her things together, hauling on her coat and following. The woman in the middle desk looked at her in exactly the same way. She was exhaling another great gasp of smoke, but as she ran out of smoke Eleanor was sure her smile turned into a sneer.

'Hey,' the large boy at the desk nearest the door, the one who'd been making faces, said to Paul, as Paul was stepping outside just ahead of Eleanor, 'Jenny called.'

Paul didn't slow and Eleanor had to trot for a moment to catch him up. It was still snowing and Eleanor wound her scarf around her neck and chin again, right up to her mouth, because her skin felt tender. The pavement was slippery with a substance that was not quite slush but more than rain.

'That place drives me mad,' Paul said. 'Two days I've been stuck inside with those arseholes.' They passed City Fried Chicken, Century Video and another estate agents. He said, 'Have you tried in there? They're pretty good, they might have something.'

'They didn't,' Eleanor said, lying.

Paul slowed and for a moment Eleanor thought he was going to back up and spot something suitable in the window which she should have noticed, but he said, 'That's all this street is virtually, estate agents.' He stopped altogether and looking at her, looking straight into her eyes, squinting slightly, the snow falling between them, said, 'You remind me of someone.' He spun round and shot off, as if he had just touched an electric fence. He crossed the road and turned into Theberton Street, Eleanor hurrying after him. A French-style café was advertising a set lunch for £4.95 on a chalk board which had been placed outside in the middle of the snowy pavement. Paul reached the door first and held it open for Eleanor so she had to duck under his arm, as she had done once before. She wondered for a moment whether it was the same café where she had had a coffee on the afternoon in early December when she had first looked at the estate agents in Upper Street. She wasn't sure.

'How's the photography going?' she said, after they had sat down.

'I haven't had much time recently,' he said. 'I used to take the odd five minutes when I was out of the office, and it's always good to be driving around, you notice things, but being stuck in there – it's like everything goes blank. But, hey, I'm not going to be there for ever.' He smiled.

'No,' said Eleanor. 'I did a photography course once.'

'Yeah,' he said. 'Yeah, I remember you said you did something with photographs. And your husband sells cameras, right?'

'I used to work for a photographic library, but I was made redundant last summer.' She wasn't going to mention Clay's shop. 'This course was when I was at college. Though I don't think I can remember very much about it. I thought—' She was going to tell him she was contemplating going back to it but suddenly realised that he might take it the wrong way and think she was only interested in taking up photography again because that's what he did.

'I was never taught how to take a picture,' he said, shaking his head. 'The only practical thing I've got a certificate for is selling houses.'

A waiter brought over two menus and said, 'The set menu's on the board above the bar.'

'Maybe people can't teach you how to really take photographs, or to do things that mean a lot,' she said, and waited for him to say something in reply, but he didn't and she suddenly felt she had said something stupid, so she said, 'You know, artistically.' She glanced up at the set menu. There was a choice between grilled salmon or pork, both with salad and *frites*. Music and the sound of people chatting and cutlery on plates grew louder between them because they didn't say anything for a while, which seemed to Eleanor longer than it was, and she said eventually, suddenly, without thinking, 'I've never had lunch with an estate agent before.' She tried to laugh.

'Please,' he said, 'do me favour and try not to think of me as an estate agent. I'm just like most people, stuck doing something I don't want to do for the money.' He briefly looked at the board detailing the set menu. 'Okay,' he said, 'maybe I'm luckier. I get to have lunch with you.' He grinned.

'There must be better things to it than that.'

He shook his head. 'I tell you, buying and selling property doesn't always bring out the best in people. I've got this National Association of Estate Agents certificate thing that proves I know how to measure a fucking room, but I'd be better off with a degree in psychology. It's not so much about whether a place has two bedrooms or three, as helping people to sort out their lives, to make decisions – to understand why they actually want to move. Think about it. I'm having the pork. I'm not big on fish.'

'So why do I want to move then?' Eleanor said.

'I'll tell you when I know you a bit better.' He leant forward. 'I still can't think who you remind me of. I wouldn't forget a face like yours.'

She rang him as soon as she got home and said yes, she would like to see the house on Battledean Road, because she thought he would be able to show it to her. And she wanted to see him again, already.

'Where the hell now?' Clay said later. 'Where the fuck are we off to now?'

The light was cold and distant and drifting ceaselessly over Highbury Fields in fading bands. She had driven up Baalbec Road and was pausing by the top of Highbury Place, shortly before the Highbury Crescent turning, so she could look at her *A-Z*. A black cab was parked in front of her – the cabby was eating something, chips perhaps. He had a thick neck and was hunched forward. The trees running down Highbury Place – with their web of spindly bare branches – were making the air there look more misty than it was, but directly over the lower section of Highbury Fields the late afternoon light was coming down clear, and the grass was an even, frozen, pale green. She wanted to get out and walk across it, but she was already late. The appointment was for three and it was getting on for three fifteen. She pulled out slowly and crossed over to Highbury Crescent. On her right, at the far end of the upper half of Highbury Fields, she noticed a large school building and in front of it some tall wire fencing. Wondering what it enclosed, she found she had missed her turning so she carried on towards Highbury Pool, with the houses fronting Highbury Crescent becoming grander. She stopped by Fieldway Crescent to look at her *A-Z* again, discovering that she could either turn off here and try to cut through – though it looked as if she might get stuck in a one-way system – or she could go the whole way round the lower half of Highbury Fields and start again. She'd come too far to back up and there didn't look much in it so she carried on, thinking she'd stick with the view at least.

However, Highbury Fields took on a darker perspective as she approached the pool, which was surrounded by bottle-banks, thick shrubs and a children's multicoloured play area. Beyond the pool she turned into Highbury Place and driving up with the grass on her left she was reminded of driving around Clapham Common, even though there was no traffic and she wasn't going anything like as fast. The trees she had looked down on only moments earlier, which had made the air seem soft and misty, now, looking the other way, shed only a starkness. And as she progressed an inexplicable sense of fate grew with the starkness. As if life was completely out of her hands. As if she were following some path, some course that had been set generations ago.

The taxi was still there and three women with pushchairs were waiting to see which way Eleanor was going to go before they crossed Highbury Crescent. Eleanor remembered to turn right into Highbury Terrace and she passed smart Georgian houses on her left, with the school building ahead and the high wire fencing just before it, which she could now see was enclosing some tennis courts. She turned left at the end of Highbury Place into Framfield Road and for a couple of seconds it seemed as if she were peering over London, with Hampstead Heath rising above the roofs of the houses at the bottom of the road – a hazy green, tree-topped horizon that promised perhaps more than it was – and her spirits lifted for a moment, and she thought, maybe the woman had to go out and he's going to be there to show me around.

And again she was facing ceaseless light, like Heaven was lowering as she crawled into Battledean Road. Though it was more channelled and harsher here than it had been over Highbury Fields and the few trees lining the pavement were in silhouette and the road was dead still. She couldn't see an estate agents' board so she let the car creep forward as she took in the squat terraces of double-bay-windowed houses, the bays being rectangular until she had gone some way up the road when they became less angular and were topped off by tiny slate-covered pinnacles – sharp against the sky. Net curtains were pulled across most windows and a number of the houses were in bad shape. She was looking for his car when she saw the board with its distinctive brown and green colouring outside a house that was more run down than any she had so far seen. She parked still not having spotted his car, eventually turning off the engine – the fateful feeling coming back, but much stronger. She knew he wasn't coming and knew she was being ridiculous for having hoped he might have – for having arranged to see the house when really she had just wanted to just see him.

She walked towards the grimy, rotted dark blue door knowing she wouldn't like the house, realising it was totally inappropriate, but knowing she had to be polite and take an interest and view it nevertheless, because she had been so stupid. That that was a small price to pay. Who did she think she was, chasing after twenty-six-year-old estate agents? There wasn't a bell or a knocker so she banged on the damp splintering wood with her chaffed knuckles – the cold spell having left them raw.

39 Woodlea Road, N16

Eleanor immediately thought of the woman she had seen in
the photograph on the mantelpiece in the Ufton Grove house,
the woman who reminded her of herself – it was the eyes, and
the mouth. She was much younger in this picture, probably in
her late teens, and her hair was longer, falling to below her
shoulders. Her face was softer-looking and less strained, but
perhaps that was because she was younger. She was smiling at
the camera, face on, standing in a garden. It looked like early
summer and the garden was dark green and wildly overgrown,
though it could have been late summer, if the summer had
been wet. It was not a bright day, or at least the camera had
not picked up much natural light. She was standing in front of
a subsiding brick wall, which was topped by the long, thick
shoots of a rose bush. The garden sloped steeply and between
the shoots the soft horizon of Hampstead Heath could just be
seen, like a smear.

'That's my daughter, Louise, in the back garden here,' the
woman said, noticing Eleanor staring at the photograph,
which had been loosely stuck into the frame of another photograph and propped against an empty vase on a filthy alcove

shelf. Eleanor, wanting to know whether it really was the same person, many years younger, asked the woman if they had always lived in the area. The woman said, 'I've been in this house for forty years.' She coughed, a low wheezing cough. 'I found that picture clearing up the other day. It was taken a long time ago now.' Eleanor thought the woman was probably older than her mother. She was certainly more frail and moved as if she were quite unsure of every step. Her voice, though quick, was reedy and would easily have been lost outside – plus she kept coughing. Eleanor asked her whether she was moving far, and the woman said, 'I should have sold up a long time ago. I was pregnant when we moved in. Forty years ago. Thought it would never happen – it wasn't meant to happen. I'd been married for fifteen years – he never guessed. Louise didn't know until they were both dead. I didn't think it was fair on anyone. I only told her when she was ill. He knew all right, he used to give me a bit of money occasionally, but we were both married and it was different then, besides he had his own family – he was a lot younger. Forty years – it goes so quick.' She shook her head and Eleanor asked her where her daughter lived now, and she said, 'You can't hang on to everything. There comes a time when you have to let go. They're putting me in a home. I don't mind. It'll be for the best. I think I'll like the company.' She coughed and when she had finished Eleanor asked once more where her daughter lived now, and the old woman said, 'She's been helping me to pack up. But she's been ill again, after her baby was born. Must have brought it back. She needs the money – she doesn't get much help.'

The woman had a dog, a mongrel with long, wiry, grey black hair. It didn't move from an armchair in the back room. The gas fire was hissing and it was hot and airless, and the dog snorted occasionally or one of its front paws would suddenly shake. It wasn't just the back room – which might once have been used as a dining room except there wasn't any space for a table any more with broken pieces of ornamental china heaped on the floor and magazines and books piled around the two small armchairs, the one with the dog in it and another which was as worn – but the whole house that smelt of the dog. Of decay. The dog's hair was everywhere also. The carpet in the back room was an orange brown and patterned, though the pattern wasn't at all clear because of the dog hair and large stains and the fact that it was worn through to the underlay in places – at the foot of the armchair which the dog wasn't curled up in and in front of the gas fire. The room was dim because the bulb was weak and a net curtain, which had gone brown with time like old newspaper, hung across the back window, covering the lower sash so that Eleanor wasn't able to see much of the garden, where presumably the young woman like her had once stood. Hampstead Heath, a smear on the horizon. 'He loves me,' the woman said at one point nodding towards the dog, 'stupid animal.'

The kitchen was at the end of the hallway and down a couple of steps. It was much brighter and the grime more apparent. The walls were a creamy yellow and heavily stained around the cooker, which was itself coated in thick layers of burnt fat. The sink was under the window looking out on to the garden, though again not much of the garden was visible because there was a net curtain over this window too. It had not gone brown with time, however, but green, blotches of it, as if it was growing mould. The enamel on the sink was cracked and caked with turquoise calcium where the taps dripped. The sink was empty but the drainer to the right was full of plates and cutlery, though Eleanor couldn't tell whether these had been washed or were waiting to be washed. The door to the garden was to the left of the sink. It was bolted and there was a pool of drying yellow liquid, of dog piss, just in front – some having splashed on to the bottom of the door – its sweet, acidic smell unmistakable. Eleanor could see the bathroom was beyond the kitchen, the door was open, but she didn't cross over to it and stood where she was for as long as she thought polite, thinking, at least my kitchen's not as bad as this.

The woman said to her, 'I can see you properly now. You have the same eyes.'

'Yes?' said Eleanor, knowing the woman was referring to her daughter, but not able to understand what it meant, so she said, stalling for time, trying to order her mind, 'The same eyes as who?' However, the woman didn't answer and carefully climbed the two steps leading back into the hallway.

She slept in the front room on the ground floor and Eleanor didn't go into that room either but peered only briefly around the door. It was as cluttered and worn as the back room, but cold. The cold came out into the hall, though it was not refreshing. Cold stale air was worse than warm stale air, Eleanor decided, because it was more unexpected and hit you harder. The woman shadowed Eleanor as best she could, but said, when they were at the foot of the stairs, 'You had better go up on your own. My legs aren't what they used to be.'

There were two bedrooms on the first floor and a short narrow stairway led to a third bedroom in an attic. This room had a small window with a spectacular view over Holloway and Tufnell Park, and on towards Parliament Hill and Hampstead Heath. From here the Heath was much clearer than from the top of Framfield Road where Eleanor had first seen it. There was a sense of how it undulated, and there were spires and masts and the odd roof visible among the trees and the shrubs and the grass. The room was empty except for a row of large cardboard boxes lined against one wall. They had been taped shut and *Louise* had been written on them in blue marker pen. Eleanor didn't stay in the room long. She had to find out if the young woman in the photograph downstairs was the same person as the woman in the wedding photograph on the mantelpiece in the Ufton Grove house. Paul saying, *You remind me of someone*, suddenly coming to mind. *I wouldn't forget a face like yours*. Wondering whether he'd seen the photograph, the photographs – or whether he had met her. The woman had said, *You have the same eyes*. Was it as simple as that?

A dark mahogany dressing table stood in the bay of the upstairs front bedroom. There was a chair before it but there was nothing on the table except a piece of stained lace the size of a tea towel. There were two single beds with bedspreads pulled tightly over them and a chest of draws matching the dresser. The wood was going grey with dust. Net curtains covered the windows and Eleanor didn't bother to hold them aside – the outline of the street, the opposite terrace was clear enough. There were more sealed cardboard boxes in the back bedroom and a single bed. There was no bedspread on this bed but a heap of crocheted woollen baby clothes. Eleanor made out an angel coat, a cardigan with pink buttons, a bonnet with a pink ribbon, and pairs of tiny socks and mittens. Eleanor picked up the angel coat and smelt it – it smelt of dust and mothballs. Of wool that might never have been worn or washed and could have been years, decades old.

Downstairs Eleanor asked the woman how old her grand-child was, and the woman said. 'I thought she'd packed every-thing up up there.'

'I saw some baby clothes,' Eleanor said.

'When you get to my age you forget what generation everyone belongs to. They all mix up. Where's the dog gone to now? I keep losing the dog. Stupid animal.'

'Do they live near?' Eleanor said, trying once more.

But the old woman was shuffling towards the back room in the dimness, so Eleanor said quickly, resignedly, 'Thank you for showing me around.'

Though before she disappeared the old woman turned slowly, Eleanor could see her small, sunken eyes glistening – flickering light must have been reaching her from somewhere, the gas fire perhaps – and she said, at last, 'South London, Clapham. Too far away.'

It wasn't until a few minutes later, however, when Eleanor was pulling out of Ronalds Road into Highbury Crescent, seeing a woman with a pram hurrying along the pavement, that she realised the woman in the photographs was the woman with the pram she had nearly knocked off the pavement outside the house on Lillieshall Road. The woman who had shouted, *careful*, and who had then hurried away, with the pram wobbling from side to side and the wheels ticking over the pavement slabs going *tickety tick*. She had not forgotten her face, the way her nose had a small crook, and how, of course, it was her eyes that were so like hers, and her mouth and hair and figure. And driving home Eleanor felt seeing this woman must have been a premonition, though of what she didn't yet know. She understood only that life, the path, the course she was on, was going round, when it should have been straightening out. That she had got no closer to moving in the direction she believed she needed to go. That life was still collapsing in on itself, not opening up. Was it because she was not impulsive enough? Because she had always stuck with what she knew?

Clay said, 'I met an old friend of your father's today. Very dodgy.'

'What makes you think he was a friend of Dad's?' Eleanor said. 'Because he was dodgy?'

'He was at your father's funeral. You couldn't mistake him. He's massive – got a large mole here,' Clay pointed to his temple.

'You've got a better memory than me.'

'Surely you remember him. He even came back to the house. He and your father had some business together at one point, I think. Toby Wilson?'

'No,' said Eleanor, shaking her head negatively.

'Well he's sniffing about Clerkenwell, has been for a while. He's buying up a load of property.'

'And?' said Eleanor.

'And he's after the shop. The whole building.'

'Oh,' said Eleanor. 'What will that mean exactly?'

'I'm not sure. I've got to get in touch with the solicitor to go over the lease.'

'Christ, Clay, you mean you could be pushed out?'

'Not, I hope, unless he pays me one hell of a lot of money.'

'Maybe that's just what we need.'

'It depends.'

'You could find new premises elsewhere easily enough, couldn't you?'

'In Clerkenwell now? You must be kidding. And I don't know whether I'd really want to set up another shop elsewhere.'

'Clay you're only fifty-three.'

'I'm nearly fifty-four.'

'That's not very old. You've got to do something with the rest of your life – you can't just retire.'

'Like what? Work my bollocks off so I can live in a poncey house in Islington?' He looked at her, but Eleanor could see he was having trouble focusing. It was nearly ten and they had just finished supper and he was trying not to have another glass of wine. 'I wonder where you get it from – this idea that you've always got to be doing something else. Your father? He was never content, always moving about, trying to pull off some new deal – spending money he never had. He lived in a dream world. Yeah, you just have to look at your eyes to know where it's coming from.' Clay gave up and poured himself another glass of wine, saying. 'I can see why your mother got sick of him – all that bluff and running around as if everything was going to drop at his feet. And when it didn't he just clammed up. He was a failure, Eleanor.'

'What, and you're a success? You'd be surprised by the number of people who think you're just like him – with your marvellous head for business and great social dexterity. But they're wrong. Do you know why? Because at least he tried. Christ—'

'Well, it didn't get him very far, did it?'

'And, unlike you Clay, he was kind and good natured, and loving,' she paused, too angry to continue. Also, she knew that Clay was right in a way, he had pretty much given up trying towards the end of his life. He was staying with them for weeks at a time, which infuriated Clay, because he didn't have much money then, and came regardless of whether Eleanor and Clay said it was convenient or not – he was meant to be living in Chelmsford but claimed he needed to be in London for business. He seldom went to Rose's because she had just started seeing Mark and Eleanor suspected that Mark made her father feel insecure, besides Rose had never been as close to him. He used the phone constantly without ever offering to pay and bought only cornflakes and packets of stale white bread. He didn't clean up after himself, or even wash himself properly. He smelt rotten. Eleanor tried to do his washing for him but he seldom put his clothes out and she eventually realised he was too embarrassed to – he had piles and wasn't entirely continent. But he never drank Clay's wine, so she said, 'At least he didn't grow into a bitter old drunk.'

It was a still night and groups of people could be heard coming out of the the King's Arms sounding as if they were leaving an office party, that or it had been quiz night. Others were cutting through Roupell Street to the station having worked late, or been drinking at any one of the pubs and bars off Upper Ground or Blackfriars Road – their footsteps and laughter amplifying Eleanor and Clay's growing stretches of silence. So it came as a relief to both of them when a train pulled into Waterloo East, like a gasp of oxygen, or being shaken back to sense – the slap of its departure hitting the house moments later. An alarm started to go in Brad Street. It could have been the garage's or the scrap metal merchant's, or the health club which had recently opened – the trains often set them off. Or it might have been a burglar breaking a lock or smashing his way through a skylight, Eleanor thought. 'I'm putting the house on the market tomorrow,' she said.

'Shouldn't we patch the place up first,' Clay said. 'You know, get a load of fancy new units, some spotlights that actually work. New lino. We could get Rose over, let her sort it out. That's her job, isn't it?'

Eleanor began to laugh, nervously, wearily, because she was tired and it annoyed Clay when she laughed at him. 'Let's just sell it, Clay, okay? And start again. Please. I can't bear this any more.'

'Oh sure, why not? Save all our energy for doing up the next place. That's something to look forward to.'

'We're not going to find another place at this rate. You could help, you know. Don't you want to live with me any more? Have you had enough? Is that it?'

'I don't think I know you any more,' Clay said. His cigarettes were on the table and he reached for the packet. 'I certainly don't feel I can give you what you want.' He lit a cigarette. 'It's not another house you want but another life.'

'I want a child, Clay. I want to have children.'

Clay looked at her for a long time. He pulled his head back, the way he did, which made the tendons in his neck stand out. He drew hard on his cigarette before exhaling slowly. 'It's a bit late for that, isn't it?' he said, and walked out of the room.

There were advertisements for breast enlargement, reduction and augmentation. Liposuction, tummy tucks, classical face lifts. Eye improvement, nose refinement, ear enhancement. For love toys, videos, books. Condoms and abortions. There was an advertisement from one clinic that said, *Family Planning, Well Woman, Menopause and Gynaecology.* Eleanor wasn't sure whether this was what she was looking for or not, but Tina arrived and helped her into her gown and led her off to the chair before she had time to even think about writing down the number.

Tina said, 'We haven't seen you for a long while. Everything all right, is it?'

'It wasn't that long ago,' Eleanor said, trying to get comfortable. The gown was caught on the foot rest and was pulling tight across her breasts. 'November I think.'

'That's ages ago if you ask me,' Tina said. She started to run her fingers through Eleanor's hair, flicking the hair out to see how it would settle. Clucking.

'Maybe it could go a bit shorter this time?' Eleanor said. 'I don't think we went quite far enough before.'

'It's going to look pretty radical.'

'Good,' said Eleanor.

'Okay. Lovely. Shall we get you washed then?'

It was the only estate agents' hoarding in the street and there were no other signs currently in Cornwall Road, Theed Street or Whittlesey Street – Eleanor realising she couldn't remember the last time she had seen the one outside number 38. She thought the man with his mean lips and pointed nose and the woman with her friendly round cheeks and fluffy grey hair must have moved to their retirement home in Hastings – taking the memory of their daughter with them, but not her empty bedroom, so maybe the memory would be less painful, softened by the sound of the sea. It had been attached to the wall between the two first-floor windows at the same height as the sign for the King's Arms. The background was bright red with white lettering spelling out for sale in capitals. FOR SALE. It was definite now, Eleanor thought. Bold and unmissable in the sun. No going back. She ran her hand up her neck and the back of her head, the tips of her fingers stroking the shaved hairs on the nape of her neck, bristling them going against the grain. It didn't feel that much shorter than the last time but she was more confident with it now and was holding her head up, taking in the whole street. FOR SALE blaring.

She knew she should have put the house on the market months ago, still the estate agent had assured her that the demand for property in the area was increasing all the time, that they had hundreds of proceedable buyers on their books, that there was an excess of demand over supply and that she would have absolutely no problem selling in just a few weeks – despite the fact that the house needed a significant amount of work to bring it up to scratch. He had mentioned a new kitchen and bathroom, a possible damp-proof course, reroofing, and there might have been some subsidence at the back. He was only telling her this, he had said, so she understood why he thought she should put the house on at two thirty, and not two four five – as she had said she wanted a quick sale.

Eleanor had been told that the average prices of property in the Waterloo/Kennington area had gone up by seven per cent in the last quarter alone, traditionally the worst time of the year, and for three and four bedroom houses the rises were in the region of twelve per cent. The estate agent had said something about larger houses leading the recovery, aided by low interest rates and the continuing battle between the building societies and the banks, which had kept the mortgage market highly competitive. He had said he hadn't seen rises like these for almost a decade. 'Funny how things always come round,' he had added.

Eleanor had agreed to put the house on at two thirty and she could still feel his clammy hand, having finally shaken it, thinking at the time of Paul, how different he was. She didn't know why estate agents in south London seemed to be so much more unattractive than those in north London. This man was a younger, fatter, just as leery version of the person who had shown her round the Whittlesey Street house – he, she had been informed, was no longer working for the company.

A car had perhaps been in the way because Eleanor saw that someone was standing under the for sale sign. A few paces further on and Eleanor realised it was her mother and that she had forgotten her mother had said she was coming up. Her mother was theatrically looking at her watch, her handbag dangling awkwardly from her crooked left arm, the buckle sparkling elaborately. Once Eleanor realised that her mother had noticed her she felt very naked, like a child who had done something wrong. The for sale sign in the glare announcing more than it was. As if it was something to be ashamed of – an admission of failure. Eleanor had to tell herself it wasn't any such thing. It's my life. Christ, I'm nearly forty-three. I do know what I'm doing. Fuck it. And when she reached her mother she no longer felt so naked, or embarrassed, or that she had failed – as if, somehow, she had taken many more than just a few steps along Roupell Street.

Eleanor smiled and her mother smiled back the way she usually did when she was displeased – her lips clammed shut and the lines deepening at the corners of her mouth with the effort. She looked up at the for sale sign, and said, 'I do hope you're doing the right thing.'

'Sorry, I got held up in town,' Eleanor said, searching in her bag for the front door keys.

They entered the house and the warmth of the day was suddenly missing. There was a stale, damp smell, not of food particularly as of airless bathrooms, of bad chests – Clay liked to keep the windows shut. They walked straight through to the back room, which was dim with dust and bad light, softening the look of the worn furniture – the sofa strewn with bits of old newspapers and auction catalogues, the TV on a round table in a corner with its control flap open because the remote control had been lost years ago, the pine dining table with its red wine and roast meat stains that neither Clay nor Eleanor had bothered to wipe off before they became indelible. There were two pictures on the walls – a not very good painting of a Suffolk beach scene, unsigned, which had belonged to Clay's parents and which Eleanor had long suspected had been done by Clay's mother, and a photograph of New York by Berenice Abbott. The photograph had been taken in the thirties from the Rockefeller Centre, looking downtown into the sun with steam coming from the rooftop heating vents and there appeared to be a thick mist rolling in from the sea, so most of the city was undefined and in some form of shadow. Eleanor thought there was something terribly sensual about the light, as if a great yearning had been captured. It was an original gelatin silver print. She had picked it up for a bargain when she was working for the auction house.

'I've always liked this room,' her mother said, walking over to the window. 'You have got a sweet little garden. I expect that'll go to ruin when you're gone. No one has any time for gardening any more.'

'Have you ever sat out there for long, Mum? There are the trains for a start, then there's the fumes from the garage's respraying thing – the scrap guy's forklift truck crashing around. Oh, and a gym has just opened which pumps out dance music all day. That's the garden from hell.'

Eleanor's mother backed away from the window and headed through to the kitchen. 'I'll put the kettle on, darling,' she said. Eleanor heard her fill the kettle and the click of the switch, followed by cupboards and drawers being opened and closed. 'I hope you're going to do up this kitchen first. You'd get a much better price for the house. Perhaps Rose could help.'

'No, we're not,' Eleanor said. 'It's staying how it is. I don't see the point. The next people can do what they like with it.'

'Well, if you think that's wise. How much are you asking?'

'For the house? Two hundred and thirty thousand.'

'Two hundred and thirty thousand pounds, for a house as small as this – in the state it's in? That's a ridiculous amount of money. What did you pay for it, not half that was it?'

'That's London for you.'

'I knew it was expensive.' She breathed in loudly, shaking her head, making a whistling sound. 'I could understand Rose and Mark's house being worth something like that – Rose is marvellous with interiors. But two hundred and thirty thousand pounds for this?' She came out of the kitchen and started to flick through the unopened mail on the pine table, most of which was Clay's – bills and official-looking letters he had uncharacteristically let gather for a number of days. 'I can see why you want to sell it now.'

'That's not the reason. Besides we can't just cash in – we've got to live somewhere.'

'Rose said you were interested in some place in Hackney. Do you really want to live in Hackney?'

'Mum, we're still looking.'

'I do hope you're not wearing Clay out with all this.'

'Hardly.'

'Has his chest cleared up? I hate the thought of him being dragged around hundreds of draughty old houses. I shouldn't think he has much time anyway. He must be frantically busy at work. They say business is picking up, that we're heading for another boom. Rose is certainly rushed off her feet.'

'I don't think it's come Clay's way.'

'She's never at home. I do think she should spend more time with those children. James is not getting on at all well at school.' She paused to stack the unopened envelopes into a neat pile with the largest at the bottom. 'I'm not surprised. You can't bring up children and work full time. I always put you and Rose first. There was no question of doing things any other way. They grow up so fast, you know. She's going to regret it later.'

'Times change Mum. I'm sure Rose is doing what she thinks is right.'

Eleanor's mother reshuffled the letters. 'I wonder whether she's seeing someone. She hasn't been herself recently – she seems very distracted, and Mark is away an awful lot.'

'Oh God, really. First it's Clay, then Mark, now Rose – oh and me. You think everyone's at it.' The phone went and Eleanor rushed out of the room, saying, 'Probably because you were.'

'Times don't change that much,' Eleanor's mother said, but Eleanor didn't hear her.

A half moon of sunlight was sitting two-thirds of the way down the hall, picking out the thinness of the fifteen-year-old needle cord carpet – the fawn of the undyed backing coming through the faded scarlet. The carpet was one of the first things Clay and Eleanor had bought together for the house. They had intended to sand down and varnish the floorboards, but when they had ripped up the old carpet the floorboards had been in such a state they would have had to replace most of them. The carpet was a cheaper option and the man in the carpet warehouse had said it would last for a good twenty years, a timespan Eleanor had then thought of as an eternity. Now it was nearly up. For the same reason the scarlet carpet, or perhaps it was more a rose, carried on through to the front room – the room they hardly ever used. The carpet in there wasn't as worn, but it was stained with drink and cigarette burns, and black shoe scuff. The result of a number of parties Eleanor and Clay had given – when they had first got the house into shape, for Clay's fortieth, her thirtieth, their wedding, and her father's funeral. Eleanor found it hard to go into the room without one of those occasions coming to mind, which was why she avoided it, perhaps why Clay did too. Eleanor picked up the phone and said distractedly, 'Hello?'

The voice said, 'Hello there.' It was male and friendly – the person speaking expecting Eleanor to know who it was immediately.

Eleanor said again, 'Hello?' For some reason she suddenly remembered the property developer Clay had recently mentioned. Clay was right, he had come back to the house for a drink after the crematorium. She could clearly picture him in the front room talking to Mark. He did have a large, ugly mole just by his left temple – thick black hairs were growing out of it. He was broad, tough-looking, though the mole softened him somehow, making him look as if he were incapable of being malicious or of doing anyone any harm –

because he would have known what it was like to live with people laughing at him. It was that sort of blemish. Which was why her father had probably befriended him, she thought now. He had always fallen for people who were scarred or flawed, or who were just not as good or blessed at getting on in life as others.

The voice said, 'Hi, it's Paul.'

'Paul – sorry, I was miles away,' Eleanor said, feeling her pulse quicken. 'Hi.'

'Battledean Road – too much work? I said it was a pit. But I thought it would be worth your while having a look. For that price.'

Eleanor couldn't think of the house at all but the photograph of the young woman in the garden with a thin stretch of Hampstead Heath in the background, and the photograph of her twenty or so years later at a wedding that had been on the mantelpiece in the Ufton Grove house, and the person with the pram she had nearly knocked off the pavement outside the Lillieshall Road house she had suddenly wanted so much because it had reminded her of the house she had been brought up in, until she was twelve anyway – the old woman saying she had the same eyes – all this in a split second. And she didn't understand it any further, thinking, surely, she must have just put it all together from fragments that didn't belong in the same picture, because she wanted there to be a connection, wanted to feel part of things herself, so badly. She wondered again what Paul might have noticed. She found her throat had gone completely dry, so she couldn't swallow and didn't know whether she would be able to say anything. But she managed to say, 'Did you see anything there?'

'Did I see anything there? Sorry?'

'You know, anything odd?'

'That old woman you mean?'

'No, not her.'

'The dog? The kitchen, the bathroom? You don't often see them like that any more.'

'It doesn't matter.' Eleanor tried to suck up some saliva to swallow.

'One hell of a lot of work.'

'Yes,' Eleanor said, 'probably too much for me.'

'I hope it wasn't a wasted trip,' he said.

'No, I'm very pleased I saw it. It all helps.'

'I had thought I might have been able to show you around myself – that woman shouldn't be there on her own – but things are going really mental in the office. Offers are coming in hours after we're putting places on the market. They say it's like the eighties all over again.'

'That's good for business, isn't it?' Eleanor said.

'We can't get hold of enough property, at least not the right sort of property. We've got plenty of studios and one beds, but no one wants them.'

'Same story south of river,' Eleanor said, 'or so the estate agent selling my house tells me.' She wanted Paul to know that she had put her house on the market, that she was still serious about moving.

'Look, I'm ringing because I've just seen this place in Stoke Newington we've been asked to sell. We don't normally take on property there but we're having to spread out. It's a great little house. Three beds. Most of the original features. I thought of you when I was valuing it. I know it's not quite the area you wanted, but it's cheap, one nine seven and a half, and you wouldn't have to do much to it – you could move straight in. Stoke Newington's really only just north of De Beauvoir. The buses are good and there's the mainline. There's a pretty vibrant scene up there too – you know, health food cafés, Thai restaurants, second-hand bookshops, that sort of thing.' He paused briefly. 'Crack dealers. No, just kidding. You've got to see this one, I think you'll love it. I'll tell you what, I can keep quiet about it until you've had a look. We're the sole agents and I'm in charge of the sale.'

'Urrgh – okay,' Eleanor said, 'Thanks. I can't see it today, my mother's here. Maybe tomorrow?'

'Tomorrow's fine,' Paul said. 'This house doesn't exist until then as far as anyone coming in here is concerned. No problem.'

'When?' Eleanor said.

'When it suits you. Say lunchtime-ish.'

'You'll be there?'

'Oh yeah. The owners work all day. We've got the keys. Excuse me a second.' Someone was saying something in the background, but Eleanor couldn't make out what they were saying – Paul must have had his hand over the receiver. 'Say, twelve thirty?' he said shortly.

'Fine,' Eleanor said.

'Great,' he said. 'I'll meet you there – 39 Woodlea Road, N16. It runs off Stoke Newington Church Street, just past the library. There's an Oddbins on the corner. Look forward to seeing you then.'

Eleanor put down the phone and walked through to the kitchen with a tingling sensation surging through her. So strong she pressed on her abdomen to see whether she could stop it, because that was where the feeling seemed to be coming from.

'You've done that thing to your hair again,' her mother said.

Rain was sweeping on to the glass in flurries sounding like sprays of grit, and the windows were intermittently moaning and shuddering, making a low-pitched noise. The curtains kept lifting away from the window with the draught, letting in faint, flickering orange light. It was two thirty-three according to the bedside clock. Eleanor sat up a little, feeling the draught in waves across her face and on her skin not covered by her nightdress, which was pulled low because she had hauled herself up the bed a little without lifting her bottom. She saw the patterns the light was making on the floor below the window, like city lights on water.

Clay was lying on his side turned away from her, so the snoring wasn't as bad as it might have been. The hair on the back of his head was scraggly on the pillow and there was warmth coming from him, filling the gap between them.

Eleanor wiped her right eye – it felt irritated – and found she had been crying. Knowing this she felt her eyes burn harder and more tears well, and she felt her bottom lip go and the tears begin to run down her cheeks, some finding their way into the corners of her mouth. She licked them tasting salt. She didn't have the energy or the inclination to get up so she lay there crying, thinking, this can't go on – thinking, I can't keep saying this. It's my life I'm throwing away. But the emptiness, the sense of slow death balling in her stomach was more painful and distracting than anything else at that moment, and she slid back down into the bed a little and turned on to her side, so she was facing away from Clay, both of them facing away from each other, and she brought her knees right up to her chest, filling some of the hollow.

She pulled into Woodlea Road and immediately saw Paul leaning against the gatepost of number 39, looking at his watch. Though as soon as he spotted her he dropped his wrist and began scratching his leg distractedly, as if he hadn't been looking at his watch. Eleanor was nearly twenty minutes late because she had missed the turning and there were road works on Stoke Newington Church Street – and she had not known what to wear and had taken too long getting ready. She had finally settled on a dress that came down to her knees and was too summery for the day. Though when she was getting dressed it had been bright sunshine and felt like spring, from indoors anyway. The sky was now thick with shifting clouds so Eleanor was thankful that at least she was wearing a cardigan and thick tights. The dress was a light green and fitted her well. Paul was wearing black jeans again, she noticed, but a different jacket. This one was made of tweed but fashionably cut, with a pink thread woven into the predominantly ginger brown fabric – the pink standing out in the blank light. A camera was hanging from his shoulder. It was a black SLR, a Nikon, and Eleanor thought he looked much more like a photographer than an estate agent, even the way he was leaning against the gatepost – nonchalant, yet fully aware of what was going on around him, like another sense was working, sizing things up. She didn't consider the possibility that this was how she wanted to see him.

The trees lining the road had been brutally pruned – the stumps knobbly and bulbous. They prodded at the sky accusingly. The houses were two storey with pitched roofs and ground-floor bay windows. The small first floor triple windows had Gothic-style arches, which gave a churchy effect. They appeared mostly well-kept. Eleanor parked the car and got out straightening her dress. She didn't look in Paul's direction until she was ready, having tried to pull the back of her cardigan down too, though it was meant to be short and rode well above her waist. As she was walking towards him he pushed himself off the gatepost and came out on to the pavement to meet her – the awkward way his limbs were sprung apparent in those few steps. They stopped a foot or so apart, close, and for a long moment Eleanor didn't know what to say, overwhelmed by his presence. She looked into his eyes, fleetingly, then over his shoulder in the direction of the house behind him, taking in little detail – the vacancy of middle distance – except the fact that there was no estate agents' for sale sign. No brown and green logo.

'I was beginning to wonder whether you might have changed your mind,' he said.

'No no,' she said. Her voice was breathy, urgent.

He laughed, turning to face the house. 'This is it. What I've dragged you all the way up here to see.'

'So far so good,' she said, a weight of emotions running through her like treacle. She followed him to the front door.

'Okay?' he said, sounding as if he didn't expect an answer. He pulled the keys from a jacket pocket. There was an orange plastic label on the ring, a white sticker on this label with the address of the house written on in blue Biro. He found the right key for the right lock quickly and they were soon stepping into the house, she right behind him, so close that her face brushed the tweed when he paused abruptly. There was a smell of cleaning fluid, and his smell again, stronger than the Domestos, or Flash or whatever it was. The narrow hallway was light – there were two antique glass panels in the top half of the front door. He didn't switch the light on and walked to the end of the hall, ignoring a door to his right and the stairs in a kink on the left, walking as if he knew the house well. A thin rug had been placed along the bare floorboards and it was badly rucked just before the already opened door to the kitchen. He tried to straighten it with his feet before moving into the kitchen, but he seemed in a rush and didn't succeed and Eleanor stepped over it after him. 'I must just have a glass of water,' he said, at last. 'I've got something in my throat.' And to Eleanor his voice did sound as if he had something stuck in his throat. 'I'm sure they won't mind.' He went to the sink, found a dirty mug, swilled it under the tap and gulped from that. When he finished he wiped his chin with the back of his hand.

Eleanor tried to take in the room. It was bigger than her kitchen, though surprisingly similar. The cabinets could have been made by the same people at around the same time, except they were not nearly as dilapidated. The front of one was being used as a notice board with bills and takeaway menus pinned to it, another had postcards Blu-Tack-ed on. A number of the postcards were from Australia, with depictions of surfing kangaroos and lifeguards with orange bathing caps and Ayers Rock glowing purple, obviously having been taken through a strong filter. The floor was covered in a black- and white-checked lino, slightly larger checks than in her kitchen, and which, though worn, did not appear to be coming away anywhere. There were no indelible fat stains at the foot of the cooker either. A strip of spotlights ran across the ceiling, with the lights angling over the units and surfaces and the dining table to one side. They were not on so she didn't know whether only half of them worked, but she suddenly remembered how nice her own kitchen had once been, and could still be if only Clay and she had made an effort to keep it clean and in working order, rather than having let it go to pieces.

Paul put his camera on the table and it rocked forward on to the tip of the lens with a thud. Eleanor realised he didn't have a clipboard or folder with him, no details of the property. 'Urrm, do you want to have a look at the garden now?' he said. 'It's pretty compact.' He made to go towards the back door, which was at the side of the kitchen by the doorway to the hall, but as he was passing Eleanor he stopped in front of her, close up again, and said, looking straight into her eyes, unflinching, 'I keep thinking about you. Your eyes.' He jerked his hands up, so for a second Eleanor thought he was going to grab hold of her by the shoulders – and she wouldn't have minded, she wanted to feel him against her. She wondered whether her eyes betrayed that thought – but he turned as suddenly as he had stopped and made for the door, saying, hurriedly, 'Sorry, I didn't bring the details with me, they're still being prepared. It always takes a few days. I was taking the picture of the front before you showed up.' He nodded towards his camera on the table. 'The light wasn't much good, not that anyone's going to care about that.' He got the keys with the orange plastic label and white sticker on the ring from his pocket and picked out the Chubb for the back door. The door was bolted at the top and bottom as well and he undid the bolts and opened the door to the instant sound of birds and traffic and a plane droning through the clouds – the clouds somehow pitching the whine of the jet engines an octave or two higher than normal. He stepped outside and Eleanor followed, gingerly, because her heart was thumping so hard she thought she might lose her footing.

Half the garden was covered with pavement slabs, tinged green with slime. The other half was flower bed, the plants either dead or smashed flat by the weather, though there was some jasmine and euphorbia against the back wall. The remains of a brick barbecue were heaped in a corner. 'It could do with a bit of attention,' Paul said.

'No garden's going to look good at this time of year,' Eleanor said. 'It's a decent size. Bigger than my garden.' She glanced at him. The house was mid-terrace and backed on to a similar terrace of two-storey houses. Some of the overlooking windows had net curtains or pieces of brightly coloured or tie-dyed material hung across. Eleanor thought the air seemed much cleaner than in her garden. It was certainly much quieter – the noise of the traffic and the planes nothing compared to the garage and scrap metal merchant, or the bloody gym. Paul had his hands in his pockets and was digging the toe of his right shoe into the black flower-bed, like a small boy might. Eleanor thought he was trying hard not to look at her, so she said, 'I don't know what to say. I feel confused.'

'You don't have to decide this minute,' he said.

'I didn't mean about the house.'

'Oh,' he said, looking up.

'You see—'

'Should we go inside, it's pretty chilly, isn't it?'

'Sure,' she said, following him in.

'Why don't you just finish looking at the house and we'll leave it at that? I know you're married and everything. I'm sorry, I shouldn't have said what I did.'

'No, I'm glad you did.' She brushed his arm with the back of her hand, feeling her hairs catching on the fabric, a charge there, before walking past him into the hall. For a moment she thought she would walk to the end of the hall and let herself out and get into the car and drive home and never see Paul again. But she hovered by the door to the front room too long, her mind impossibly split, feeling his presence behind her, her heart racing again, and she turned fleetingly – he was staring at her with his light green eyes, almost the colour of her dress, frowning slightly, looking disappointed – and she opened the door to the front room because, however torn she was, she couldn't leave this minute. It's my life, she said to herself.

There was another rug on bare floorboards, but it was thicker, cosier, harder to ruck up than the one in the hall. There were a couple of worn sofas and an armchair, none of which matched, a stack of newspapers beside the armchair and a large television in a corner with a video machine underneath it. There was a simple fireplace with a cluttered mantelpiece and a fake gilt mirror above that. The shutters on the front window were folded back and there was a clear view on to Woodlea Road – the parked cars and stumpy trees. The room had probably once been divided but if there had been another fireplace it was now well bricked up. The back window looked out on to the garden. On the wall running adjacent to the hall, above a long radiator, was a Bill Brandt photograph. Eleanor knew it was called *Sky Lightens over the Suburbs*, she had seen it before. It showed a hill of terraced houses, their slate-tiled roofs glistening with the chimneys casting short thick shadows. Eleanor looked around the room again, thinking I wouldn't need to change a thing, and back at the Brandt.

'I love that photograph,' Paul said. 'I think in many ways he was better at landscapes and cityscapes than portraits and nudes.'

'Maybe,' Eleanor said. 'I suppose people are always harder,' she laughed. 'Christ, I've been with my husband for fifteen years and I don't think I really know him. I don't even know whether I love him any more.' She walked out of the room and he followed. 'You were right about this house,' she was by the front door, feeling somehow that this was her last chance to leave before it was too late, 'I think it's great. But I—'

'Are you not going to see upstairs?' Paul sounded as if the thing in his throat had come back. He coughed.

Thinking, I can't keep looking, thinking, I'm not going to get anywhere if I'm always so bloody hesitant, she said, 'Yes. Yes, of course.' And she turned and started to climb the stairs quickly, hearing Paul stepping up behind her. She was breathing short hard breaths and could hear her footsteps on the bare floorboards, echoed by Paul's, making her go quicker. She ignored the bathroom and the separate toilet running off a short corridor on the split level, which was nearer the top than the bottom, and carried on to the top with her breath getting shorter and Paul closing in. The door to the front bedroom straight ahead was open and harsh, flat light was coming on to the faded pastel-blue landing carpet. Eleanor's footsteps were suddenly lost and she might have floated into the room, only aware of a tingling sensation growing in her lower stomach, spreading all over – she could sense his warm breath on the nape of her neck, through the shorn downy hair.

The room was large, larger than her and Clay's bedroom, and bright with the triple window and the walls painted brilliant white – she thought, suddenly, of how Rose would have approved of the colour, of what she was about to do. The carpet was still the pastel-blue – a seaside shade. Against the far wall was a pine chest of drawers and the bed came out from the back wall, so it would have been possible to lie in bed and stare straight out of the window – into the space once taken up by the trees – and to spot a plane, perhaps, coming through the cloud. There was a small white table on the far side of the bed. Standing on it were a wind-up alarm clock – its metallic bells catching two tiny, fat reflections of the window – a box of tissues, a couple of magazines and an anglepoise lamp. A photograph was propped against the base of the anglepoise. It was a dusty colour snap, Eleanor could just see, of a young blonde woman with a thick – purple? – hair-band. There were no other photographs or pictures in the room.

'Plenty of light,' Paul said, coughing.

'I've thought about you, too,' Eleanor said, turning, facing him, stepping closer. Their arms touched first, finding there way around each other. Their lips next. Urgently, passionately coming together. She felt his tongue on the insides of her lips, on her teeth, probing deeper into her mouth. His hands under her cardigan. His right leg trying to spread her legs, blocked by her dress, pushing against it, bending his leg slightly, making the dress ride up, so she suddenly felt his thigh against her. And she pressed down on it, parting her legs further, pressing harder – because she wanted to feel him there.

53a St Mark's House, Clapham Road, SW9

She could still feel him inside her. Like it had been the first time. His fingers. His penis, not ripping but grazing. The urgency. His vigour. More potent than Clay had ever been. And the pain, because she wasn't ready. Because she was too dry. They had fallen onto the bed and he had run his hands up the inside of her dress, lifting the dress and then tugging at her tights with his thumbs and pulling them off with her knickers in almost one go, so later she found her knickers balled in the crotch of the tights. His face between her legs for a moment – his cheeks rough on the soft skin of her thighs – forcing her legs further apart. His warm breath and wet tongue, which left a cold trail running up the middle of her stomach. But she hadn't wanted to slow down as that would have given her time to think what she was doing. He had unbuttoned his jeans and got himself half out of them and she had felt his penis, hard against her pubic mound. He was sort of grinding it on to her and it caught in her pubic hair, twisting and pulling it. And his breathing was fast and loud, as if that were enough, as if he didn't need to say anything. Easier than words at this stage.

Clissold Park was under solid cloud now, cold and unmoving and ominous. She turned left into Green Lanes feeling something of him dripping out of her. She had tried to wash herself in the bathroom but the sink was too small and too high, there wasn't a flannel and she was getting water everywhere. She had stuck some folded toilet paper into her knickers, though not enough – the wetness was growing between her legs and she thought it was probably beginning to leak through to her dress. It was her fault. He had wanted to get up to search for a condom, but she had clung on to him, knowing she couldn't pause. And she had said something like, *It's not necessary. Don't stop.* Then it was too late, anyway. With his head on her shoulder, his lips clamped to her neck, he had shuddered powerfully. When his breathing had slowed and the full weight of him was on her, he had said, lifting his head so his mouth was right by her ear, *I don't normally do this*. It had sounded as if the sea were in the background.

The lights just before Newington Green seemed to take forever to change, and when they did she had to wait for a drunk to stagger across. He was clutching a crumpled can of lager. It looked as if it had been empty for a long while. She knew there would be a damp patch on the back of her dress when she got out of the car and stood up. A cloudy, viscous smear of Paul. A blatant sign of her betrayal. She had always felt so good in the green dress. A car in front didn't know where it was going and stopping blocked her way into Newington Green Road, and the car behind her hooted as if it were her who didn't know where she was going. The car got out of the way eventually and she accelerated but shortly had to brake for a 73 bus moving extremely slowly. It was only when she had overtaken the bus and was back on Essex Road that she felt she was getting anywhere. She passed the hardware shop again, but the bins lined up outside were not glistening this time.

The sky above the shops running along Upper Street between the Business Design Centre and the Angel, was even heavier than over Clissold Park, blotting out any hope of the sun breaking through – seemingly for ever. Looking right to pull into Upper Street, Eleanor saw through the useless branches of the Islington Green trees hanging over the road, beyond the Slug and Lettuce and in between cars coming at her, the wall of spot-lit estate agents' signs – a shrinking flash of them. Then she was facing the other way, passing the place where, she remembered for some reason, she had dropped Rose off after they had viewed the Ufton Grove house together. And the thought came to her that maybe her mother was right, maybe Rose was having an affair. *What on earth do you buy a ten-year-old?*

The lights across Pentonville Road turned to red a few cars ahead of Eleanor. She found herself alongside a scaffolding truck. There were three men in the front and the man at the wheel winked at Eleanor. She looked away feeling self-conscious and that the wet was everywhere and unbearable, stinging her. She took her foot off the accelerator and lifting her leg slightly and pressing against the door shifted sideways in her seat trying to get more of the toilet paper, the bits coming out of the sides of her knickers, back between her legs. She knew she looked flushed, and that the men in the truck were laughing at her. And she couldn't cry because she was too angry. Because nothing inside her seemed to work how it should. God, she had been stupid. The lights went green and the cars ahead were slow to get going and the truck finally cut her up changing lanes. She hadn't had an orgasm. It had been so quick and painful she hadn't enjoyed any of it. Was that her punishment?

The Royal Festival Hall. The Hayward. The National Theatre. Eleanor would never forget walking along the wide, sun-soaked concrete walkways of the South Bank that morning. Walking east from St Thomas'. The clatter of skate-boarders. Remembering thinking she would never treat Clay in the way her mother had treated her father. Driving over Blackfriars Bridge now there was no trace of late winter sun to halo a cloud, or a crane, or the glinting belly of an aeroplane. There was no setting light raining on the Savoy or the Shell Building, or Charing Cross Station – their great façades blankly, listlessly lining the curve of the river beyond Waterloo Bridge. The Thames, a wide strip of steel grey. The office blocks south of the river without lustre or mystery and looming. Leaving north London she wondered whether he might have ruptured something inside her.

'Come here sweetheart,' Clay said. He put his glass on the table behind him and Eleanor walked over, shuffled really, stopping just short. He reached out with his right hand and tickled her under the chin – something he hadn't done for a long while. He moved his hand over to her shoulder and raising himself on to the tips of his toes leant forward and kissed her on the forehead – he was helped by the fact that her head was already bowed. 'I'm sorry,' he said. 'I've been a selfish bastard. If you want us to live in Islington that's fine. Wherever you want – De Beauvoir, Canonbury. I'd even give Stoke Newington a go. I would. They say it's good value and that there are some interesting pubs and places to eat. There's a bit of life left in me yet, Eleanor – I'm only fifty-three. I've been thinking, a different scene, a new part of town would be good for us. We need to get out more.' He stepped back. 'Shut your eyes for a second. I've got something for you.'

Eleanor did as she was told, listening to Clay walk out of the room, the pounding silence which was left, her head split-ting, thinking this is worse, this is torture. Shortly she heard him coming back, his wheezy breath. He was carrying a plastic bag, she heard it rustle. Then heavy things being taken out of it and put on the table.

'It's not new, of course,' he said, 'but it's in great nick. There's a Summicron f/2 50 mm, and a Elmar f/4 135 as well. I don't know what you're going to shoot, I suppose this equipment might be more suited for portraits, but it'll certainly get you going. Hey, open your eyes.'

'Clay, I don't deserve it,' Eleanor said, finding fading black dots drifting across her vision.

'Eleanor,' he said, 'I don't deserve you.'

'Clay, I—'

'I've been a complete bastard. I haven't helped you look for a new place, or put this house on the market – I haven't exactly been hugely sympathetic about you losing your job. I haven't helped you with anything. Quite frankly I'm surprised you didn't leave me a long time ago. I'd have deserved it. Eleanor, I realise how much I've been taking you for granted, and not pulling my weight, but things are going to change. This is nothing,' he said, picking up the black Leica M6, turning it over, opening the back, blowing in it. 'You were right, we need to move. We need to start again.' He closed the back and wound the camera on, depressed the shutter, and wound it on once more.

'Clay—'

'I know that I've got to be more understanding and that we've got to make more time for each other. We could go on holiday when we get this house thing sorted out. Your choice. When did we last go away – was it three years ago, that awful trip to France? Didn't you say you wanted to go to America, to New York?' His nose was sweating and he wiped it with the back of his hand, as if it were running.

'It's not all you, Clay. It's not all your fault. I can't be much fun to live with at the moment. I don't know what's wrong with me.'

Clay put the camera on the table next to the lenses in their original boxes. He looked at her for a long moment. 'You're still lovely Eleanor, even with that ridiculous haircut. Hey,' he said reaching for her. 'Come here, I need you. It's not too late. Don't say it's too late. We can still make it work.'

'Can we?'

'Of course. We have to. We owe it to ourselves, to the last fifteen years. Sixteen nearly, isn't it?'

'Thanks for the camera, Clay.' Eleanor felt his arms enclose her and she let her head fall on to his soft shoulder, in the nook by his neck. She shut her eyes again. Tight because she didn't want to feel anything, though his neck was hot and rough, and smelt of him, of a sweaty staleness, of cigarettes, and she kissed his salty skin, wondering how much she still smelt of Paul – of hurried, unfulfilling sex. She had had a long bath with cheap, pungent bath oil, washed her hair, sprayed herself with deodorant and perfume, put on clean clothes and underwear, but she still felt she smelt of him, that he was on her skin – coarse, boyish, indelible. Sure Clay would pick it up.

'We don't have to live in Islington,' she said, lifting her head and pushing away from him. 'I think you were right. It's not us. We wouldn't fit in.' She knew she couldn't see Paul again. She wanted to forget him, everything about him – her stupidity. De Beauvoir, Highbury Fields, Stoke Newington – they were all now places she wanted to erase from her mind, from the *A-Z* somehow. The Woodlea Road house might have been more suitable than anything she would find, it might have been almost perfect, but that bedroom with the pastel-blue carpet and the brilliant white walls and the pine chest of drawers and the bedside table with a wind up alarm clock on it and an anglepoise and propped against that a snap of a young woman, with the empty space left by the branch-less trees hanging outside the windows – she would never be able to sleep peacefully in there. It would be full of his breath, the words he said and didn't say. 'No, there must be plenty of other places,' she said. 'Perhaps we should stay south of the river. We don't really have that much money, do we? I think I've been kidding myself.'

'We should have enough,' Clay said. 'We'll be all right.' He pulled her back against him and his hands were suddenly all over her, tracing her sides, her breasts, her bottom – his fingers plucking at the elastic of her knickers through her skirt, playing at the tops of the backs of her thighs, trying to scroll up the loose wool skirt. His mouth was on her neck now, wet, sucking, the flick of his tongue. She wasn't wearing tights and he suddenly bent over her and grabbed at the bottom of her skirt and lifted it up. While one hand gathered the material the other ran up her bare legs, trying to get between her thighs – stubbing with his short, fleshy fingers. But he couldn't get his hand in between because her legs were clamped shut and tensed. She was biting her lip. 'You know,' he said breathlessly, letting go of her and standing back, a broad grin on his puce face, 'I think we're in luck.' He found her hand and unclenched her fist and placed the opened palm on his crotch. 'Let's go upstairs.'

Eleanor felt his erection, the tip of his penis pushing against a fly button. 'Clay, I—'

'Quick,' he said, pulling her by the hand. 'Quick.'

Was this later? Was she conscious? There was the sound of someone snoring, and something else – a thick, heavy thudding. She could feel it, thinking perhaps it was a train, or a helicopter. Out of the corner of her eye she saw a blue beam run along a wall. She was lying on her back and her limbs were unbearably heavy. There was cool air on her face. *She could still feel him inside her*. Fierce, hot. The friction. And the sudden ease after he came. The instant softening. The way he slipped out, a slurping sound, and everything else that followed.

She struggled with her senses, trying to bring them back to the present, to get them in some sort of order. I am alive, she thought. I am here. She lifted her head, taking in more of the darkness. The darkness where the blue beam had traced. There was nothing unusual. And the reality was suddenly blinding, so for a short moment everything was awry again. She knew where she was – where she always was.

But she knew something else. The strength of this conviction startling her. She knew that she was stronger, that she was her own person, and that she didn't need anybody. She tried to hang on to this feeling, though exhaustion – a sense of relief perhaps – quickly overcame her and she fell back to sleep. As if she had dreamed it.

They walked out of the house into a day which was neither warm nor cold but thick somehow, and Rose said, 'You can never park in this bloody street.'

'You can normally find a meter on Whittlesey Street,' Eleanor said, seeing Rose had double-parked her car, a midnight-blue Mercedes estate, in front of her house.

'I didn't have time to look all over London,' Rose said, making for the driver's door.

'What time do you have to be there?'

'No particular time. I've just got a lot to do this afternoon.'

'You didn't have to pick me up.'

'No, stupid me for being so bloody thoughtful.' Rose unlocked the car using a button on the keyring that made the car beep and the indicators flash. 'I know you won't be in the least bit interested, Eleanor, but I wanted you to see this project. It's a new departure and it means a lot to me.' She paused beside the car. 'If you were to consider a unit I could get you in ahead of the queue. The architect's a friend.'

'Let's just see it first. I can't imagine I'd want to live in a unit. I shouldn't think Clay would for one minute. Especially if it's all swanked up. You know what he's like.'

'Oh fuck Clay. It's not all swanked up anyway. It is an old children's hospital for God's sake. Besides you can take a shell and do exactly what you like with it – some of the spaces are enormous. I'm only doing the show apartment for the moment. That's the beauty of accommodation like this. It's so versatile.' She opened the car door, talking to Eleanor across the roof. 'I'll tell you, it's a breath of fresh air compared to bloody Victorian terraced houses. It's not surprising stuff like this is so popular at the moment, especially with younger people and couples who don't have kids.'

They got into the car and Rose drove to the end of Roupell Street ignoring the sleeping policemen. She swung it round Konditor & Cook into Cornwall Road, the huge dark bonnet gleaming and seemingly floating away on its own – the gleam momentarily dulled under the railway bridge. She turned right into The Cut by the Old Vic and immediately left into Waterloo Road.

'You could have gone straight ahead,' Eleanor said, 'you'll have to go round the Elephant now.'

'Shit,' Rose said. The car silently gathered pace and they passed an empty Bar Central and a closed Master's Super Fish. Edging towards the first Elephant and Castle round-about, Rose said, 'Don't people know how to drive around here?'

'Rose,' Eleanor said, 'you're sounding like Mum, shut up.' And she suddenly thought of the time she had driven her mother to Dulwich, a few months ago – this same route from Roupell Street so far and getting angry herself with the traffic, or perhaps she had been angry already. She wasn't sure which, though she could remember how depressing Dulwich had been – the pizza place, the park, Druce Road. And she clearly remembered the distraught blonde woman whose husband had obviously just left her. He was an architect. What was her name?

'Look at that guy. What the hell's he doing?' Rose said.

'Who's this architect?' Eleanor said.

'I suppose you're used to it. I can't believe you've decided to stay in south London. How many places did you see north of the river, two, three, was that all? And you had that cute, young estate agent going out of his way to help you. You didn't give it a chance. I'm not surprised. It's you all over – you're never going to do anything.'

'If south London's so awful, how come you're doing all this work here?'

'Because I was offered it.' They were passing Kennington tube, with an ugly sixties estate on one side of Kennington Park Road and a row of large, scruffy Georgian houses on the other.

'By who, this architect?'

'Yes.'

'You know him well?'

'Are you getting at something?'

'No – what do you mean?'

'Look, you'll probably meet him in a minute. God, I don't know why I bothered to bring you.'

'I'm sorry. Are you all right? You don't look great. You look a bit tired.'

'Thanks, that's just what I wanted to hear.'

Eleanor was sure she could see buds on the trees in Kennington Park. She knew they should be there because it was mid-March, suddenly realising that in another two months she would have been out of work for a year. Small groups of people were walking in the park, mainly women with pushchairs and young children, though there were a few lone men and large dogs. The air looked smoky and damp. She said, 'Do you like being self-employed?'

'I don't really have any choice,' Rose said. 'It seems to be the only way I can manage with the kids and running the house and everything. I suppose we could have a nanny.' She paused. 'I don't know whether I'd really want to work full-time for someone else. I like the flexibility of working for myself. But then I don't have to rely on it. I could get by on my own, if I had to.'

'You mean without Mark?'

'I should think I'd have to move. I'd probably end up living in south London.' She laughed.

'I can't imagine you without Mark,' Eleanor said. 'I've really got to find some work.'

'You must be running out of money.'

'Yeah. It's been nearly a year – ridiculous, isn't it? It's only recently that I felt I could face it. I don't know, it really dented my confidence. And then I got obsessed with moving, that I couldn't get a job until we'd moved – I had to sort that out first. Not very realistic of me really.'

The park came to an end and they went straight across the Camberwell New Road junction. There was a drab Methodist church with a vacant bell tower on their left and the Oval tube on the right with a shoe repair outfit next to the entrance and a little way on from that a closed-up newspaper stand. The old children's hospital was visible now, on the left, rising beyond the church and the few mature trees in the churchyard, which was clear of gravestones though thick with rubbish. Rose turned into a side road running between the graveyard and the hospital and parked almost immediately on a single yellow line, the tyres squeaking against the curb. 'This is it,' she said, undoing her seat belt.

The building was Victorian and appeared to Eleanor to be top heavy with steep pitched roofs and balconies and upper-storey open-walkways. It was large, but not overwhelming and had clearly recently been renovated – the brickwork reren-dered and the sandstone sills in the many elaborate windows replaced or spray-cleaned. Getting out of the car, Eleanor said, 'It's smarter than I thought it would be.' The traffic was suddenly very loud.

'Shit,' Rose said, 'the bloody dogs round here.' She had stepped into some dog shit and she was dragging her shoe along the pavement trying to get it off. She finally stuck her foot through the railings and wiped it on the long grass in the graveyard. She was wearing a pair of jeans and a white polo-neck. Both were tight-fitting and Eleanor thought Rose looked liked she had put on weight since she had last seen her. 'I'm always doing this.' She retrieved her foot and crossed the side road making for the Clapham Road. 'The entrance's round the front.'

The entrance was covered in scaffolding and above it was an estate agents' board advertising *Real Lofts*. There was a wide, arched porch. A man was fiddling with the intercom. He didn't look up or say anything as Eleanor, following Rose, walked past him and through some double-doors, which were wedged open, into the hallway. Mounds of rubble and plaster dust lay on the floor, though small, worn black and red square tiles were coming through in places – they looked as if they had always been there. The walls were covered in bare new plaster and there were a number of thick electrical wires dangling loose. Light was coming from a bulb clipped to the top of a step-ladder. 'When's all this going to be finished?' Eleanor said, surprised by the mess.

'A week or so. One person's moved in already.' Rose walked carefully around the step-ladder. 'I could show you a few of the shells first, or the one I'm kitting out?'

'Whatever you think.'

'Urrm – wait here a minute, I'll just see who's about.' Rose turned right at the end of the hallway and disappeared.

There was the sound of building work, a deep, resonant clanging, and the traffic, quieter but still unremitting. Eleanor was left looking at the disorder and the man fiddling with the intercom, who was now in silhouette because the natural light hitting the porch was much stronger than the bare bulb clipped to the step-ladder. A distant siren rapidly grew in strength before it faded just as quickly. Eleanor thought it sounded as if whatever it was – a police car? – had passed directly outside. And when the clanging, the sound of build-ing work came back Eleanor noticed other sounds she hadn't picked up before, like a radio and a low, wavering electrical whine. Shortly she heard footsteps and talking and Rose reappeared with a man. He was tall and thickset, with a heavy face. He had a sweaty, reddish complexion and he was almost totally bald – the hair he did have at the sides and back of his head was neatly trimmed. He wore thick glasses and a smart, single-breasted suit with a white shirt and floral tie. He wasn't good-looking, but Eleanor could see that there was something attractive about him. Maybe it was his build, the sense of power he gave off. There was something ruthless, something very calculating about him. Yet at the same time Eleanor thought she discerned a weakness. As if he had never been properly understood. She thought he was about forty-five, maybe fifty, and that he had aged badly.

'Eleanor, this is Brian, Brian Wilson,' Rose said.

'Hi,' he said, holding out his hand, beaming.

Eleanor took it. It was surprisingly soft. Not at all clammy. 'So this is all your doing?' she said, feeling strangely shy.

'I wouldn't say that,' he said. 'I'm responsible for a fair whack of it, but the buck doesn't quite stop with me. I'm in partnership with my father – he puts up the money. Rose has been pretty useful, as well.'

'Oh rubbish,' Rose said, tapping him on the arm with the back of her hand.

'Rose will show you around,' he said, smiling at her. 'Rose, I've got to do something in town, I hope you'll still be here when I get back.' He looked at his watch. 'I'm not going to be more than an hour. There are a couple of things I'd like us to go over. Perhaps we can have some lunch?'

Rose nodded but didn't say anything and he turned, still smiling, and made for the opened double-doors, his bulk cutting out much of the daylight. 'Okay?' Rose said, when he had gone, checking her own watch and moving the other way. She reached the end of the hallway, this time going left. Eleanor followed and almost immediately they came to a wide staircase with a wrought iron banister. 'They've installed the lifts, but they haven't got them working yet,' Rose said. The steps weren't steep and Rose started to go up two at a time. 'I'll show you what I'm doing first before we look at some of the other spaces so you can get an idea of the potential. It's at the top I'm afraid.'

'That's okay,' Eleanor said, climbing after her, thinking how hard it must be to go up two at a time wearing such tight jeans.

'So what did you make of Brian?' Rose said. They were reaching the second floor and Rose was becoming short of breath and starting to slow.

'Brian?' Eleanor said, 'I don't know. I only saw him for a second. He wasn't quite what I was expecting,' realising she must have pictured Rose with someone other than Mark, and that perhaps he was exactly who she had been expecting. She wondered whether it really could be him – the architect, the property developer, whatever he was, from Dulwich, from Druce Road. The man who had abandoned his wife – the woman she'd actually met – for Rose.

'What do you mean?'

'I don't know. I don't know any architects. He's big.'

'There's not a size restriction.'

'Rose, why are you so concerned about what I think of him? Why do I think you're not being quite straight with me?' But Rose didn't answer and Eleanor was too out of breath and too confused to repeat what she had just said.

They got to the fifth floor and when they could breathe more easily and the walls stood still it became apparent how faint the clanging now was, and the other noises, as if they were in a different building. The builders appeared to have finished this part. Eleanor and Rose were in a wide corridor, the walls of which were painted a grey industrial colour. Lights ran high up along the walls – they were encased in heavy glass with chicken-wire running through it, and Eleanor thought they must have been designed for outdoor use. There was a smell of newness, of paint, of adhesive.

Opposite the lift that didn't yet work there was a heavy steel door with the number 53a stencilled in black on the buffed front. Rose got a key from her bag, inserted it in the lock, turned, put her shoulder to the metal and pushed. The door opened slowly with a drawn-out hiss – a train sound.

'They've got to do something about these bloody doors,' she said. 'They might look great but they're doing my shoulder in.'

Eleanor followed Rose straight into a vast room with a high, vaulted ceiling. There were windows at either end. 'Christ,' she said. 'It's huge. It's like an old school hall or something.'

'I think I need to sit down for a minute,' Rose said, making for a long sofa a few feet in from the back wall. That and a glass-topped coffee table with strange wing-like chrome legs were the only pieces of furniture in the room. The back wall was bare brick, but all the other walls were plastered and painted brilliant white. The floor was a light-coloured wood, perhaps ash, Eleanor thought – with a pink hue to it, though that might have been because of the way the bricks were affecting the light coming into the room. It was waxed and Rose's shoes squeaked as she walked to the sofa, which was purple. She sat on the edge and bent forward wrapping her arms around her knees. 'This used to be two rooms and when we took away the old ceiling we found those incredible beams.'

'You're not okay, are you?' Eleanor said.

'I just feel a bit sick. I'll be fine in a minute. I ran up the stairs too quickly.'

Eleanor could sense her sister didn't want to be fussed over so she walked to the furthest window from where she was – her shoes squeaking, too. It looked out on to the roof of the church and the empty bell tower and beyond that the tops of the broad, mature trees of Kennington Park. They were perfectly still. If there was any wind it was too light to sway the newly budding branches. Eleanor tried to imagine the trees in a couple of months time, the leaves, the sun on the leaves flickering. How her view, how everything might have changed. How she hoped everything might have changed.

'It's pretty quiet considering where we are,' Rose said.

'Yes,' said Eleanor, backing away from the window, 'much quieter than I'd have thought. So what exactly have you done?'

'What have I done? Eleanor, I've done everything – the walls, the floor, the lights, the blinds. The furnishings. It's meant to be like this. It's what they call minimal.'

'Oh,' said Eleanor. 'Where's the rest of it, the bedrooms and things?'

'There's a small double bedroom and a bathroom through that door to your left. And the kitchen's at the other end in an alcove, there, see? This room's the main feature.'

'How many people's the flat intended for?'

'Two. A couple.'

'Without children?'

'What do you think?'

'I can see it would be great on your own,' Eleanor said, pushing open the door to the bedroom and bathroom. She found herself in a small dim space with just enough room to turn around in. Two other doors led off from here and Eleanor opened the nearest. This led to the windowless bathroom, she discovered, having pulled the light cord – a fan had come on at the same time. The room was tiny, and the bath, Eleanor reckoned, about half normal size with a shower cubicle built around most of it so it looked impossible to sit in comfortably. There were floor-to-ceiling white tiles and a stainless-steel cabinet above the sink, reminding Eleanor of the bathroom in the Ufton Grove house – the smell of the perfume Rose had helped herself to coming back to her. Then Paul's smell, overwhelming it – rough, boyish, unmistakable. She could feel she was blushing, embarrassed for herself.

She left the bathroom and poked her head around the bedroom door. It wasn't much bigger, though it had a thin window running across the top of one wall. It was too high to get a view from and didn't look as if it could be opened. Most of the room was taken up by a double bed. It had a plywood base with built-in drawers. The bed was made, with the duvet cover, pillow slips and sheet a natural, unbleached cotton colour, not so far off the hue of the wood. There was a bedside table, also made from plywood, with a small plastic lamp standing on it. The base and the shade of the lamp were purple and looked as if they came from one pressing.

Eleanor felt herself blush again, but much more deeply this time, feeling the skin on her face tighten and prickle, because she saw – not coming to her like a flash, more a zooming in – the photograph propped against the anglepoise by the bed in the Woodlea Road house. The photograph of the young blonde woman with a thick purple hair-band. Jenny, she thought, it was Jenny – the Clapham estate agent who had never got back to her about the Lillieshall Road house. She didn't stop to think how it could have been her but immediately thought of the photo on the mantelpiece in the Ufton Grove house, of the woman at the wedding who looked so much like her. And the same woman but younger in the photo in the Battledean Road house. The woman with the pram she had bumped into on Lillieshall Road. Coincidence after coincidence. And she thought, life's not like this, it's too indiscriminate, too haphazard, too big. Surely?

She had a tremendous urge to slip out of her clothes, get into the bed, pull the unrefined cotton over her naked body and fall asleep – so she could wake in this uncluttered space fresh, where the weight of coincidence, of the world closing in, was not suffocating and she could move freely. She shut her eyes for a moment and, strangely, she had a feeling she wasn't so very far from reaching that state. It was an intense, eerie sensation, not dissimilar from déjà vu. Though as she walked back into the main room like a nave – that was what it was like, not a school hall, but a place where people might once have prayed – she knew she couldn't get there by just falling asleep, it wouldn't be as easy as that. She'd have to work at it, she'd have to be strong. She'd have to believe in herself. That this stage, this chapter wasn't over yet. And she wondered for a second whether she really was strong enough, that maybe not everyone was able to make it on their own.

Rose was standing behind the sofa with one hand pressed on the purple back for support, the other squeezed into a pocket. She sighed loudly, more a swift, sudden blowing out of air, and Eleanor knew she wanted to say something. Rose took her hand off the sofa and stuffed this too in her other pocket, and said, standing back a little, 'I'm pregnant.'

'You're pregnant?' Eleanor said – she almost spat it out. 'You're pregnant, now? Rose, Christ – that's, that's fantastic. Wow.' She rushed across the room so both of them were behind the sofa and put her arm around her sister. 'How pregnant?'

'Urrm—'

'God, I'm shocked.' And Eleanor immediately felt bad for having imagined that Rose was having an affair, with the architect, with Brian Wilson, and she knew it had been her mother's fault for putting the thought in her mind. 'Rose, how many weeks?' She pulled her tighter to her. She didn't feel jealous. She didn't. She found she was shaking.

'I'm not sure.'

'Mark must be delighted. Three's a great number. Do you want a boy or a girl?'

'Eleanor,' Rose said, struggling free, pushing her sister away, 'it's not Mark's.' She walked towards the window Eleanor hadn't yet looked out of.

'It's not Mark's? What do you mean?' Eleanor walked after her and the room seemed instantly to darken, or maybe it was just something in her head coming down.

'I've been having an affair. I thought it was obvious. Even Mum guessed the other day.'

'Rose, she's suspected for a long while,' Eleanor said.

'And you? You didn't.'

'I've had other things on my mind.' The window looked out across the rest of the old hospital, the new roof tiles and flashing, the flat grey sky shrinking away over south London.

Eleanor couldn't catch Rose's eye so she stared out of the window also. 'God, Rose, what a fucking mess.'

'Tell me about it. But I don't feel it's all my fault. Mark shouldn't have been away so much. I dread to think about what he gets up to. He's probably got mistresses, if not kids all over the world. Even when he's in this country I never see him. We don't really have a proper marriage, haven't for years. Look, it's one of those things. It happens.'

'It's that architect, isn't it?'

Rose nodded.

'I suppose you're not very subtle.'

'I'm not going to shy away from what's meant to happen, if that's what you mean. I'm not going to deny everything.'

'No? Well look where it gets you.' Eleanor had had enough of the view and she left Rose still staring out at the busy roof and the low sky squashed between a couple of chimney stacks – thinking perhaps she can see something I can't. 'What are you going to tell Mark, that it's his?'

'Eleanor, I can't remember the last time we had sex.'

'You're not going to get rid of it, are you?'

'I don't know. I don't think I have any option.'

'Leave Mark, if you no longer have a marriage. You said you could get by without him. I'll help you. I'd love to help you with the baby.'

'You know it's not as simple as that. There's James and Sarah to think of.'

'What does Brian – is it? – say?'

'He doesn't know. He'll probably run a mile when he finds out. He's already got two kids who are a real pain in the arse, I'm sure he doesn't want any more.'

'So how pregnant are you?'

'About two months. There's still time.'

Eleanor was suddenly jealous now. She wouldn't have cared who the father was or what he would have thought – she simply wanted a child, to be a mother, to curb an unremitting feeling of failure and loss. And Rose was thinking of having an abortion. She tried to shut her mind to it and looked about the large uncomfortable room – at the beams, the squeaky floor, the flat, unsteady daylight fluttering almost on the waxy surface. But the longer she looked the more the room seemed to be shrinking, to be closing in on her, and she wanted to leave. 'So what are they trying to flog this flat for?' she said.

'About a hundred and eighty thousand, but if you are interested I'm sure Brian could sort out a deal.'

'No thanks Rose. If I were single and had that much money, who knows. He lives in Dulwich, doesn't he?'

'Brian? He used to. His wife and kids still do. How did you know?'

'I think I met her,' Eleanor said, 'when Mum dragged me to Dulwich that day. We saw their house – it's for sale.'

'Yes,' said Rose, 'that's right. But how extraordinary.'

'My life seems to be full of coincidences at the moment.'

'What's she like? Is she attractive? Apparently she gets very hysterical.'

'Wouldn't you in her situation?' Eleanor suddenly wanted to punish Rose – for having so much and still fucking it up.

'Eleanor, don't get all moral on me. Anyway he had left her before I met him.'

'That's what he said. No, no you're right. It's none of my business.' She knew she hadn't behaved much better, and she wondered for a moment how much she had been trying to compete with Rose. 'I think I'll walk home,' she said. 'I need some air and I don't want to be here when he gets back. I can see my way out.' Eleanor walked towards the heavy door, turned the handle and tried to pull it open – she had to use two hands and all her strength to get it to move. 'Have it,' she said, red and breathless after the exertion, stepping out, hanging on to the opened door for a moment. 'I meant what I said – I'll help you to look after the baby, and James and Sarah. Brian doesn't even have to know.'

'You don't understand, do you? It's not the baby I want, but Brian.'

Eleanor cut through Kennington Park on a thin path of cracked tarmac – the odd tree root breaking the surface looking like a diseased limb. There seemed to be more women with prams and pushchairs and children about than when Eleanor and Rose had driven past earlier. Many of the children were rushing on to the unkempt grass with footballs – some were on small bikes, the stabilisers getting stuck in the soggy ground. Eleanor tried to imagine how she would feel if Paul had made her pregnant. But she found it hard to think of anything other than just how unlikely that would be. Despite her ovaries probably having packed up she knew you had to work at it. She had once read that it took the average couple six months to conceive. She had probably spent twelve years not using contraception with Clay without success – okay, half that time might not have been worth counting, but that still left six years – and under six minutes with Paul on a bed. *I don't normally do this*, she remembered him saying. They hadn't shut the curtains and she could still picture the stumpy trees of Woodlea Road, stark against an uncertain, shifting sky. The day hadn't known whether it was winter or spring.

Eleanor watched a young boy on a bike without stabilisers tear off the path on to the grass. He went a few yards before coming to a sudden stop and toppling over. He ended up face down in the dirt, because he was under a beech tree and there was no grass there. He remained motionless with the bike tangled on top of him. No one seemed to be going to his help so Eleanor rushed over and got the bike off and picked him up. He was lighter than the bike. She stood him on the ground, letting go only when he seemed able to stand on his own without wobbling. She gently brushed the dirt from his dark skin with the back of her hand. He had huge brown eyes, the whites unchecked by blood vessels and glistening. The boy didn't appear to be hurt. He wasn't crying or whimpering – he didn't say anything at all, his huge eyes just following hers. Eleanor stood up and looked about her. Two other boys on bikes had stopped a few paces away. When they saw Eleanor had noticed them they started to peddle off. The boy she'd helped climbed on to his bike and raced after them, his legs working as hard as they could, with the bike slipping on the dirt and grass until he got it on to the path, then the dirt started to fly from the soft, fat tyres, leaving a trail of mud-flakes. Eleanor thought he couldn't have been more than five.

And if she had got pregnant Eleanor knew ironically that unlike Rose she could have told her husband that it was his, because later that day Clay had managed to ejaculate something inside her. Though nothing like the amount Paul had produced – nor shooting it anything like as deep. She was sure she had felt the tip of Paul's penis slamming against her uterus.

When she left the park the boys were long out of sight. She crossed Kennington Park Road by the pedestrian lights and walked along the north side of the road going roughly east. She paused when she came to a hardware shop, noticing it was called M. P. Moran & Sons, saying Moran to herself over and over again. Then *Eleanor Moran*. She shook her head, not believing how stupid she was being. Three homeless people were slumped outside an off licence. Two of them had recently peed and Eleanor had to step over the trickles of urine running across the pavement. A terrace of tall Georgian houses split into flats and offices led up to a zebra crossing and just past the crossing there was a side street which Eleanor thought could be going in a slightly better direction – she knew she needed to get over to Kennington Road if she was to cut out the Elephant and Castle – so, sick of the traffic already, she took it. It was Ravensdon Street and a few paces on it began to look peculiarly familiar. The street was lined with terraces of boxy, square-fronted, three-storey Victorian houses, rising to four storeys mid-terrace. The brick was greyer than normal London brick and the houses had an oddly utilitarian-look. A short way further and she realised why it was familiar. Clay and she had looked at a house here before they settled on Roupell Street, fifteen, sixteen years ago. If they had not discovered Roupell Street they probably would have bought it.

She knew there would be a for sale sign, and sure enough, scanning ahead, she saw one three or so houses from the end. She couldn't remember whether this was the very same house they had looked at, and she knew it didn't really matter. It was enough to have found herself on this street. And writing the number of the estate agents on a piece of card she found at the bottom of her bag, it occurred to her that maybe these coincidences weren't really coincidences at all, but echoes somehow of what might have been, and perhaps what was to come.

She dropped the card into her bag and increased her pace, feeling a brightness surge through her. She was eager to tell Clay what she had just found. She wanted to look at the house with him. Not because she really thought that they should move here and start again – she knew you couldn't go back that far, that you couldn't really start again, from scratch – she just wanted confirmation that she had actually been here – full of hope, full of herself. To be reminded of that, a reflection she had once seen in his eyes. Because she was beginning to believe that to take control of the rest of her life she not only had to understand where she was coming from, but also piece together how much she had lost on the way.

Perhaps loss, perhaps wanting wasn't so difficult to live with, she thought. At least she wasn't in a mess like Rose – maybe it was only those who had so much who didn't know when to stop. She came to Cleaver Street – the roar of the traffic on Kennington Road and the whip of wind jumping back from a bus hitting her with force. She forged ahead, smiling, with her lips pressed tight together – the way she smiled when she felt confident – shaking her head, wondering how far she could go feeling so positive. As far as Roupell

Street, as far as home? Was that the end of the journey? An image of her former self coming through – a sense of who she was to become. She felt she was reconnecting with her core somehow, her self. And that was where the power was. And the freedom.

The answerphone said, 'Hi, this is Paul Moran. I'm trying to get hold of Eleanor Mitchell. I'll call back.'

'Eleanor, have you seen Rose? It's me darling, I'm at home. Do give me a ring.'

'This is a message for Mrs Mitchell. This is the Coronary Care Unit at St Thomas's hospital. Could you telephone 0171 928 9292 as soon as possible. I repeat – 0171 928 9292.'

'Hi, this is Paul Moran again still trying to get hold of Eleanor Mitchell. I'll be in the office for the rest of the day.'

'Clay, just checking you got home okay. You're probably in bed. I'll try you tomorrow – Charles. Oh, that guy came back, but he said it could wait.'

41 Ravensdon Street, SE11

West St Leonards, St Leonards Warrior Square, Hastings. She caught the last few stations, the drawn-out door closing, but no hurried footsteps, as if it were the dead of night. A ghost train. Then the accelerating engine, as if someone were frantically winding it up. The shudder as the train pulls out of Waterloo East. The shudder bounding back, rattling the windows, Eleanor feeling it running right through her – hearing the distancing crackle of electricity as the train shifts up a gear. And she wished she were on that train as it gathered pace, shifting away on an elevated track giving splendid views of Southwark back streets – Wotton, Isabella, Joan, and on past Gambia, Union and Great Suffolk. The heating turned right up when it needn't be and with no windows to open the temperature getting uncomfortable already – the air short and soporific, smelling of stale crisps, spilt Coke and day-old socks. Cutting through Borough, London Bridge, Bermondsey. Unsure of the route to Hastings from there, Eleanor thought it would have to go through Deptford, Blackheath and Lewisham. She'd see. Before they moved. *They*. She hadn't forgotten the promise she'd made herself.

And this was one she wasn't going to break. Clay, what the hell have I done to you?

Eleanor hadn't moved from the hall, unable to make that call, or even switch the answerphone off. The ancient machine was playing blank tape, making a faint whirring sound, audible once again since the train had sunk. And yet a terrible sense of excitement was surging through her, like an electrical charge, as if she were connected to the track. And the longer the empty tape lasted the worse it grew, terrifying her. Because there was something behind it she knew she didn't want to contemplate – a thought that just wasn't her. And it was playing havoc with her breathing, and her body temperature. She pulled her blouse away from her chest and even in the dim hall light saw that her skin between her bra straps, on the tops of her breasts was blotchy. Wondering whether it was worse than usual.

'He's drifting in and out of consciousness. We're trying to stabilise his condition. He's not in any particular danger at the moment,' the doctor said.

So he's not dead. And it was like exhaling air. Coming down to earth.

She remembered leaving the hospital and walking away that last time, of course, but not walking there. Funny, she thought, how easy it is to forget dread, that sense of empty time before you know where everything stands. She'd had no idea what to expect then, she supposed. She wondered whether Clay would have an oxygen mask strapped to his face, an electrocardiogram taped to his chest. Whether he would be able to conceive her presence. Whether there would be harsh neon strip-lighting beating on to a germ-repellent plastic bubble, making the sort of patterns on his chest you see at the bottom of a swimming pool – or perhaps that was only after other organs had begun to fail. Whether there would be a blind caught in an air-conditioning down draught flapping against a window, making a sound like a trapped bird. She had an idea what to expect this time, but she couldn't remember how she'd actually felt making her way to see her father after his heart attack, stepping out of the house now, into a day that should have been dimming, but had sprung back to life with a surge of late sun. Maybe she'd just been numb.

She didn't feel numb, however. Her mind was racing ridiculously – everything was more real than ever. And strange, too, she thought how your worst, how your most significant experiences seem to come round again. Out of the blue. So she turned right into Cornwall Road heading for the South Bank, not going the way she thought she'd taken to St Thomas's all those years ago, the shortest way, but retracing the route she had taken home having left her father there for the final time – her hand still tingling from the flutter of his warm, stale, last breath. As if by going this way she'd not exactly reverse time, but catch up, possibly, with the right sort of emotions. Because she was certain she shouldn't be feeling the way she did – not quite so alive.

She crossed Stamford Street, building up with rush hour traffic, not bothering to go out of her way for the zebra crossing and continued along Cornwall Road, passing the old redundant printing plant on her left and the temporary car park on her right, which was occupying the deep, rambling foundations of a raised building. Ahead, sun was shafting over the National Theatre making straight for the white facing of the London Television Centre, hitting it smack on. Much of the IBM building and the National were in shade, but as Eleanor made her way on a narrow service road beside the National, having crossed the fancily repaved Upper Ground heading for the river, sun was coming from somewhere and making it on to Denys Lasdun's grained concrete shell, highlighting the damp patches and areas that had turned a milky, fungusy white. She cut under an echoey walkway which smelt of wet cardboard, increasing her stride, hearing her quickening footsteps fading in the cold shade.

She stepped out from under the walkway on to the embankment, spotting a group of people near the railings enjoying the sudden spring warmth. The tide was low and the river didn't come into view until she had almost reached the railings. She'd been looking across the river at the trees of the Temple gardens, which, even from where she was, appeared far more advanced than the ones she had seen only earlier that day in Kennington Park – but perhaps that was because of the sudden change in the weather. There was a slight breeze and they shimmered with green. The Thames was a metallic mauve and an empty sightseeing boat was ploughing upstream, against the current. Eleanor could see ripples piling against the buoys and moored barges and other sightseeing boats all pointing towards Westminster, because the tide was still going out. Gulls sharp on the water, like litter, were being swept back to sea, bobbing stupidly. There was a smell of salt, of summer even, and the sound of gulls piercing the groan of distant traffic.

There were more people west of Waterloo Bridge, mainly tourists. Eleanor paused briefly by the closed off entrance to Festival Pier – a chain and padlock securing the gates – and looked back at the way she'd just come, seeing the growing spread of sun-soaked concrete. She carried on. The great windows of the Festival Hall picking up the metallic river and the flecks of gulls, and, faintly, incredibly the shadow of a plane on the water. A flurry of pigeons shot out from under Hungerford foot and railway bridge as Eleanor stepped into its gloom. They were frightened by an approaching train and the explosion of noise as the train passed overhead sparked something in Eleanor. She knew the train would have just gone through Waterloo East, perhaps having come all the way from Hastings, and that her house was probably still feeling an aftershock of sea air, which had been suspended in the slipstream all the way up from Hastings, perhaps. She suddenly knew how things could bury themselves deeper with each passing, only becoming clear once they had worked their way right through. She emerged into the low sun believing she wasn't retracing her steps. She didn't need to hunt around for old emotions. She had a whole new set to contend with. She was covering new territory, facing ahead – St Thomas's just beyond County Hall, coming into sight, like someone stepping slowly out of a shadow.

'Your husband's had a coronary thrombosis. We haven't been able to assess the full damage yet, we'll be conducting some tests when he's a little more stable. Don't worry, he'll pull through. The heart's a tough muscle. Bit of rest and he should be out of here in no time. You'll be surprised. Just go easy with him now.'

Eleanor hesitated. Clay looked worse than her father had straight after his attack. He wasn't in a bubble or attached to oxygen, but his face was waxen, doll-like. Making it hard to remember his normal ruddy complexion.

'He was awake a few moments ago,' a nurse said cheerfully.

'Oh,' said Eleanor, surprised because he didn't look like he could have been. She pulled up the chair and the nurse disappeared. His chest was exposed and the thick grey hairs seemed oddly curly and vibrant. A couple of wires were taped to the left side, above and below his nipple. They trailed off to the electrocardiogram, which was perched on a stand across the bed from Eleanor so looking up she could clearly see the hard, seemingly distressed pattern of his heart in bright, cathode green. His right hand was lying outside the bedclothes, slightly crooked, as if his fingers had frozen while clawing at the sheet, and she covered it with hers, balling hers on to his, balling his up more and out of its frozen, frantic gesture. His hand was cool and stiff. And though the shape of it, the form of his fingers, was perfectly familiar she didn't feel she was really touching him, that she was getting through. It was as if he were elsewhere, already. Or maybe it was she who was elsewhere, having left him behind. Yes, it was she who was moving forward, but she felt the momentum was beginning to snag, already.

The nurse had pulled the curtain around the bed and Eleanor didn't have anything else to look at but Clay's ridiculously pale face or his flashing heart up on the screen in wild contrast. She pinched the skin on his middle finger, between the knuckle and the first joint, catching the hairs there – for a moment wanting him to wake up and be who he always was, wanting to be her old self, too. How things always were. It was this feeling of space, of freedom that she found so exciting, and terrifying. Because she knew how close it was. She let go of his hand, pushed the chair back so that it squeaked on the thick, over-cleaned lino floor and stood up. Can there ever be the right moment to let go, she thought, turning to walk away, however certain you are that that's the right thing to do? She felt she was on the end of a piece of elastic, a bungee – every time she got a little further away something pulled her back. She bent over Clay's plastic face, he didn't smell of cigarettes or alcohol, or dried sweat – he was always sweating, especially when he ate – he didn't smell of himself, but of air-conditioning, of disinfectant, of hospital. She ran her fingers down his face, tracing a wide line from his brow over his eyelids and nose, cheeks, lips, chin, running them under his chin. She turned her hand round to get at his chin from an easier angle and tickled him there gently, the way he used to tickle her. Her fingernails caught on his bristles, lifting them. His head moved slightly and his lips parted and closed making a smacking sound. There was white stuff around the corners of his mouth. She pulled her hand away and holding it behind her back leant further forward and kissed him gently and quickly on the forehead. She returned to the chair and once seated took a handkerchief from her bag, dabbed at her eyes, because there were tears welling there, and blew her nose hard.

Clay coughed. 'Look's like I'm banged up just like your old man was,' he said. His voice was rough and faint, as if he badly needed a sip of water. He was blinking, getting used to the strong light.

'Clay,' Eleanor said, 'it's all right, don't say anything.' She took his hand again, feeling him move his cold fingers to fit hers. 'Do you want some water?'

185

'I only just got over the river,' he said. 'I didn't feel that ill when I left work. I would have taken a taxi but there weren't any, no buses either. It wouldn't have made much difference, the traffic was terrible.' He tried to clear his throat.

'Let me get you some water.' There was a plastic jug with a blue lid and a scratched glass on a locker beside the bed. Standing, she poured him some water and tried to tip it into his mouth. Most seemed to miss however and dribble down his cheeks, taking with it some of the white stuff. She wiped his face with her hand.

'Went down on the pavement. I couldn't breathe, the pain in my chest was so bad. Felt like I was being crushed.'

'Clay,' Eleanor said, 'don't talk so much. You're meant to be resting.' She glanced at the ECG, the vivid flickering. 'The doctor told me you'll be out of here in no time.'

'I'd give anything for a cigarette.'

'That's probably what did it,' she said, thinking it had more likely been her.

'I've been cutting back for years.'

'You didn't cut back your drinking. And you've never exactly eaten healthy food.' Seeing him look so ill brought back her sense of guilt about Paul, her sense of betrayal, and she wondered whether he knew. He couldn't, she reasoned with herself, could he?

'Well you cooked it.'

'You demanded it.'

Clay paused to get his breath. 'What worries me is what's going to happen now? How incapacitated I'll be. Laid up for months. I know what happens to people with conditions like mine. Can't even get to the toilet on their own.'

'Don't think about it.' And it occurred to Eleanor that she would have to look after him, that she couldn't possibly leave him now. She felt surprisingly calm, a warming feeling, because she knew it would be easier than leaving him – she wouldn't have to make that break, she could stick with what she knew. But her mind raced on, to a place that was tougher and more determined, where there was will, and anger and resentment, and she thought, obviously I haven't been punished enough for sleeping with Paul. A faintness overcame her and she reached for the half full glass of water she'd helped Clay to moments earlier. She finished it in one gulp. The water was tepid.

'I was thinking, it must be our wedding anniversary soon,' Clay said quietly.

'It was,' Eleanor said. 'Last week.'

'Oh God, sorry.'

'It's all right. Look, you really shouldn't be talking.'

'So we've been married for what, twelve years now?'

'Yeah.'

'That's not so very long. It's not even half a – what is it? – a silver.'

'Clay, do you remember that house we looked at in Kennington, the one we would have bought had we not found Roupell Street?'

'No.'

'You must remember, it was on Ravensdon Street, near Cleaver Square.'

'I'm tired, Eleanor.' His voice was going.

'Sorry.' She thought she ought to help him to some more water, but she didn't get up.

'Why?'

'I came across Ravensdon Street today, by accident – there's a house for sale. I don't think it's the same one, though I thought you might like to look at it.'

'You've seen all those other bloody places without me, why this one?' Clay sounded suddenly stronger. 'Eleanor, this moving thing's up to you. Houses are all the same to me. Take Rose.'

'Yes, but I thought – oh, I don't know – that it might bring something back. That it could help us somehow. Stupid really.'

'There's not much that can help me at the moment. I shouldn't think I'll be able to go anywhere for a while.'

A nurse came through the curtains carrying a small, translucent plastic beaker with three or four large, brightly coloured pills in it and a clipboard. He smiled at Eleanor, placed the beaker by the jug of water, walked to the other side of the bed with the clipboard and wrote down some readings from the ECG.

'I should be going,' Eleanor said, rising.

'You'll be fine for a little longer,' the nurse said, looking at his watch. 'Just don't get him too excited. These'll probably knock him out anyway.' He came back round to her side of the bed and refilled the glass and helped Clay take the pills, much more apt with the water than she had been. He disappeared as swiftly as he had appeared, sweeping closed the curtains behind him. They took a while to settle, billowing and rustling, and when they did they left a gap a few inches wide through which a heavy stillness drifted.

'There was a message from Charles on the answerphone,' Eleanor said, remembering why she thought he might have known about Paul, that perhaps he had gone to the shop and said something. It wasn't inconceivable – he knew her husband sold cameras and obviously knew the name. 'He said that some man had come back?'

Clay tried to nod, his head barely moving, but enough to show Eleanor he knew what she was talking about. He said, his voice going again, 'Have you used that camera yet, because I don't think there are going to be many more from where that came from?'

'You haven't lost the lease? That man, Dad's old friend?' Eleanor knew there must have been relief in her voice and how inappropriate it would have sounded.

'I tell you, these fucking developers can get round anything.'

'Clay, look don't worry about it, not now,' Eleanor said, thinking of Rose. Everything will be fine. You must get some rest.' She stood and kissed him again on the forehead, noticing the whites of his eyes looked dry and yellow.

'Thanks for coming,' he said, lifting his hand, reaching for her, but she had already moved away and when she turned to wave goodbye, with the curtains of the cubicle half swept aside, his hand was back on the bed, crooked up, and his eyelids were closing.

'What did you expect? Clay, I am your wife.'

'Eleanor,' his voice was urgent, as if he had just remembered something important. She moved back a step, the curtains wrapping around her, but with her head and upper body in his space. Clay struggled to open his eyes. 'Eleanor, I – you know I'd have liked us to have had children too. I'm sorry we couldn't. We did try, didn't we? Perhaps we didn't try hard enough.'

'Maybe not.'

'It makes you think about it, lying here. Who you're leaving behind.'

'Clay, having children is not just about carrying on the great Mitchell name.' She could sense her anger now. It wasn't far away. 'People have children for other reasons, like love. Like fulfilment. Because you begin to feel empty and useless without them. Because you're programmed to have them. But why should you understand any of that, you're a man.'

'And by accident,' he said, coughing.

'Yes,' she said, 'yes.'

'I'll tell you what Eleanor, we're going to make that silver. That's my ambition – I don't care about the shop. I'm only fifty-three. I'll cut out the fags and the booze. Take up jogging or something. You can cook me healthy meals, can't you sweetheart?'

'You're fifty-four.'

'Whatever. Oh Christ, I suppose I've missed your birthday as well.'

'No, it's not for a couple of weeks. You've got to get some rest, or you'll never get out of here.'

'We've stuck together, haven't we, Eleanor? That's the important thing.'

189

Gazing out of the window with a tiredness pressing behind her eyes, making them feel swollen and heavy, trying to focus on the shrubs and mossy brickwork, working out how bad her eyes really were, Eleanor thought, why do I feel so guilty – about Paul, about wanting a new house, about not being able to have children? And it occurred to her – as she managed to focus on a particular brick with half its face missing, so that it sat well back from the others immediately surrounding it, lighter than them because the clay couldn't have been exposed to the elements for as long – that she had always felt guilty about something, about the way her mother had treated her father even. She had assumed what she thought was some of her mother's guilt, because her father had always maintained that she was much closer to her mother than him, that she was in league with her. He'd never really accepted her for who she was. Was it because she was the daughter of the woman who left him? Simply because she was a woman, and that he'd never had much luck with women?

And she thought, why are women made to feel so fucking guilty all the time? Fuck it, I'll go on my own. Because I don't need Clay's presence, I don't need to see myself in his jaded, yellowing eyes to be reminded of who I was. Life's messy and confusing and contradictory enough looking through your own. But at least it's not a reflection. Sticking together isn't the important thing. No. The important thing is knowing whether you really want to. Knowing yourself. And who knows, the house might be all right. As surely it wasn't just chance that led me there.

Her handbag was on the table – the front flap worn and crinkly, with wear on the sides by the straps where they rubbed too. It had once been black and the brass-coloured coating on the buckle had mostly flaked off leaving a duller, lighter-looking alloy. The bag was becoming unstitched in two of the bottom corners – a piece of thick, black thread, three or so inches long and frayed at the end, was coming away from one of these corners. Clay had given it to her for a birthday or Christmas present, she'd forgotten which, years ago. She reached for it, feeling it cave in on itself, flopping almost in half in her hands. It did this when it wasn't full – which was most of the time because she hated hauling about a heavy bag – the scuffed leather was more like cloth. It made it awkward to get to the buckle. Undone she began going through the contents blind. Despite the bag not being full she couldn't feel what it was that she was after so she started to take everything out, one by one. Car keys, mini-Filofax, eyeliner pencil, Biro, compact case, damp handkerchief, hair brush – which she'd hardly used since she'd had her new hairstyle – purse, lipstick, cheque book, moisturiser, packet of Anadin, a single Tampax losing its wrapper, and a clump of paper and cards. She put the empty bag back on the table beyond the spilled contents and started to sift through the pieces of paper and cards, eventually coming to the one she was looking for.

She realised she couldn't have been pressing against anything when she wrote down the estate agents' number because her handwriting was worse than normal. She wasn't sure whether a 6 was a 6 or an 8. She'd try both. She turned the card over, finding that she had written on the back of someone called Steve Brett's card. *Steve Brett*, it said, *Designs*.

It gave the address and phone and fax number in smaller letters running vertically up one side, so she had to turn the card round to read it, holding it close. *63 Lillieshall Road, London SW4 8ER*. Steve Brett, she thought, Steve Brett. He suddenly came to her. His dark wavy hair and fine strong face. Her dream of him, of getting into his bed in the house she had wanted so badly, because it had reminded her of the house she had grown up in. She tried to picture that house, only managing to see the Lillieshall Road house, as if that had simply and irreversibly replaced the memory of her first home – the Virginia creeper, the bay window, the rickety gate – and she thought, no, her childhood hadn't been that happy or special. Perhaps she'd just been carrying around a grossly distorted view of it – the way everything seems bigger when you're a child.

And she pictured the woman with the pram she had nearly knocked off the pavement – Louise? Had she been looking at the house too? Trying to peer through the windows, which were catching the sun side-on making it almost impossible to see beyond the faint reflection of yourself and the road, on that October morning? So it was his house. Of course. Perhaps the woman, Louise, knew him. Perhaps she used to live with him there and they had recently split up. Or he had been having an affair with her – they'd even had a child – and he was splitting up from his wife to live with her elsewhere, except she had changed her mind and wanted to bring up the baby on her own, because she didn't trust him and really only wanted a baby anyway. Eleanor remembered him saying that thing about children, how the tricky thing was who you had them with. How that had been where he'd gone wrong.

Eleanor couldn't believe she had not looked at his card before putting it in her bag while standing on the pavement outside the café in Clapham. That she had forgotten about it altogether – wedged in there, unread, the surface fuzzing up. She went to the phone.

Eleanor's mother said, having put on one of her knowing looks, so Eleanor knew that she was going to say something annoying, 'I'm not surprised in the least. You can't expect people to pay all that money – what is it, two hundred and thirty thousand pounds? – for a house this size. There's only two bedrooms. And let's face it, it's not in the greatest area. Personally, I could never see what you and Clay saw in it.'

'Apparently the market's going through a temporary blip,' Eleanor said.

'That's what the estate agent told you, is it? They're full of crap. You should know that by now.'

'Mum, the man said that the market's stalled because there's so much demand for property all over London, and not enough houses for sale, people aren't able to move even if they want to, so they've stopped looking.' Eleanor paused to turn off the kitchen light, which she'd just noticed had been left on – it had been overcast earlier in the morning but sun was now reaching the garden, tipping on to the rosemary and making the back door window look grimier than ever. 'Plus, there's some worry that interest rates are going to shoot up, which is not helping matters.'

'More crap. Has anyone even viewed it?'

'No.'

'Eleanor, quite frankly you should forget about moving until Clay's better. All that running around looking at houses, all that pressure probably put him in hospital. You know I've been worried about his chest for a long while. He's not as strong as you think.'

'He's had a heart attack, Mother, not pneumonia.'

'Men need looking after. That's where I went wrong, I suppose. I never had enough time for them.'

'He's going to be fine. He's coming out at the end of the week. The doctor said he just has to have a quiet couple of months then he'll be back to normal.' Eleanor leant heavily against the wall by the light switch, bumping her shoulder blades on the cold, damp-feeling plaster.

'You take care of him,' Eleanor's mother said. She searched for some cups, looking in the wrong cupboards as usual – opening them with unnecessary force so there was a cracking sound when they were as far back on their hinges as they could go. 'You've got to do something about this kitchen.' She gave up looking and faced Eleanor again, folding her arms in front of her. 'I feel like I've been through all this before.'

'I don't remember you being around when Dad was ill.'

'It wouldn't have been appropriate. But that doesn't mean I wasn't thinking about him. I always felt for him in a way – he was weak.'

'Oh come on.' Eleanor got the cups her mother had been looking for. 'Besides Clay's not dying.'

'I suppose you haven't seen Rose lately?'

'Not for a week or so.'

'Too busy with that architect chap, I imagine.'

'What do you mean by that exactly?'

'I'm not blind. I've known about them for a long while.'

'Oh. Rose did say you knew.'

'How serious do you think it is? She won't let me see her.'

Eleanor breathed out, sure her mother didn't know that Rose was pregnant as well. 'Serious,' she said quietly.

'I thought it might be. Eleanor, darling, I really ought to stay up here for a few days. I can help you with Clay when he gets out. He'll need a lot of attention. And I should be around in case Rose or the children need me. I've brought some things, they're in the hall.'

'Mum, it's not necessary. I'm quite capable of looking after Clay – I have done so for the last sixteen years. And Rose has got me if she needs anyone. I'm sure she doesn't want us getting involved. She's pretty tough.'

'I know, I know darling, but I'd feel a lot happier if I was on hand. You've got no idea how much I worry about you both – I am your mother.' She turned sharply away, for effect Eleanor thought, her thin body hunched, pathetic-looking –

reminding Eleanor of the old woman in the Battledean Road house. She went to the back door and ran a finger down the inside of the window, like an embarrassed child might. 'You've made this garden awfully nice.' She stepped away and studied her finger, the smudge of black dirt she'd picked up. She searched for something to wipe it off on, finding a tea towel hanging on the back of a chair. 'Perhaps you and I can have a jolly good go at getting this house in order. Clay doesn't want to come back to a tip. Let's make him feel really special.'

'Mum, life doesn't just revolve around Clay. I have got one or two other things to do this week.'

'Right,' she said, either not hearing Eleanor, or choosing to ignore her and moving towards the sink, 'let's get cracking.'

'Mrs Mitchell, his condition is more serious than we first thought. There's a large clot in the right coronary artery which we can't get to dissipate, as well as widespread muscle damage. Matters aren't helped by the fact that his aorta's pretty furred up. We've got to get more blood to his heart. We're still hoping the drugs will reduce the clot.'

The cafeteria was bright and smelt of fat and floor cleaner – an odour that stuck in the back of Eleanor's throat like glue, too heavy to sting. It was virtually empty and Eleanor got a tea without queuing and sat at the table furthest from the hotplate area. She was by a floor-to-ceiling window which looked out on to a wide concourse leading from the North Wing entrance of St Thomas's through to Westminster Bridge Road. She could see the traffic passing and was able to read the advertisements on the double-decker buses, the 109 and 53. She found she was by a heating vent and the warm air was churning the fat and floor cleaner smell about. Her tea seemed to taste of it – a hard, twangy, metallic taste. It made her gag.

Even though the cafeteria was largely empty and Eleanor was the only person at a table for four with unmovable seats it soon seemed stifling. She stared through the window wishing she were outside. That the glass would simply shatter. She would have got up and left but she felt too faint – her own heart was out of step, perhaps in sympathy with Clay's, or it was just reacting to a rising, uncontrollable feeling of excitement again, a giddiness. She clasped the plastic rim of her maroon seat, her hands making the plastic moist. She concentrated on the outside, the people on the concourse, their sense of purpose, the steady traffic on Westminster Bridge Road, the slow clouds no longer looking like rain – thinking there was certainty there. Movement, breath. Waiting for the skin on her face to go taut and a searing wet heat to tear through her. But the moment simply passed and with it, oddly, the feeling of hollowness, of emptiness she had been carrying around inside her for so long.

She stood slowly holding the table for support, with the rim of the seat pressing into the backs of her legs so she couldn't stand completely straight. She left the cafeteria by an exit which brought her into an atrium. A NatWest, a newsagent and a florist lined the sides with the large, automatic doors leading to the concourse directly ahead. Behind her was the bank of lifts – eight in all – one of them having, some twenty minutes earlier, brought her down from Clay's floor. He hadn't yet been enclosed in a germ resistant bubble – there was no fractured light beating on him, or any blind drumming against a window pane – but he was being given oxygen. Not through a mask this time but by tubes taped to his nose, which made him breathe with a rasping sound, or perhaps that was just the noise the oxygen made filtering through. He hadn't been able to say very much, or move his hand even, leaving it crooked on the cotton blanket for her to try to squeeze some life back into. Except she had felt like a fraud, his cold, stiff fingers wrapped in hers, avoiding his sunken eyes, his waxy, pale face. She hovered by the news-stand, eyeing the tabloid front pages and the magazine covers – the skinny models, the number of headlines incorporating the word sex. *Sex*. Yes, she thought, we stuck together, without passion, without love, because we were scared of being on our own. Scared of change. She hoicked the strap of her handbag on to her shoulder more firmly and headed for the open air, where life was. Movement, breath. And unshakable echoes.

Eleanor hadn't reached the end of the rubber mat which led through the parted automatic doors on to the concourse when she saw her. She couldn't have been more than twenty feet away, coming straight towards her. She was walking quickly, looking up at the sign above the door. She was carrying her baby in a sling this time, face out. The child's blue eyes and full red cheeks were clearly visible, heightening the fact that Louise looked so pale. She was wearing a denim jacket and a long blue skirt, perhaps made of linen. She looked to her side momentarily and Eleanor caught her crooked nose. It had to be her. Eleanor froze, one foot on the concourse, one still on the rubber mat, waiting for her to reach her, knowing she had to say something. Louise slowed as she passed – for a split second she even looked straight at Eleanor. But she didn't stop and Eleanor found she was unable to say anything. All she could do was turn and watch the automatic doors close after her, waiting for her to turn too, because she was sure she had seen a flicker of recognition in Louise's eyes. Every bit as dark as hers.

'Oh, urrgh, Mrs Mitchell, and, urrgh, your mother, if you'd both like to carry on through to the end of the hall and take the stairs down to the kitchen, perhaps we can start there?' the estate agent said.

'It's Mrs Davidson,' Eleanor's mother said. Eleanor had only introduced her mother to the estate agent as her mother.

'Pardon,' he said. He pulled a crumpled handkerchief from his pocket and blew his nose. 'I always like to start with the kitchen,' he said, wiping his nose, 'when I show women round a house. Helps them get the size of the place straight away. Can save a lot of time and disappointment. Now men – you'd be surprised with the number of men who want to have a look at the toilets and bathrooms first. A few go for the bedrooms.' He winked, nodding as well.

Eleanor followed her mother, who had marched ahead, to the end of the hall and down a short flight of stairs leading directly into the kitchen/breakfast room area in the basement – or the *lower ground floor* according to the particulars Eleanor had been handed. The estate agent was close behind her, taking short, loud breaths. Eleanor wasn't sure whether he had remembered her from showing her the Whittlesey Street house or not – he kept looking at her with an odd, leery expression – so she said, 'Didn't you use to work for a different estate agents?'

He had manoeuvred himself in front of Eleanor, his body brushing hers, and was now standing by the sink, wearing, Eleanor was sure, the same pair of badly creased grey trousers and soft brown shoes – she could see him in the tiny kitchen of the Whittlesey Street house. He was also wearing a maroon V-neck pullover so she couldn't tell whether he had on exactly the same – pink striped? – shirt that had had the terrible sweat stains. 'I've worked for a number of estate agents over the years,' he said. 'I've been around,' he winked and nodded again. His hair was wiry and thinning, a grey brown, and needed cutting. 'Mostly in south, south-east London, that's my patch – not quite as far as Bromley or Sidcup, but I can find my way round Bexley and Catford. Of course, you don't get the sort of quality period properties out there as you do here.' He turned to study the kitchen, which was set against the side wall opposite where they had entered and part of the back wall, so it was L-shape. He began to fiddle with the appliances built into cheap-looking sage-coloured cabinets and the marble-effect plastic work surface. 'As you can see, everything's here – Hotpoint dishwasher, washing machine, and fridge freezer. Zanussi oven – got one myself – and hob. Quality gear. It's all staying, I believe.' He paused to catch his breath. His nose sounded as if it was blocking up again. 'We all shift around. In my mind you don't want to stick with one company or one location for too long. You go stale. The thing about selling houses is that you've got to keep fresh. On your toes.'

Eleanor's mother said, 'Can you unlock the French doors, please?'

'Been looking long?' the man said, ignoring Eleanor's mother. 'You look familiar.' He rubbed his hands together, as if they were cold, frowning quizzically.

'Oh, a while,' Eleanor said, not sure she wanted him to remember her now.

'And we're no nearer, are we darling?' Eleanor's mother said.

'I'll just find the keys,' the estate agent said, turning to her. He extracted a large bunch from a pocket, bringing the soiled handkerchief out with them. He walked over to the French doors where Eleanor's mother was still waiting, stuffing the handkerchief back into his pocket and wiping his hand on his trousers. 'It should be one of these,' he said, 'I've only been here a couple of times before.'

'It hasn't been on long then?' Eleanor's mother said, making way for him.

'Two or three weeks. The market's gone a bit stale lately. Interest rates aren't helping. They're obviously trying to dampen down the market. But if you ask me it's probably a blessing. It was beginning to get silly again. People forget how precarious property can be, even when they've been burnt before. I suppose they think it won't happen to them again. I wouldn't bet on the property market. Though that's not to say you'll never find a bargain. This house's a cracker, that's for sure.'

Eleanor thought the kitchen/breakfast area was about the size of her back room and kitchen knocked together – which it suddenly occurred to her was something they perhaps should have done – but it seemed much darker than that part of her house ever did. The French doors, though large, were almost north facing and there were a couple of steps up to the garden which cut out more natural light. The room was a bright yellow, as if that would compensate for the darkness, and numerous spotlights had been set into the ceiling. The floor was lino made to look like wood. It was beginning to lift in places – against the cabinets and in a corner and there appeared to be a number of air bubbles further in. Eleanor thought it couldn't have been that old and that maybe it just hadn't been stuck down properly in the first place. There was a battered pine table, much like Eleanor and Clay's, standing in the middle of the eating area, which was towards the French doors at the end of the room. Similar aged pine chairs were scattered around it. On the table were piles of letters and newspapers shoved under candlesticks and a two-thirds drunk bottle of wine – the cork having been pushed a small way back in. A box of empty wine bottles stood next to a bin by the short end of the L, and there was a drying rack towards the back of the room, just to the left of a closed door, which, Eleanor presumed, led to the *lower ground floor toilet/utility room*. It was hung with large wrinkled T-shirts, odd coloured socks and fraying boxer shorts. Eleanor decided that the room had been recently done up by someone who wasn't entirely competent. Either that or they didn't have the energy or the inclination to see it through properly. A couple, perhaps, who were splitting up and wanted to get shot of the place as quickly as possible.

The estate agent had found the right key for the French doors – which surprised Eleanor, remembering his failed attempt to open the back door in the Whittlesey Street house – and was stepping outside with her mother. 'I like to see a few more plants myself,' she heard him saying. 'Patios might be easy to manage, but a little gardening never did anyone any harm. No one has time for it any more. Look at these climbers – coming out nicely. I do love a good garden. Have a bit of a knack for it myself.'

Eleanor's mother said, 'It's a little overlooked.'

'You could always put up a trellis,' the estate agent said. 'It would hide most of those first-floor windows and they're a great security measure.'

'What's the crime like?' Eleanor's mother said. 'Is it safe at night?'

'Round here? You're not going to get anywhere safer in south London. The police keep a pretty good eye on it – the place is crawling with MPs.'

'Any subsidence?' she said.

'None that I can see, Mrs, urrgh, Mrs Davidson. Doesn't look like there's any damp either. Look at that rear wall – straight as an arrow. I've never seen a more solid-looking terrace. Last for ever.' He shook his head.

Eleanor stepped outside, having hung back, thinking I've heard all this before. The garden seemed smaller once she was in it. It was completely covered with paving slabs going green with slime and looking as if they would be as slippery as anything in the wet. The air was warm and stagnant, which might have contributed to the feeling that the garden seemed smaller outside. There was a charge to the air also, making Eleanor think the weather was going to break. She had found nothing particularly memorable about the house so far, nothing to draw her back sixteen years – to a time when her life had been going where she thought she wanted it to go, full of expectation. It was very unlikely that it was the same place Clay and she had viewed anyway, she decided, not that that mattered. It simply appeared to be another house occupied by another unhappy couple who were coming to terms with the fact that their marriage had failed. It could have been anywhere. She didn't want to view the garden, or any other garden at that moment, feeling she was slowly suffocating here – walled in with the heavy, unbreathable air.

'Mum,' she said, 'can we get a move on? I should be at the hospital by four.' She had a sudden, compelling urge to confront Clay. It was her chest that needed clearing. She wasn't going to be bound by guilt. She wasn't Rose or her mother. She was herself. She was going to tell Clay about Paul, about why she thought she could no longer have children – how she had been planning to leave him. Because she believed that if she were ever going to make something of the rest of her life she was going to have to do it on her own, and that she had to get the past straightened out, out in the open first. As if telling Clay would lend weight, an authority somehow, to her decision. Christ, Clay was never going to do or say anything. She needed a new order, independence, freedom. Coincidence, faint chance, familiarity weren't enough. Clay, I did love you once, terribly. Was it life that let us down, or each other?

'Nothing serious, I hope?' the estate agent said. Neither Eleanor nor her mother replied, and the estate agent, realising he'd said something he shouldn't have, limped inside, his face reddening, leaving a strong smell of cheap aftershave again – it had to be aftershave. Shouting, once he was in the kitchen, 'It's amazing the difference a lick of paint can make. Change a place around in no time.'

'Eleanor, it's only just gone two,' her mother said. 'There's not that much of a rush, surely? I'm rather enjoying myself. I love looking around other people's houses.'

Eleanor stepped back through the French doors and waited in the kitchen for her mother to come inside before saying quietly, but firmly, 'Mum, I'd like to go. I've seen enough.' She knew that there was no point in looking at the rest of the house – the double reception room with its *decorative coving and ceiling roses*, the *part tiled* bathroom with *Servoflow power shower*, *pedestal washbasin, low flush WC, Bedroom 1* with *its range of fitted wardrobes, alcoves with shelving*, its bedside table supporting a blinking radio alarm clock, an anglepoise, a box of tissues, a half drunk glass of water full of tiny stationary bubbles. Books, dust and dreams losing their colour and going faint like old photographs. She'd seen it before. Perhaps all houses assumed a familiarity once those who lived there couldn't bear to do so with each other any more. Was that it?

'No, Eleanor, I think you should see all of it. We're here now. It will be good for you to keep your mind off Clay for a little while longer. Concentrate on something else.'

'I don't know why I brought you.'

'Eleanor, come along.' The estate agent had already left the basement and Eleanor's mother shot up the short flight of stairs with the vigour of a much younger woman, saying again, once she had reached the top, 'Eleanor, come along.'

The estate agent was at the back of the hall holding open a door. 'They've put the bathroom on the ground floor,' he said, his nose now badly blocked up. 'Each to their own. You could, of course, move it upstairs at a later date which would leave you with the possibility of knocking through to make a double reception room. You'd lose a bedroom, however, unless you wanted to have the bathroom on the lower ground floor. Nothing's undoable. That's the beauty of these properties. I can recommend a great builder who works locally.'

Eleanor's mother pushed her way through to the bathroom while Eleanor remained by the stairs to the kitchen, trying not to catch the eye of the estate agent, who she thought was about to say something to her. The hall was a dusky pink, perhaps more a coral, or a rust, or possibly what a paint manufacturer might call a peach. It was pictureless and lit by the narrow, rectangular window above the front door.

'Where are you wishing to move from?' the estate agent asked Eleanor, shifting towards her.

She faced him reluctantly. 'Urrgh, not far. Near Waterloo, Roupell Street.'

'Roupell Street. That's in the conservation area, isn't it? Great location. Classy street too.' He nodded, looking down at his feet. 'Got it,' he said, suddenly raising his head. 'I knew

I'd seen you before. I showed you round a property on Whittlesey Street, a few months ago.'

'Yes,' said Eleanor, 'that's right.'

'I never forget a face.'

'What did it sell for in the end?' Eleanor said. She heard a toilet flush.

'It was taken off the market. The owners changed their minds. Happens all the time.'

'It's a neat little bathroom, Eleanor,' Eleanor's mother said, emerging into the hall behind the estate agent. 'Though I don't know why they have to make toilets so shallow nowadays. It's a German thing apparently so they can—'

'Upstairs?' the estate agent said. 'I usually leave the reception rooms until last. I like people to go away with the most impressive aspect of a property fresh in their minds. You'd be surprised at the amount of psychology that goes into selling houses. We're not all as daft as we look.'

'Mum,' Eleanor said.

'You lead the way,' her mother said to the estate agent.

'No, after you,' the estate agent said, motioning her up and waiting for Eleanor.

But Eleanor didn't move. 'Mum,' she repeated sternly, watching her mother head up the stairs and the estate agent rush after her.

'How much is the house on for?' Eleanor's mother asked, reaching the top.

'Two two five,' the estate agent replied. 'It's a terrific price if you ask me. The vendors want a quick sale. Not that properties on this street normally hang around.'

Eleanor waited in the hall for a while longer before she went up too, finding them in a small back bedroom. The room looked as if it was in the process of being decorated – old backing paper had been stripped off leaving creamy shreds stuck to cracked plaster. A dismantled cot was propped against the wall under the window, which had a thin yellow blind pulled most of the way down making the air glow. Next to the bits of cot were piles of baby clothes, girls' clothes, some still in their wrappers, and a box full of toys and cuddly animals.

'Funny,' the estate agent said, 'my daughter's just had a little girl. Good as gold.'

'Mrs Mitchell, I'm so sorry, your husband passed away shortly after three. We only got your answerphone when we rang. We weren't expecting—'

89 Roupell Street, SE1

There is no wind. All is stillness. A light, airy stillness which she glides through. It is dusk, there are no street-lamps, no shadows. She hovers in the middle of the street, a faint tingling sensation running through her body, not sure if her feet are on the ground. In each direction the street slips away into darkness. A darkness that becomes blacker the longer she looks into it. She thinks she should at least see the pub, the King's Arms, people entering and exiting, but the pub is not there. She waits in the easy thin air, air that might not be air at all but space, the tingling coming on stronger, welling in her stomach, her womb, a fluttery feeling. She looks into the black distances at either end of the street. She can hear nothing, cupping her ears alternately. A thickening silence. She's wearing only her nightdress and finds she's making swimming movements with her legs. She starts to circle, her arms tight against her sides, her legs kicking as one, as a diver might. It takes no effort and the circles become bigger, making her shiver because it tickles.

She swims into a whirl of bubbles. Instinctively she puts out her hands, bracing herself, seeing nothing but the bubbles, which make her shiver more, the bubbles rubbing against her. It's an intense, almost sexual feeling. Someone grabs her hand and pulls her through the churning back into the clear. There is a tight sucking sound and she finds she's standing next to the young woman she saw in the photograph in the Whittlesey Street house, the daughter who had died. Except she's not wearing her graduation gown but a denim jacket and a blue linen skirt – Louise's clothes. Her hair is no longer bushy and wild but straight and bobbed and darker than before. She's also older and thinner. There are rectangles of light in her brown eyes. It is not dusk now but bright – daylight. The woman smiles, increasing her grip on Eleanor's hand. Pulling her towards the end of the street. There is an urgent look on her face. Quick, she mouths, and as they go the houses behind them start to collapse into the road, one after the other, like a pack of cards. Except they are not now the normal Roupell Street houses but houses from all over London, from Clapham, Dulwich, De Beauvoir, Highbury Fields, Stoke Newington, the Oval, Kennington, Waterloo. Some with bay windows, some flat fronted. Mostly Victorian.

The woman leading her is clearly Louise now, the crook of her nose sharply defined against the gathering brightness. They struggle to keep ahead of the collapsing houses, the rubble dust and shattering glass – their path made harder by people coming out of the houses yet to collapse, blocking sections of the street off like bollards, so they have to weave and shimmy. She spots the estate agent still in his sweat-stained shirt and creased grey trousers. Jenny with her fair hair pulled sharply into place by the purple band. Mrs Wilson shifting nervously from one foot to the other. The old woman from Battledean Road muttering to herself. Her mother linking arms with Rose. Brian Wilson, red and puffy in the face like Clay used to be. Clay, faint and smoking a cigarette. Paul leaning nonchalantly against a lamp-post, her father next to him, younger than she can ever remember him being, as young as Paul, laughing with Paul, as if they're sharing a joke. Just beyond them a baby is crawling into the middle of the road, a little girl. Avoiding the baby they slam into something solid. Looking up Eleanor sees a tall, slim man with blue eyes, a fine strong face and wavy dark hair. They are suddenly outside her house – 89 Roupell Street. The brass numbers buffed and glinting like never before. Louise has seemingly evaporated into the thin air and Eleanor falls back against this man. He stoops and she feels his cheek against her cheek. Wet from rain, because it's raining and she hears the baby begin to cry.

Eleanor woke finding broad daylight and room to stretch. She was lying on her side and her nightdress was rucked up around her waist. It was uncomfortable and she pulled it off, throwing it to the floor. She stretched again, feeling freer, feeling the clammy sheets against her skin and a dull ache at the bottom of her stomach. She rolled on to her back and kicked out to get fresh air under the duvet. She pressed on her stomach, relieving the ache, scratching her pubic hair with the tips of her fingers at the same time. The curtains were thin and had never been a good fit, lifting away in the slightest draught, so she shut her eyes, letting her head sink into the pillows, seeing orange, thick with hastening particles, feeling warmth on her face, and the first tremors, more a whispering, of a shocking, full, calmness.

But she knew she wouldn't be able to go back to sleep. She wasn't tired. There was the sound of people walking along the street, a car parking. She pushed her hand further down, to between her legs, pushing her right index finger a short way into her vagina. She was surprised by how moist she was. She lifted her hand out of the bed quickly, carefully keeping her fingers from touching the duvet cover, wondering whether she had been bleeding. She opened her eyes to see – taking a moment to focus – that she hadn't been bleeding. Still there was the ache, a pressure, a need really, and she returned her hand to the base of her stomach, letting it lie there while her fingers crept on, and with the tips of her first finger and index finger tight together she pressed lightly on her clitoris, thinking of the tall man with dark hair, her first dream of him, of being in bed with him. She arched her hand up and started a slow, circular motion. Bringing tears to her eyes. Tears of sorrow and relief. I'm still a woman, she thought.

The camera was heavy and cold and Eleanor turned it over in her hands. She had never used a M-series Leica before – its weight, its double-image focusing, its aperture setting ring, the sound of the shutter, were all quite unfamiliar. Wary of it she put it to her eye, aiming at a mug on the table, seeing, once she had positioned the camera against her eye correctly – she'd always had a problem with her eyelashes or getting the eyepiece up too close – two mugs out of focus. She started to turn the focusing ring, watching the mugs begin to merge and the picture come into sharp detail. She stood back a little and aimed at an envelope on top of a pile of unopened letters further away, bringing that into focus much quicker. She adjusted the aperture finding the exposure and depth of field she wanted, using the shutter speed the camera was already set on. She depressed the shutter release, wound on and depressed the button again. There was no film in the camera but Eleanor liked the sound the shutter made, a quiet ratchety clunk.

Quickly becoming more confident with the feel and mechanics of the camera she focused on other things in the room – the television, a leg of the small round table the television stood on, a patch of wear on the arm of the sofa, the empty wastepaper basket, empty ever since her mother had cleaned the house in preparation for Clay's return from hospital. She found she didn't create much mess on her own. She picked out the brass catch on the window, plants in the garden through the window – the rosemary, the jasmine, the acacia. She could even catch a faint reflection of herself holding the camera in the glass, like a shadow, the plants still coming straight through her. But she knew she was real and solid and breathing.

A train went past without stopping and she paused waiting for the timbre of its slack motion to subside before continuing, trying to pinpoint the stem of a creeper. It was too in the shade and she gave up turning into the room with the camera still to her eye, so everything seemed to be going round, not her, quicker than it actually was – the kitchen door, the bookshelves, the dirty cream walls, the awful beach painting by Clay's mother. She realised she really had to take it down. She stopped on the Berenice Abbott photograph of New York, remembering it must have been something she'd had before she lived here, before she'd even met Clay, when she'd been working for the auction house. Maybe she'd get rid of that too, thinking surely it isn't good to hang on to everything. Not all memories can be worth keeping.

She knew how easy it was to look back, how important it was to remind yourself of where you came from and what aspirations and dreams you once had but she also knew that she couldn't live with regret for ever if she wanted to make the most of the future. Yes, she thought, there are plenty of things that should go. Besides, she might even make some money in the process, certainly from the photograph. Until Clay's debts and insurance, the mess over his business was sorted out, she couldn't be sure of what she was going to be left with – except the house. Their solicitor had informed her that it had been put solely in her name some years ago, to avoid them losing it if Clay's business went under – that no one could now touch it whatever Clay's debts. She didn't remember signing the papers, but then Clay had often asked her to signs things to do with the house or money which she'd never studied properly. She vowed to herself that she wouldn't let anyone take control of her financial affairs like that again – even though it might have worked out in her favour this time. Christ, she wasn't innumerate.

She put the camera back on the table, the lens looking purple and dreamy tipped away from direct light. She wasn't going to get rid of the camera. It might have taken Clay fifteen, sixteen years to have given her something of use, but he had in the end. And she liked the idea of carrying around this reminder of him, of making her mark on the next stage in her life with it. Because it meant that something good had come out of that time. No, she thought, that's unfair, there were other good things. Clay could be funny and tender towards her. He was never deliberately hurtful, or abusive, except perhaps to himself. She pictured him, how he was before he was ill – his soft body stuffed into ill-fitting clothes – clothes that always stank of cigarettes, of stale sweat. They'd obviously have to go.

But there was a sorrow inside her that she knew wouldn't be as easy to get rid of. Sorrow for a man who had spent his life avoiding any real responsibility, any real emotion. She would always love him in a way – like you might love a wayward parent – and she wondered whether it had been his very hopelessness, his lack of ambition, which she took for a contentedness with life and had found so attractive, that she had grown so weary of, because life just wasn't like that. He'd never faced up to reality. Perhaps he had had as strong an urge to have children as she'd had. Was it possible for a man to feel that way? But he'd never talked about it – okay, once when he was dying. He'd never talked about anything that had really mattered to their marriage, to their life together. She'd betrayed him no more than he had betrayed her. She didn't feel guilty now – about Paul, about her inability to have children, about her lack of perfection as a wife, as a woman. Clay was the one who'd been flawed.

Since Clay's death she had been experiencing odd, swift feelings of incredible energy which made everything seem extraordinarily light, as if she were able to float. It was more than a freedom of movement, it was the ease and power with which she could do so. And she thought how heavy guilt must weigh. She put the camera in its case, with the other lens already packaged up in its original maker's box, knowing Clay would probably have been more interested in the box than the actual piece of equipment inside – how he'd always looked at things the wrong way round. She made a mental note to buy some film the next time she went out. She knew she had to make a start, she was forty-three tomorrow. She also promised herself she would ring her old work colleagues at the photographic library – it had been almost a year, she could handle it – knowing they'd be able to give her some pointers at least. She needed a darkroom, studio space, contacts. She was going to make a success of it. She'd surprise Rose, her mother. Besides, she had all the bills to worry about, car insurance, council tax – although she'd now be eligible for a single occupier's allowance, of course.

Eleanor said, 'Mum wanted to come. I only just managed to put her off. I couldn't bear it.' They had been given a table in the front of the restaurant. The doors had been concertinaed back, so it felt like they were more outside than in – an awning kept the sun off, though the glare from the river was bouncing on to the embankment and rose up like a wall an arm-stretch away. They were sitting side-on to the view but both were having difficulty looking at each other despite the fact that they were wearing sunglasses, and they kept glancing at the river instead – the barges and sightseeing boats moored to bright buoys, the sparkling stays of the larger party boats permanently tethered to Victoria Embankment across the river, the broad, shimmering leaves of the soft Temple trees and the silver skylights and pale spires stretching up into Holborn and beyond. Eleanor felt uncomfortable, because they had barely spoken since Clay's funeral, since Rose had told her she was pregnant really. However, Eleanor thought that Rose looked much better than she had the last time she had seen her. She wasn't as pale and there was no puffiness in her face. She'd had her hair cut a little shorter than normal and was wearing a summer dress

Eleanor hadn't seen before. It was a deep rust colour and probably made of a silk linen mix, because it glistened more than if it had just been made of linen. The colour and fit suited her well, making her look younger than she was, or maybe that was the haircut. 'You know what she's like,' Eleanor said, 'going on and on. I'm not sure what's worse, Mum blaming me for not looking after Clay properly, or her feeling sorry for me?'

'She doesn't think men are capable of looking after themselves,' Rose said. 'Maybe she's right.'

They had ordered and a waiter offered them the bread basket. They each took a roll, Eleanor immediately breaking hers open and tearing a piece off. She popped it in her mouth without buttering it. The crust was hard and hurt her gums. 'Actually, I can't bear her feeling sorry for me, that's worse,' she said, still chewing. 'I've always hated people feeling sorry for me. Look at me, Rose, I seem okay, don't I? I'm still in one piece. I'm tougher than you think.'

'I've never doubted you.'

'Oh no? Not like most people. Mum has always thought I was pretty useless. You were the one who did things. She always somehow made me feel inadequate.'

'You had Dad. He doted on you. I never had anything like the relationship with him that you had.'

'It wasn't that special. He never really accepted me you know. I might just have tried harder with him than you.'

'You've always blamed Mum for them splitting up, haven't you?' Rose said, 'But I don't think he treated her so brilliantly. From what I can gather he played around a bit, too. I've always suspected something went on that we've never been told about. He wasn't blameless.'

'You're as bad as Mum. She's always thinking things like that about people.'

'Well she's right most of the time. Maybe you should try to look at people a little harder. You've never been a great judge of character.'

'Thanks. Maybe I just don't think the worst of everyone all the time. Perhaps I give them more of a chance.' The tide was going out and Eleanor could hear small waves breaking on the patch of dirty sand immediately below their stretch of the embankment, that and the throaty reverberation of a diesel engine driving a slipping propeller. But she couldn't see the boat it was coming from. There was no boat moving on the river then. 'You know, the odd thing is I was going to leave Clay anyway.'

'Eleanor, you'd never have left him.'

'Rose, it's true. I promise you.'

'Why? It wasn't so bad, was it? God, poor Clay. Fifty-four – it's not fair, is it? I'm going to miss him.'

'Why? Why, because there was nothing holding us together any more. Apart from habit. We weren't helping each other. There was no understanding. Passion – ha. We just got on each other's nerves. We didn't have a marriage, whatever that is – it had ended years ago. It was lifeless.' She finished her roll, nervously, feeling the hard crust against her sore gums. 'And I needed to do something for myself. I wanted a new start. Christ, I'm forty-three.'

'You think you'd have been happier on your own?'

'I am on my own. There's no choice about it now. But, yes, for the moment certainly. Of course I wish it hadn't come about this way. Don't think I'm glad Clay died for a minute. He shouldn't have died.' She looked at her watch. 'He should still be in his shop fiddling around with cameras – except he wouldn't be there because some property developer was about to take his lease. God, Rose, it's like a part of me's gone, too – a chunk of my life. But, strangely, I suppose it's something I was preparing for anyway.' She ran her tongue around her gums, tasting salt. 'I'm getting things organised. I'm trying to sort out some photography work. I'm meeting an old colleague from the library next week. I feel I've suddenly got all this energy – like there's nothing holding me back.' She took a sip of water, pushing the water around her mouth, freeing specks of crust.

'The house?'

'It's still for sale – waiting for the market to pick up. But what about you? How have you been? I haven't been much help.'

'For God's sake you've had enough to deal with,' Rose said. The wine came and Rose was made to taste it. She nodded distractedly and the waiter filled up her glass and Eleanor's, placing the bottle in an ice-bucket on a stand next to their table. It was followed almost immediately by the starters – Eleanor had gone for the chargrilled aubergine salad and Rose the sardines. Rose began pulling pieces of blackened skin and flesh from the bone, arranging them next to shreds of lettuce in rough forkfuls. But didn't eat any. 'I thought you realised. I had a miscarriage.'

'I'm sorry,' Eleanor said, quietly. She looked beyond Rose to Blackfriars Bridge, focusing on the cars going north, because she could only see that lane, catching spots of dazzle as the sun hit a wing mirror or a splash of chrome. She followed the traffic over, her gaze lifting and being immediately taken with the gold cross topping St Paul's. It was radiant and made the sky over the City appear darker than elsewhere, giving the other buildings and cranes a more dramatic backdrop. It almost looked stormy behind sunglasses. 'I'm sorry,' she said again.

'It's all right. It wasn't a big deal.' She started to eat now, rapidly, talking at the same time, so bits of sardine were sent spinning into mid air. 'It was a bit like having a heavy period. I went to hospital, but I was only there for a few hours.'

'Oh God, Rose.'

'In a way it made things much easier. It was decided for me. Plus Mark never knew. I think he suspected I was having a thing with Brian, not that he was in a position to make a big deal about it anyway, but he never knew I was pregnant. The stupid thing is, before it happened I told Brian. He went berserk. So he's sort of gone too. I would have had an abortion. I'd have left Mark.' She swallowed. 'I thought I really loved him. Maybe I wasn't thinking straight. Pregnancy plays havoc with your emotions – things get out of proportion. Believe me, I've been there twice before.' Using a fingernail she picked a piece of fish from between her lower front teeth, wiping it on her napkin. 'Everything's much clearer now.'

The aubergines were warm, but bitter and Eleanor was glad when she had finished them. 'So, what, you're staying with Mark, after all this? God, life goes on, doesn't it?'

'It's not perfect but it'll be much better for James and Sarah. And we have got a pretty nice house. It would be awfully expensive to split up. I couldn't live in a little place in south London. It wouldn't be fair on the children.'

'I was going to leave Clay, Rose. You do believe me, don't you?'

'Eleanor, what difference does it make now?'

'I want you to know. I want you to realise that I've changed – you of all people.'

'Of course you were going to.'

'Don't you see, it's part of being able to get on with the rest of my life?'

'I understand,' Rose said, nodding unconvincingly.

The main courses came and Eleanor could immediately see she'd made the right choice. Her grilled swordfish on a bed of leeks looked vastly preferable to Rose's salmon, which appeared overcooked and with a grey, bitty dollop of mushroom sauce on the side beginning to get a skin. A double portion of chips was placed between them.

Having tasted a mouthful of food and finding it was as good as it looked, Eleanor put her knife and fork down. 'Clay would never have left me,' she said. 'He hated any sort of upheaval. He always went for the easy option. He spent his entire life deluding himself about one thing or another.' Clay saying, *We're going to make that silver*, suddenly came to Eleanor's mind and she smiled to herself, a knowing smile, thinking, no, we never would. She took a long sip of the cool white wine. She liked white wine, she realised – she never normally drank it because Clay had always refused to and she drank so little they rarely had any in the house. If they went out Clay had liked her to have red with him, because he didn't want to be seen ordering a whole bottle for himself, even though they would normally go through two bottles with him drinking most of both of them. She took another sip, the wine tingling the back of her throat, numbing her gums.

'Come on Eleanor, we all kid ourselves from time to time,' Rose said.

Eleanor picked up her cutlery again and started to eat. 'Perhaps part of the problem with Clay was not having children. I thought I had come to terms with the idea. Then, I don't know, a year or so ago I suddenly felt that there was this huge thing missing, like I was hollow somehow, a failure. I'd see women with young children everywhere and think why can't that be me, I'm a woman too? It was as if they were mocking me. There was this one woman in particular – she even looked like me.' Eleanor was thinking of Louise. Was that her real name? Maybe there was nothing real about her, maybe she'd just imagined her – the conclusion of too many coincidences. 'Talk about your emotions playing havoc. There've been times when I've felt I can't even trust what I'm seeing. Your eyes stream and you feel your head's going to blow off.'

'You've still got time, surely – with someone else,' Rose said, pushing her food around the plate. Eleanor thought her sister looked embarrassed, but it was hot and Rose was drinking.

'No, I don't think so,' Eleanor said, shaking her head. 'Even if it was Clay who was infertile, I haven't had a proper period in months. I've been getting these hot flushes. I wake up in the middle of the night sweating. My bones ache. Rose, I'm too old. I'm menopausal.'

'Nonsense. You're just stressed – don't forget you lost your job. Lots of women your age have children. Plus there's all that IVF treatment and things you can get nowadays.'

'Not if you're forty-three – well not easily.' Eleanor finished her glass and poured another, it was her birthday. 'Besides, I think there comes a time when you have to accept the fact that you're not going to have children. People manage without. Surely there's no right to a child.' She looked at her sister, thinking we don't even look alike. She turned away, spotting a red boat in the middle of the white river – the words, *This is an official London Sightseeing boat*, written on the side. 'Rose, remember the estate agent who showed us that house in Ufton Grove, who you thought was rather cute? I slept with him one afternoon.'

The back of Eleanor's dress was damp because she had sat on a solid chair in the heat for so long and as she walked she felt it cool and drying against her bare legs. She waited until she had got to the end of Gabriel's Wharf, past the colourful stalls and cafés, the clumsy wooden sculptures and people lingering in the fantastic early May weather, and was on Upper Ground, by the London Studios, before she tugged at the elastic on her knickers – pinching the band through her dress – because her knickers were cutting into her bottom as they always seemed to do when it was hot. There was less breeze away from the river and the air smelt of tar and drains, and humidity. Eleanor had said goodbye to Rose at the restaurant, because Rose was heading the other way, across the river.

Eleanor would normally have carried on along Upper Ground until the beginning of Cornwall Road but they were widening the pavement ahead so just before the London Television Centre she decided to take Coin Street through to Stamford Street and walk that way around the temporary car park and join Cornwall Road there. She paused for a moment looking down Coin Street to the backs of the buildings lining that stretch of the river, from the top of the Oxo Tower to the National Theatre, the Hayward and a fragment of the Royal Festival Hall – the sun flicking over the bold, flat roofs, some with flags depicting company logos or advertisements for exhibitions or plays, or concerts. And she realised how little she had used the South Bank, or Gabriel's Wharf for that matter, living so near. Which made her think of the other amenities close by – the Old Vic, Waterloo, Eurostar. She thought of the restaurants that had sprung up in the last few years and which had remained largely untested by Clay and herself – Livebait, Bar Central, the Fire Station, the two in the Oxo Tower she kept reading about. There was the market on Lower Marsh, an excellent greengrocer's on The Cut, Tesco's at the Elephant. The ease with which you could get into Covent Garden or Clerkenwell, Westminster or the City. How you never appreciated what was on your doorstep.

No one seemed to notice Eleanor waiting by the zebra crossing on Stamford Street just before Cornwall Road – in her sunglasses and simple cream A-line dress which she had bought years ago from Hobbs because it was comfortable and timeless. She had got the stain out of her favourite summer dress, the green one, but she hadn't felt like wearing it since the time with Paul, and she was beginning to wonder whether it wasn't quite her anyway, that she might look as if she were trying to be someone else in it trying too hard. She had to step on to the crossing before a taxi stopped, and then a lorry and a motorbike in the far lane. Another fitness centre had recently opened in the building on the corner of Cornwall Road and Stamford Street – it had been unoccupied for as long as Eleanor could remember. Passing she heard loud thumping music and someone shouting above it and she thought, perhaps I should join a gym. She knew she never got enough exercise and that it would be good for her circulation and might even help her concentrate when she was working.

Walking up Cornwall Street she felt the sun on her back, knowing her dress would probably look see-through to people in front of her, the light silhouetting her legs, but much to her relief the men sitting at the pavement tables outside the White Hart didn't stare at her as she approached. Small children were coming out of St Patrick's across the road – it had just gone three-thirty and there was the usual cluster of women and a couple of men waiting by the entrance. The parents who had already been handed their children were trying to sort them out, their bags and drawings and other loose belongings. One boy was screaming and his mother seemed to be running out of patience with him. Another boy, he couldn't have been much more than two, had climbed on to the back of his pushchair and was shaking it furiously. It looked to Eleanor as if it might topple backwards at any moment, but his mother was unaware of the situation, talking to someone facing the other way. And Eleanor suddenly thought, of course it would be worse to lose a child than never to have one. However much of a sorrow, a grievous-ness, a tragedy childlessness was, surely you would never really know what you were missing. That bond would never have formed. There would be no memories, no record of their first day at nursery school, or the time they fell off the back of their pushchair, and without memories you would have nothing to mourn. Would you?

She was turning into Roupell Street and saw the door to Konditor & Cook had been propped open, so she skipped across the road and entered without hesitation – it always smelt so appealing and, what-the-hell, she hardly ever went in. Besides, it was her birthday and Rose hadn't even given her a card. The people who worked there were always very friendly and she spent a long while looking at the cakes and savoury things, far longer than was necessary, because she knew what she was was going to have before she'd even entered – a piece of banoffee pie. They put it in a small box for her complete with a ribbon, as if they had sensed it was for a special occasion, just the single slice, and she carried it out into the streaming sunshine, which was only on her side of Roupell Street – hitting the edge of the road with a zigzagging pattern of light and shade, as it did when the sun was only so high in the sky, skimming the opposite rooftops.

She had to step into the road to let an elderly couple pass, only realising a few moments later that they were the people who had been trying to sell the Whittlesey Street house – the woman with her round, friendly cheeks and fluffy grey hair, the man with his thin lips and pointed nose. He had even nodded to Eleanor as she had stepped out of their way – he hadn't appeared mean at all, not like in the photograph. And Eleanor wondered, looking over her shoulder – the woman had her arm through her husband's – why they might have changed their minds about moving. Had they realised their daughter wasn't going to come back, whether they moved to the south coast or not? That their loss would be just as palpable there as here – maybe more so, because they would be in an unfamiliar place and unfamiliar places were always harder to occupy? Eleanor looked at them for one more second, thinking they'd obviously found some sort of peace, of acceptance. Whether it was through their God, or trips to Konditor & Cook, which they were entering, she didn't know.

She reached her house with its for sale sign still attached to the wall at first-floor height – the front door desperately needing a coat of paint and the brass numbers dull and grimy as ever. Holding the cake box in one hand, she managed to find a tissue in her bag. She spat on the tissue and began rubbing away the dirt.

The answerphone said, 'Mrs Mitchell, this is Jenny from Clapham. The Lillieshall Road house you enquired about a few months ago is back on the market. If you're still interested I'd be delighted to fix up a viewing. Please call me back, we want to get this property moving again as soon as possible. Thank you so much.'

'Mrs Mitchell, we've got someone who's very keen to view your property. Could you give me a ring as soon as you get this message, cheers.'

'Eleanor, Eleanor darling, where are you? There's something I've got to talk to you about urgently. I'll be in all evening. Bye. Oh, I hope you had a nice lunch with Rose.'

'Hi, it's Paul, Paul Moran – I'm glad you're still there. I heard about your husband from his shop. I'm very sorry. I imagine you still don't want to talk to me but if you do I'd love to hear from you. I've got some photographs in an exhibition in a space in Clerkenwell at the end of this month – why don't you come to the private view if you're feeling up to it? I'll send you an invite.'

She got into the bath and let her body slide under the hot water, just bearing the heat, feeling grit on the bottom as she sunk up to her chin – her hair getting wet at the back and the water lapping against her ears, into them, cutting out most sound, with her knees out of the water and her feet pressed against the end of the bath, her toes playing with the plug chain and the scaly chrome-fitting the plug chain was attached to. She'd always been told that she had nice knees and wet they were glistening. She noticed, too, that her legs, the parts of her shins that she could see, were hairier than ever – the hairs dark against the white enamel of the bath. She knew she should shave them but she hated shaving her legs – she always cut herself and it took ages, and it wasn't as if Clay were there to make remarks like, *Christ, your legs are getting hairier than mine*, so she thought, I'll leave it for another day, when I feel like it. And with that in mind she let go of the thought that she should shave her armpits as well.

She hadn't soaped herself yet, or added any bath oil, but she found the water unctuous, running her fingers and thumbs together, rubbing her hands on her thighs and forearms – maybe it was because of the moisturiser she had applied all over herself earlier in the day, or the bath was already dirty. She hated cleaning the bath, though it was a damn sight easier now. Clay used to leave a soapy scum which dried hard on the sides. It was worse when he shaved in the bath, then the cake of dirt was thick with tiny bristles like iron filings. She stopped feeling the water, its unctuousness, and let her arms rest on her body, her hands falling on the insides of her thighs, her fingers crossing, with her elbows wedged between the sides of the bath and her. She pushed herself up a little so the water wasn't tipping into her ears, though water was still trapped in there, impairing her hearing. Adjusting her head slightly, getting perfectly comfortable, she shut her eyes. And warm and relaxed like this she couldn't think of anywhere she'd rather be, or anything she'd rather be doing. And she felt a sense of stillness, of fullness overwhelm her.

Despite the water in her ears she heard the phone go, the ringing seemingly getting louder. She thought, it's bloody Mum. Always when I'm in the bath. How she disturbs everything. She let the phone ring, thinking the answerphone would pick it up – remembering only as the phone rang and rang that the answerphone wasn't switched on and that perhaps whatever it was her mother had been wanting to talk to her about for the last few days really was important. It wouldn't stop so she sat up, the water rushing off her in one slab, and climbed out of the bath knowing she couldn't ignore her any longer. She grabbed a towel and wrapping it around herself ran out of the bathroom – because now she was out of the bath she was damned if she was going to get to the phone too late – taking the stairs two at a time. 'Hello,' she said, breathless, picking up the receiver.

'Eleanor, darling, are you all right?'

'Mum, I was in the bath.'

'Sorry darling, do you want me to ring you back?'

'I'm out now.'

'I can easily ring you back.'

Eleanor sat on the stool by the phone, pulling the towel over her legs. 'What is it?'

'Was it hot up there today?'

'Mum, it's been hot all week. Since my birthday anyway.'

'It's been sweltering down here. I can't think it's going to last for much longer. It's been terrible for the garden.'

'Mum, please, I'm dripping.'

'Look Eleanor, there is something I need to talk to you about.'

'Can't it wait?'

'Not really.'

'What? You're not getting married again?'

'No. God no. It's about something that happened a very long time ago – between your father and I.'

'Mum, I really don't think I want to know. Surely it can't make any difference now?'

'Maybe not,' said Eleanor's mother, 'but I should tell you anyway.'

'Why, after all this time?'

'Because I don't want you to find out from anyone else. You see, I received a letter from her. She wants to meet you, and Rose. She hasn't been well.'

'Who?'

'Your father's other daughter. He got someone pregnant when we were married. He didn't tell me about it for a long while, for years. I'm not sure when even he first knew. She's younger than you, not by much. She's Rose's age.'

'You're not being serious? Why didn't you tell me before?'

'I always thought he should have told you. And I suppose I was embarrassed about it – I didn't want to think about it, I didn't want it to be a part of our lives, and the longer it remained unmentioned the less important it seemed to be. You didn't need to know. What difference could it have made? I don't think he ever saw her. Certainly not when I was with him. Apparently she wasn't told who her real father was until after he died.'

'What's her name?' Eleanor wasn't shocked. She felt surprisingly calm. Relieved in a way – that her eyes, her mind hadn't totally misled her. Of course she might have seen it earlier, had she been more astute, more canny, a better judge of character like Rose. Maybe underneath she had always known – her female intuitiveness kicking in, something every woman would have sensed sooner or later. But it didn't change a thing, it didn't change where she was at now. And in a way she was glad of what she had seen – the reality and the illusions, how people can deceive, how they can deceive themselves. People so close to you. Because otherwise she might not have been so determined, so strong, the person she had become. 'No, don't tell me. I know it.' She stood up and saw she'd left a trail of dark footprints on the fading carpet.

Eleanor thought, God, I'd better run through the house – I suppose I'll have to show them around, they'll probably want to see everything – wondering what it would be like to be an estate agent, realising how much easier it must be if it's not your house, dealing with complete strangers. She wasn't sure where to start. There really was no best bit, or worst bit – well, maybe the kitchen was in the worst condition, but at least it was tidy, as was the back room. She had cleared away her breakfast things, she had even managed to sort out the pile of correspondence. She stood admiring the empty table – the stains, as permanent, as characterful as the knots in the wood. She decided she was going to keep it, she'd aged with it. She walked to the hall, imagining coming into the house for the first time.

She found herself opening the door to the front room, last used for Clay's wake – the party room. She went over to the window and drew back the net curtains, bringing fresh daylight into the room, making the scarlet carpet look rose. The carpet wasn't so bad, she thought. The walls would do for the moment, too – they were an inoffensive magnolia and went okay with the carpet. There were no pictures but she knew she had some framed prints of the Thames in a cupboard upstairs she could hang, and there was the Berenice

Abbott from the back room she could always bring through. She thought she might as well try it in here before selling it – it might not look so tired in a new setting. In fact there were a lot of things she could move about. Clay had picked up the sofa and matching armchair from an auction. They were very seventies-looking, covered in fawn corduroy, but Eleanor could see there was still plenty of life left in them – she didn't like things that were brand new anyway. She bent down to remove a piece of tissue caught between a cushion and an arm of the sofa. A standard lamp was positioned next to the sofa so it could shed light on whoever sat there, but neither Clay nor Eleanor had ever sat there for long. Eleanor turned it on to see if it worked and it didn't.

A couple of ebony candlesticks, a wedding present from a relative of Clay's, stood on the mantelpiece. Eleanor couldn't remember when they were last used, what dinner, what special occasion. She wished she had some flowers to put alongside them, perhaps a photograph or two as well. Clay had never liked having family photographs about the place, he said they depressed him because they were always so contrived – how they hid so much. Soot had fallen on to the grate and the floor tiles immediately surrounding the fireplace. Clay had talked about getting a coal-effect gas fire put in, saying how much easier it would be to manage than a real fire, but he'd never got round to organising it, not that they'd ever lit many real fires. She tried to sweep the soot off the tiles and under the grate with her foot but the soot was getting everywhere and she left it turning to walk out of the room, thinking, yes, this room could be all right – with a bit of attention it could be lovely. The light shade would have to be changed, though. It was a wire-rimmed paper orb, which had once been pure white but was now a yellowy grey, like wood ash.

She glanced at her watch in the hall and hurried up the stairs, missing out the bathroom, thinking she'd save that for the way down. She opened her bedroom windows further, feeling warm air slide on to her arms – hearing footsteps on the pavement below, a car starting, a siren way off, the steady trill of the city. She tried to get the old, pale blue and brown Habitat rug to sit smoothly on the floorboards – it never had. And although she had shaken the duvet cover earlier, she shook it again, eventually getting it to float evenly on to the bed and the already plumped up pillows. She rearranged the books and magazines and alarm clock on the small chest of drawers on her side of the bed for the second time that morning, thinking, why am I doing this, it's ridiculous? Still, she went round to Clay's side and blew on his side table, blowing a faint film of dust from the peeling varnish, ringed with dark watermarks, into her face. She thought she was going to sneeze.

She had left her dressing gown draped over the chair and she picked it up, wiping her face on it, wondering whether she should hang it in the wardrobe. She noticed she'd left a pair of knickers underneath so she grabbed the knickers and lay the dressing gown back on the chair, thinking she'd throw the knickers in the dirty-washing basket in the bathroom after she'd checked the rear bedroom. She paused by the door for a second, knowing the room couldn't look any better, with sunlight beginning to edge in, without a great heap of Clay's clothes mounding on the floor – or the overpowering smell of cigarettes and stale sweat, because he never wanted to have the windows open more than a crack.

As she was entering the small spare bedroom – the room her father used to sleep in, with his secret, his inability to face up to life, so like Clay – the room their child would have had, had she had a child – a train came clattering into Waterloo East. The back of the platform was visible from the window and she heard the psst and squeal of its breaks, the hydraulic hiss of the doors, the rush of late commuters, suddenly thinking, I still haven't caught a train from there. I still haven't got to Hastings. Though she knew there was plenty of time. That there would always be time. *Orpington, Sevenoaks, Tonbridge.*

The room was small, with just an unmade single bed, an empty chest of drawers and a built-in cupboard she hadn't gone through in years, where she thought the prints of the Thames were. There was the original fireplace and a view over the garden and Brad Street, and the back of Waterloo East of course. It might have made a decent bedroom for a small child, though it occurred to her that she could always use it as an office. She'd have to get the phone line moved upstairs, and she'd have to put up with the scrap metal merchant's forklift truck and the garage's respraying thing and the new pounding gym. But in a way, she thought, the sound of people working nearby might help her, besides she realised she had grown to love the trains, the sound of them, their fleeting presence. She listened to the closing doors, like someone gasping with surprise, the whine of the accelerating engine and the train's rapid departure followed by the echo of clanking electricity trying to keep up. Not noticing, until she'd left the room and was descending the stairs to the bathroom on the split level, that someone was knocking at the door.

Still holding the knickers she dashed into the bathroom, dropping them in the wicker basket, which bulged whether it was full or empty. Catching herself in the mirror she ran her fingers through her hair, thinking she'd let it grow a bit, knowing it hadn't really been her so short – she wasn't twenty. She walked carefully down the rest of the stairs suddenly feeling sick. She opened the front door and, squinting slowly focused on a pair of blue eyes belonging to a tall, slim man with a fine, strong face and wavy dark hair – Steve Brett. He smiled showing perfect teeth. She had been expecting him – her estate agent had told her the name of the person who wanted to view her house. But it was only a few moments ago, coming down the stairs, her eyes taking in the cosy narrow hall with its cheap scarlet carpet, a wave of nausea sweeping through her, that she had finally changed her mind.

'I had a feeling I'd run into you one day,' he said.

He was better looking than Eleanor remembered from the café in Clapham. Or maybe that was because he was slightly tanned. He was wearing a faded blue shirt with the top two buttons undone – perhaps it was the one he'd been wearing then. 'I'm sorry,' Eleanor said, standing back, knowing she was going to be sick, trying to swallow, 'the house is no longer for sale. I'm taking it off the market.'

'But—' he said, edging forward, cutting out the light.

'Sorry,' she said again. 'Look, I'm not feeling well, I can't talk now.' And she closed the door before he could come any further.

HENRY SUTTON

Gorleston

'In this odd, touching, beautifully written first novel he lays out for us with rare sympathy the frightening and exhilarating fact that age does not necessarily bring serenity. Or even respectability'
THE TIMES

'A wildly original, funny and affectionate first novel'
ELSPETH BARKER

'A finely judged first novel ... [a] wonderfully inventive and moving finale'
THE SUNDAY TIMES

Bank Holiday Monday

'Quivers with irritation, sexual tension and half-suggested danger; it is an acute, discomforting portrait of ordinary damage and the English talent to repress ... Sutton captures perfectly the nuances of ordinary unhappy relationships. His descriptions of the shifting landscapes are similarly precise and evocative ... an intelligent and unusual novel'
THE TIMES LITERARY SUPPLEMENT

'With the successor to his accomplished debut *Gorleston*, Sutton continues to mine the rich stream of domestic drama and the tender parochiality of family life. Like the best of Alan Bennett this is satire at its most affectionate'
ARENA

S

SCEPTRE